Hills of Nevermore

Montana Gold Series

Hills of Nevermore

Montana Gold Series

By

Janalyn Voigt

Hills of Nevermore
Published by Mountain Brook Ink
White Salmon, WA U.S.A.

© 2017 Janalyn Voigt
ISBN 9781-943959-26-6

The Team: Miralee Ferrell, Susan K Marlow, Nikki Wright, Cindy Jackson
Cover Design: Indie Cover Design, Lynnette Bonner Designer

Mountain Brook Ink is an inspirational publisher offering fiction you can believe in.
Printed in the United States of America

Reader Bonuses

For a map showing locations in this story plus exclusive
features to enhance reading this book, go here:
http://janalynvoigt.com/hills-of-nevermore-readers.

Dedication

Dedicated to the man who knows me best and loves me most,
my sweet husband John Voigt.

Acknowledgments

Resurrecting a by-gone era requires epic research. Thanks go to historian Jim Peterson who aided my understanding of Montana history; Billie Ratcliffe of the Virginia City Preservation Alliance for taking her time to let me into Robbers' Roost; and Karen Fisher of Virginia City's The Gingerbread House bed-and-breakfast. She took in my husband and me on a cold night in the off-season, fielded our questions, and regaled us with stories from the town's history.

No work of fiction reaches publication without the help of many publishing professionals. Those who offered solid advice on development of this story include Nick Harrison, then a senior editor for Harvest House and now an agent for Wordserve Literary; best-selling, award-winning authors Miralee Ferrell, Tracie Peterson, Susan May Warren, Angela Breidenbach, Lynnette Bonner, and Lesley Ann McDaniel; Barbara Johnson, celebrated editor and an early agent and mentor; Greg Johnson, president of Wordserve Literary and the founding president of FaithHappenings; Chip MacGregor of MacGregor Literary, and Sarah Joy Freese, my talented and inspiring agent at Wordserve Literary.

I'm grateful in particular for Miralee Ferrell of Mountain Brook Ink, publisher of this book. We met several years ago as featured authors at a Montana book festival and hit it off. I asked Miralee's advice about a work of fiction I was writing, never realizing she would later become its publisher. Miralee is the recipient of a Will Roger's Medallion Award, celebrating her contribution to excellence in Western fiction. I am honored by her mentorship.

Miralee Ferrell and Susan Marlow, a copyeditor with a

gimlet eye, both made *Hills of Nevermore* stronger. I also appreciate the assistance of those who proofread this book.

My thanks to Lynnette Bonner of Indie Cover Design, who created a beautiful cover that sets the right mood.

Thanks and hugs go to my family for believing in me as a writer and giving me practical support so I could work on this book.

CHAPTER ONE

Idaho Territory, May, 1863

AMERICA WATCHED HER WAGON TRAIN SHRINK steadily in the distance, dust billowing in its wake. How could it have traveled so far in such a short time? Oh, why hadn't she let someone know she'd needed to stop? Her friend Addie, taking a turn holding America's baby, might not look for her unless Liberty woke and cried for her mother. Bill Baker, driving her oxen for a spell out of kindness, wouldn't notice her absence for some time.

"I can't have lost it!" Tears blurred the trail beneath America's feet. She'd been a fool to wear the locket Kyle had given her. She should have kept it stashed away. When she'd felt her necklace's chain break, she'd stopped walking at once. Why couldn't she find it? If she didn't come across the locket soon, she'd have to leave it behind. Catching up to the wagon train would take some doing even now, and every passing moment carried her baby, only three months old, farther away.

A meadowlark trilled, the song a sharp accent against the deeper thud of hooves.

A shiver ran down her spine. She jerked her gaze upward.

A spotted pony pranced on the path. The rider on the horse's back watched her from dark eyes. Beneath the quillwork adorning the brave's chest, his skin gleamed the color of robust tea. A black stripe of paint slashed across the bridge of his nose. Two tight braids fell to the sash that bound fringed leggings at the waist. Strips of cloth crisscrossed a wide forehead, and feathers fanned sideways behind his head.

A group of Indians on ponies clustered beside him. One of them called out, laughing.

The brave held up his hand for silence.

Wisps of hair escaped America's bonnet, stinging her eyes. She clawed them away with a trembling hand. One thought crashed into another, beating to the rhythm of her wild pulse. Could she outrun them? *No.* What would they do to her once they caught her? *Horrible.* She trembled at the very idea. They could scalp and murder her. Or. If they let her live, that might be worse.

With fear burning the back of her throat and her heart pounding like the wings of a canary against the bars of its cage, America walked toward the brave. Her legs shook so badly that they threatened to collapse. But she lifted her head high and pretended chance encounters like this happened every day.

She picked her way through the sagebrush and bunch grass beside the trail. The spotted pony snorted and showed the whites of its eyes. The leader's dark gaze swept over America, making the hair on the back of her neck prickle.

The ground gave way as pain shot through her foot. She pitched forward and sprawled beside the pony's prancing hooves.

The brave gave a command in his native tongue that quieted his pony. He leaned down to her. She stared at the hand he extended, then past it to his face. He watched her with an expression that told her nothing.

She pushed to her knees, drew breath, and took his hand.

The brave tugged America upward and caught her in a strong grip, lifting her to sit in front of him. She perched before him astride the pony with her skirt riding up to her knees. Heat rushed into her cheeks at being so immodestly displayed. He tightened his arm around her middle, and she fought the urge to scream. Whatever he intended, a clear head might help her survive. He'd spared her life so far, but for what purpose?

She'd heard tales of women forced to live with natives but had never thought such a fate might befall her.

The pony lurched into motion beneath her and went through its paces, finally stretching into a gallop. The wind of their passing fanned her face. The thundering of hooves told her the other braves followed. The ground sped by as they overtook the train and curved into the path it would travel.

But this made no sense. Why would the brave carry her toward, rather than away from, the wagon train? Did he mean to trade her for goods?

A shout went up from the wagons.

The pony slid to a stop, and her captor lowered her with swift ease. He wheeled his pony to face his waiting companions but looked back with a smile touching his lips. "Brave woman."

"You speak English?" The words jerked from her.

His smile broke into a grin, and the pony plunged forward as the shadow of a cloud raced over the ground.

America stared after this brave who had turned from captor to rescuer. He'd done none of the things she'd dreaded and everything necessary to help her. His behavior didn't reconcile with what she'd been told about Indians, but now was not the time to puzzle that out.

She ran toward the wagons with the prairie wavering through a sheen of tears. Two riders pulled ahead of the train to meet her. America's joy at being set free plummeted at first sight of the red-headed miner, Pete Amesly. Why would the last person she wanted to see right now ride out to meet her?

Grant Hadley, the wagon train's scout, reined in his Morgan beside her. "Are you all right?"

Pete drew in his chestnut quarter horse on her other side and peered at her with narrowed eyes. "What were you doing with those Indians, anyways?"

"I'm well, thank you," she answered Grant, ignoring Pete.

The grizzled scout squinted. "What happened?"

"I stopped for a few minutes and came across some Indians." Describing her actions made them seem even more foolish.

Pete snorted. "Why would you do a fool thing like that?"

Heat flamed across America's cheeks. She wasn't about to tell Pete about Kyle or the locket he'd given her.

The wagon train reached them then, sparing her from commenting as the oxen lumbered by on either side. Here on the flat prairie, the drivers fanned out their wagons to avoid breathing one another's dust.

"That's not important." Grant sent Pete a scalding look before returning his attention to America. "Let's get you back to your wagon."

"There's Addie now." She gave him a grateful smile and moved off to intercept her friend. Walking a safe distance beside her wagon and the oxen driven by her mop-headed son, Travis, Addie cradled Liberty in her arms.

"I was wondering where you were." Addie gave her a quiet smile. "My arms are starting to ache." She looked past America to Grant and Pete. "Gentlemen?"

America took Liberty's weight into her arms and held her daughter close. Here was a treasure more precious than any locket. She fell into step beside Addie with tears blurring her vision.

Grant kept pace astride his Morgan. "She's had some sort of mishap, ma'am." He cleared his throat. "Maybe you can ask her about it. Find out if she's come to harm in any way." His ears turning pink, he gestured with his head to Pete, and they rode off.

Addie turned a frowning face toward her. "Tell me what happened."

"He helped me." America spoke on a note of wonder.

"Who helped you?"

"The Indian brave. I thought he meant to kill or kidnap me, or else trade me for goods. But he helped me instead."

Addie shook her head. "Tell me from the beginning."

"I lagged behind the wagon train."

"You left the train on your own?"

"It was more like it left me, but yes. I meant to stop only for a short while to—well, to look for something I dropped."

"But you know not to fall behind. Why didn't you tell me?"

"Mr. Hughes was talking with you, or I'd have said something. I didn't want to call attention to myself. I was bound and determined not to slow the train."

Addie sighed. "Does this have anything to do with Pete Amesly's objections to your joining us?"

Moisture prickled America's eyes. "Maybe he's right. I can barely do my share with a baby to take care of."

"That's hardly your fault. Granted, if you had asked to join the train when we first set out, our captains might have refused, but leaving you stranded at Fort Bridger would be quite a different matter. Christian charity required us to rescue a widow in need. Under the circumstances, no one minds doing a little extra work for you."

"Amesly objects."

"Oh, pshaw! Pete is so taken with gold fever he's lost his manners. The others don't feel the same."

"I fear he may be right, though. I've slowed the train and taken others from their own chores to attend mine. I can't help feeling like a burden."

"Why, America Liberty Reed! I'm appalled you would say such a thing. I don't know what I'd have done after my Clyde—" She took a breath. "After the accident, I felt I couldn't go on. My son tried to support me, but Travis had his own grief to bear over his father's loss. Your company eased us both. You're a blessing not a burden and remember—I need your help cooking for the miners at Bannack."

The idea of cooking for miners held little appeal, but other options were in short supply. "I'm touched by your kindness, although I'm not sure why you want to cast your lot in with mine."

Addie smiled. "That's easy. Having your help makes me feel less—alone. And you need a friend. Never mind all that about not knowing you well, by the by. I'm a good judge of people, and I could tell right off you're decent folk."

Addie's judgment of people must have faltered, but no need to tell her that. Liberty stirred. Her blue eyes opened to stare at America—eyes like her father's. America hitched a breath.

No one ever had to know her secret.

Shane Hayes pulled the brim of his slouch hat lower and positioned himself in front of the enticing, tall open doors of Nell's Dance Hall. Sharp smoke and the stench of rotgut whiskey fouled the air. He loosened his string tie, which all at once seemed tight.

"Take your partners for the next dance!" a jovial voice called. A piano ground out a tinny melody, joined by a bright whistle and the seesawing of a fiddle. Laughter and the clink of glasses rode above the lively melody, spilling into the street along with lantern light.

Shane glanced inside. A lantern suspended from a ceiling beam by a rope cast a pool of light on the dancers but left the edges of the room in shadow. Miners clasped each hurdy-gurdy girl on the floor in an energetic dance. The girls' skirts glowed like jewels as they turned in their partners' arms. Whenever their gyrations allowed a glimpse of lacy bloomers or a well-turned ankle, the men crowding the bar along one side of the room cheered.

Shane turned his back on the debauchery.

Boots thumped on the boardwalk behind him, and an arm caught him across the shoulders. "Well, go on in and be done with it!"

He tried to pull away, but the arm held him fast. Laughter

barked in his ear. Casey Brogan's fleshy face crinkled into a smile. At close quarters, his breath stank. Hands in pockets and with his blond hair sticking out from beneath a black bowler, Skip Jackson grinned at Shane from beside his mining partner.

Casey blinked watery eyes. "Admit it, Irish! You're hankering to go inside. Why not live a little, eh? One of those gals would feel powerful good in your arms."

Shane jerked out of the miner's clutches. "Get thee behind me, Satan!"

Casey's smile died. "Now what did you go and call me that for?"

"You tried to tempt a man of God." Shane shrugged to throw off the feel of Casey's arm about his shoulders.

"Come now, Saint Preacher." The old miner blew out his cheeks, looking wounded. "You wouldn't begrudge me a bit of fun now, would you?"

Shane took a breath, reminded himself of his mission, and went on in milder tones. "Come away, Casey. This is no place for you."

"What? And sing hymns with you on Sundays? No, thank you."

"I only want to help you."

"If'n you weren't a preacher, I'd put a fist in your stomach on account of that name you called me." Casey pushed past Shane but turned to deliver a parting shot. "You'd best get out of this doorway, if'n you aim to stay healthy."

Skip, about to follow Casey, cocked a bushy brow at Shane. "I don't care if you *are* a preacher." He pivoted, and his fist bashed into Shane's eye.

Shane splatted face down in the street. He turned his head to spit out mud and blinked to clear his vision. Shane pushed to his feet. The world swung around him. Blurred figures loomed above him on the boardwalk. They merged into Skip.

"Nobody calls a friend of mine names when I'm around, y'hear?"

A voice spoke from behind Shane. "What's this rabble-rouser up to now?"

"Just a misunderstanding, deputy." The blond brows came down. "Ain't it?"

Shane covered his burning eye with one hand and made no answer.

Skip glared at him a heartbeat longer then turned on his heel and strode into the dance hall.

"You're going to get yourself killed, Sean."

"My name is Shane now, as I'm sure you recall." He spoke without turning his head. "I can take care of myself, Con. I don't need your help."

"Look, I know you can handle yourself in a fight." Con squatted before him in the light falling into the street from the dance hall. "I grew up with you, remember?"

"I'm a man of the cloth now. I don't fight anymore." Shane reminded him.

"That's what worries me. You've gone soft. Bannack's no place for you. A man who won't fight shouldn't put himself in the way of those who will."

Shane shook his head. "God looks out for his own."

"And suffers fools?"

Shane snatched his hat from the mud beside him. "I'm here to bring salvation to the lost souls of Bannack."

"Oh, Sean. When will you learn that the lost souls of Bannack don't want saving? At least not by you."

"They don't know what they want."

The tilt of Con's head in the moonlight gave his opinion on that subject. "Gold is the only god and savior they want." He hoisted Shane to his feet. "No matter how much they find, there's always the possibility of more. That fact can drive a man mad with gold lust."

Shane wiped the mud from his slouch hat and put it on with quiet dignity. "And you? Why do you stay?"

"Me?" Con gave a dry laugh. "I'm no better than any of

them."

Shane opened his mouth to rebuke the remark, but Con hauled him backward into the shadow between buildings. Hooves clopped in the mud as two horsemen trotted past, moonlight silvering their familiar features. Con's grip loosened, and Shane took advantage of the distraction to pull away from him. He stepped on wobbly legs into the light. "I wonder what Sheriff Plummer and Jack Gallagher are about, riding in this late."

"That's not a question to ask." Con fell silent but then clapped a hand around Shane's shoulders. "Come on, Cousin. Let's see to that eye."

They followed the boardwalk westward but left it to cross the street with mud sucking their boots. When they didn't have snow or dust to slog through in Bannack, they dealt with mud.

Con's cabin wasn't much—a simple shanty covered in tar paper—but Shane welcomed any roof over his head. While traveling his preaching circuit, he spent many a night alone and without shelter in the wilderness.

His knees gave way, and he plunked onto the wooden bench at the scarred table dominating the cabin.

Con struck a match, and the stench of sulfur filled the small space. The flame flared and receded. Con raised a lantern between them and peered at Shane's eye. He gave a whistle. "Just look at you! You'll have that bruise for a good while, make no mistake. Now stay put." He hooked the lantern on its rope above the table and crouched to rummage in a trunk against the wall.

Shane's lips quirked in a smile. "And where did you think I'd be getting off to, might I ask?"

Con retrieved a container of salve and a faded bandana from the trunk. "Hard telling, but I wouldn't put anything past you. You have a knack for bringing trouble down on your head, rushing in where angels fear to tread. What gives you the right to interfere with people?"

"I'd answer that question if I thought you'd understand. Ouch! Rub my eye any harder and there'll be nothing left to doctor."

Con continued scrubbing. "I don't suppose you want an infection. Ah, but this takes me back. Me patching you up after a scrap. You didn't use to put yourself in harm's way without the sense to defend yourself, though."

Shane sighed. "Must we go over all that again?"

"You still need convincing." Con reached for the tin of salve. "I don't want to find you in Boot Hill someday, or rotting on the prairie without a proper grave. A man who won't fight doesn't live long in the territories." After subjecting Shane to more of his ministrations, he stood back with a glint in his green eyes. "You look like death."

"Tact was always your redeeming quality, Cousin."

"Tell me, are you sure of your calling? That's something you should know for certain."

Shane's gaze fell before Con's direct scrutiny. He wanted—*needed*—to be sure of such a thing, but truth be told, he was not. He ought to summon the will to respond with enthusiasm, to cover his doubt, but no words came.

"Have you no answer, Sean?"

"Sometimes I doubt myself. No matter. I can't do less than honor my word to watch over the people in my circuit. They are my sacred charge."

"But what of *you*? Circuit preachers live hard lives and die early."

"Deputies aren't known for growing old in the sun, either." Shane couldn't resist pointing out another truth.

Con laid a hand on the back of his neck. "Yes, well. That's a different thing entirely. But now you mention it, I could be in trouble."

"What sort of trouble?"

"It's a long story. Let's just say I may need to remove myself from town in a hurry."

CHAPTER TWO

A RIFLE CLICKED IN THE DARKNESS.

America's feet hit the wagon box floor. Her hand closed on the stock of her rifle.

Liberty stirred in her rocking cradle.

America inched forward and parted the flaps that closed off the front of the wagon. A gibbous moon hung bright in the sky and reached fingers of light to touch the silver sagebrush. A long barrel gleamed, betraying the figure crouched where the front wheel of America's wagon was chained to Addie's rear wheel. That shock of curly hair could only belong to Addie's son, Travis.

Beyond the circled wagons, shadows slipped through the dimness, too slight to be buffalo. One leaped into a shaft of moonlight, revealing nothing more sinister than a herd of antelope foraging near the wagons.

She let out her breath with a sigh of relief.

Travis turned toward her wagon. From the angle of his head in the moonlight, America knew he'd seen her.

"What are you doing there?" Her voice quavered, giving away the fear that hadn't yet drained from her. "Surely the men can guard the wagons."

His shoulders slumped. Her careless words had wounded him. He jutted out his chin. "It's *my* turn to stand watch."

Travis had taken his father's place in the wagon train in more ways than she'd imagined, but it hardly seemed fair that a boy of thirteen should bear such a burden.

Liberty wailed, and America went back inside. She laid her weapon aside and lifted her baby from the cradle Richard had made before he died. She stroked Liberty's downy hair and for a time forgot all worries as she snuggled her tiny daughter against her on the narrow cot. Liberty slipped into slumber, and America soon followed.

Nate Whalen stepped into deepest shadow next to his wagon as young Travis's voice carried to him across the moonlit wagon circle. He relaxed when he caught sight of the Widow Reed talking to Travis. The boy must have made some sound that roused her.

It troubled Nate to see him guarding the wagon camp in his father's absence. He had no doubt Travis would do his diligent best to stand duty in his father's place, but anything could happen in a wagon train in these days of unrest. Why had the wagon master thought that allowing a boy to bear an adult responsibility was a good idea?

Travis didn't need coddling, but a little safeguarding seemed in order. Nate had taken to looking out for the boy without his knowledge, staying up to keep an ear out whenever Travis had night watch. Coupled with his own shifts guarding the wagon, sleep had been in short supply of late.

This had more to do with Travis than his mother, he told himself. Addie Martin had come to his notice, and he'd found himself increasingly smitten with her gentle ways. Loneliness and grief must hound her in the aftermath of her husband's death, but she carried herself with quiet dignity, never letting on that she suffered. That only made him want to ease her way all the more.

Love came without invitation at odd moments dictated by no man. It was far too soon after her husband's death to speak his mind, but he would count finding a wife of Addie's worth of more value than the richest gold strike.

The thud of hooves and rattle of chains roused America in the gloomy dimness. She untied the pucker string at the rear of the wagon and looked out. The sky had lightened toward morning while the wagon camp came alive with movement. She'd slept later than she intended. Between Liberty's interruptions and her own inexperience, it took her longer than most in the train to prepare for the day's journey. She usually liked to get a jump on the early chores.

She didn't have that luxury today. Men already moved among the livestock in the wagon circle. Young Johnny Taylor came from the river with careful steps while balancing a bucket of water in each hand. The Baker children darted about hunting firewood. Most of the women already stood over cooking fires with smoke spiraling.

Travis strode around the back of Addie's wagon. "Ma sent me to let you know the flapjacks are ready," he told America with a smile. "She says she won't take no for an answer."

America returned his smile. "I'll be right over."

As she approached, Addie poured steaming coffee into a tin cup. "Good morning. I hope you've recovered some from your ordeal yesterday."

America accepted the cup. "I'm bruised and sore but otherwise all right."

"You're lucky to be alive, according to Grant Hadley."

She took a warming sip from her cup and reflected on that. The grizzled scout's views, when he ventured them, were generally well-founded. "I'm thankful the Indians brought me back."

Addie flipped flapjacks in her three-legged spider skillet. "You must have done something to win their respect."

The image of an extended hand and a painted face flashed before her. Pulling her mind back to the present, she shook her head. "Cooperating was safer than running."

"It could have gone otherwise. Relations are tense after the army and cavalry put the Shoshone down at Bear River last winter. And then there was that incident at Bannack."

"Incident?"

"I sometimes forget you spent the winter alone on your homestead."

Another image intruded, that of buffalo wolves snarling over Richard's frozen remains. She'd fired her rifle to drive them away long enough to retrieve her husband's body. With the ground frozen after the blizzard, she'd had to pile stones over him in the hopes of keeping the wolves away until she could bury him properly.

She shuddered. "I don't like to think on it."

Addie's face held sympathy. "I'm sorry for what you've suffered."

America frowned into her cup. "I survived, anyway."

"No woman should have to birth alone. I'm thankful the good Lord watched over you and that he brought you to Fort Hall in safety."

If God cared for her, He would not have taken her husband away. America didn't speak her thoughts aloud. Addie, with her resolute faith in God, wouldn't want to hear them. "What happened at Bannack last winter?"

Addie dished up the flapjacks and offered the plate to America. "Help yourself to molasses and bacon." She poured more batter in the pan. "It was terrible. Two men took it into their heads to shoot into some tepees outside of town, and all because an Indian woman wanted nothing to do with one of them. An old chief, a young boy, and a baby died, as well as several miners who ran to see what was going on."

"What happened to the men who did the shooting?" She plucked the wooden spoon from the molasses crock and trickled a thin stream over her flapjacks.

"From what I hear, very little."

America looked up in surprise. "Just what kind of place *is* Bannack?"

Addie filled Nathan Whalen's bowl with venison stew. After watching his pathetic efforts for weeks now, she'd finally broken down and offered him food. Maybe she shouldn't have done it, but honestly, what harm could it do to feed a malnourished man?

"I'm obliged, Mrs. Martin." Warm brown eyes returned her smile with a lingering look.

What harm indeed? Had she given the wrong impression by inviting Nate to supper? Surely he couldn't think that she, barely a widow, had any interest in finding another husband. Fear of such a misunderstanding had kept her from inviting him to her fireside until now. She'd hardened her heart to his plight, despite the longing looks he'd cast in her direction whenever the smell of her cooking wafted across the wagon circle.

It was hard not to notice the unvarying portions of burnt bacon, cold beans, and hardtack Nate consumed. This afternoon, a sweet melody he'd played on his harmonica had pierced her heart. He couldn't know that "When Summer Flowers are Blowing" was her mother's favorite song. Addie's resolve had weakened, and now he sat across the fire making inroads into a plate of stew while she watched, tongue-tied as a schoolgirl.

If she was honest, she'd admit to herself she was famished too, but in a different way. She missed Clyde beside her, the touch of his hand at her elbow, his conversation. She'd never understood until now how a person could feel alone even in the company of others.

She clasped her hands together. "I appreciate you looking out for Travis during night watch."

He smiled. "Glad to do it whenever we stand guard together, but with that boy's gumption and good sense, you might as easily ask him to look out for me."

A smile touched her lips. "His father would be proud to hear you say that."

"I reckon." Nate returned his attention to his stew.

The silence stretched too long. What else could they talk about? Addie latched onto another subject. "Do you know when we'll reach Bannack?"

"Probably tomorrow." He spoke around a bite of biscuit.

"That soon? I didn't realize we were so near." She sighed. "I'll be thankful to end this journey. I can't wait for the chance to take a ba—to wash clothes."

His eyes shone with humor.

The wind ruffling the grasses lifted Addie's hair and cooled her flaming cheeks. She searched for something else to talk about. "Travis should be back soon. He's gone to fetch water."

"I see that." He nodded toward the Snake River flowing past the wagons, where Travis leaned above the grassy bank and dipped a bucket into shining water. Overhead, a heron beat its wings and opened its throat in a raucous call. Travis straightened to watch the bird. He stood outlined against the Bitterroot Mountains that jutted above the plain.

"More biscuits?" She extended the plate.

He took two. "You watch yourself in Bannack. There's plenty of hungry miners who'll want to get hitched to a good cook like you."

Not quite able to meet his eyes, she addressed her remark to his ear. "I don't plan to marry again, Mr. Whalen. Mr. Martin was a good man, and I loved him." There, it was said. She heaved a breath. "At least I still have our son."

"That's a comfort."

"Travis is a good boy, almost grown. It's hard on him, but he shoulders a man's responsibilities now."

Nate hesitated. "Must you go on to Bannack? Miners there are a rough lot."

"I didn't want to come west in the first place, but my

husband insisted after hearing about the gold strike at Grasshopper Creek. He sold everything, and now we've got nothing to go back to. In a manner of speaking, gold fever killed him." She clasped her arms about herself. "Be careful, Mr. Whalen, or it'll get you too."

The warmth in his eyes faded. "I'll take my chances, thanks all the same."

Travis walked past Nate and set the buckets down at Addie's feet. "Water's good and cold."

"It should be," Nate said. "It runs from snow melt."

Addie smiled at her son. "Mr. Whalen tells me you have gumption."

"I guess so. Leastways, I do when it comes to looking out for my own." The direct look he gave Nate left no doubt as to his meaning.

"I should go now." Nate smiled at Addie. "Thanks again. I enjoyed the food and the company."

"You're sure you won't take more?"

He shook his head, and his glance traveled to Travis. "Thank you, no. I don't want to wear out my welcome."

"So you're just going to quit?"

Shane looked up from packing his saddlebags and focused his good eye on his cousin, confronting him from across the scarred table. Early sunlight from the window behind him haloed his rumpled head. Conan wore a red-striped shirt and tan trousers, but his feet remained bare.

Shane sighed. "I don't understand you at all, Conan Walsh. Only last night you warned me against staying. Something about ending up in an early grave as I recall."

"Maybe I wanted to see if you still would. Stay, that is."

"I don't take your logic."

"I hate to see you run away."

"I'm simply moving along my circuit." Shane spoke in clipped tones, enunciating each word. He tightened his jaw, yanked open the door, and stepped outside into a fine day at odds with his mood. The contrast brought him up short. "See you next time." He nodded to Con.

His cousin offered him a faint smile. "Stay safe."

Shane pulled the door closed between them more gently than he had at first intended and turned his steps toward Chrisman's store. He shouldn't have lashed out at his cousin for being so infuriatingly right. He would return to Bannack, but right now he craved the freedom of the open road. He yearned for the chance to be alone with his thoughts and draw close to God in solitude.

He had never fit in here at Bannack, a fact his blackened eye announced for all to see. Other stops on his circuit welcomed him more, and at the moment he needed a rest from the struggle of trying to reach his flock in Bannack.

George Chrisman eyed him from behind the counter as he entered his store. "What happened to you? Come up against the wrong side of a mule?"

Shane attempted a smile. "It's nothing."

"Sure don't look like nothing from here. That eye is a mite colorful."

Shane placed a tin of hoof salve on the counter and laid his money down right when Donald Dillingham emerged from the sheriff's office at the back of the store. The deputy pushed his hat back on his head and swept a steady gray gaze over Shane. "I reckon you'll be leaving town."

Shane bristled. "I do have a circuit to complete."

Dillingham held up his beefy hands. "Now don't take any meaning from what I said. As a circuit rider, you're already bolder than most in this town, including the coward who blackened that eye. Who did it?"

"I'm surprised no one's told you." Shane's voice held a dry note. The male residents of Bannack enjoyed swapping stories in Chrisman's store.

Chrisman's eyes lit. "It's early yet."

"True enough." Shane squared his shoulders. "I'll be on my way before it gets any later."

Chrisman gave a nod. "Yes, go before the jawing starts. Miners can be a rude bunch."

Dillingham grasped Shane's hand. "God speed, Reverend. Remember to keep eyes and ears open, and you'll live longer."

Shane smiled. "I suppose a man can pray with his eyes open." He picked up the tin of salve, pushed through the door, and stepped onto the boardwalk.

Gunshots punched the air, and Shane skidded to a halt. Confusion broke out everywhere at once as men brandishing firearms spilled into the street.

"Indians are killing whites!" someone shouted.

"Watch out for the Injuns!" another voice warned.

Several dark-skinned natives that had been visiting the town rode into the hills.

Gunshots ricocheted.

One of the Indians turned at the top of a hill and shook his blanket in a message of fury. His pursuers took aim, but he disappeared over the crest of the hill before they could shoot him.

A shriek tore through the willows lining the creek.

Men carrying guns pursued another Indian escaping up the hill. When they came within firing range, the fleeing man turned back to his pursuers with hands raised. "Good Injun!"

They fired anyway.

He staggered, screaming, into a stand of trees.

"For the love of God, stop this!" Shane shouted. He might as well have whispered for all the impact he made. No one heeded him.

Running footsteps pounded toward him, and he stepped aside barely in time to avoid a collision with Dillingham. He hurried after the deputy. Dillingham turned down a street. A small crowd parted for him.

Shane followed with a sinking in his gut. The scene that met his eyes made him shudder. Dillingham stood in silence looking down at a prostrate figure. Shane recognized the features of the dead man with sorrow.

Dillingham swung back to the crowd. "Who killed Chief Snag?"

No one answered.

"Tell me what happened!" he thundered.

A miner Shane knew as John Carroll pushed through the crowd. "Buck Stinson shot him in cold blood while the chief was talking with his daughter, Jimmy Spence's Indian wife." Bitterness edged his voice. "Buck said he'd learn Indians not to kill whites. Afterwards, he and his pals shouted about Indians killing whites to cover what Buck did." His jaw worked. "I say hang the murderer."

"You would say that." George Dalton, a young miner with blazing red hair, shouted at John Carroll. "What with raising Snag's granddaughter like your own and all, everybody knows you're an Injun lover. When are you going to paint your face too?"

"Now, now." Dillingham put up a hand. "There's no call for rudeness."

Dalton snorted. "Indians were mighty rude, I'd say, when they killed those miners last week."

"That's only a rumor, so far as we know." Crossing his arms, Carroll glared at Dalton.

Angry voices snarled at one another within the crowd.

"This isn't about loving or hating Indians." Shane found his voice. "It's about what's decent."

"That so?" A big man, one of the town's merchants, leaned over the body. His hunting knife flashed. "I thought it was about keeping my scalp." He straightened and held aloft a hank of skin and hair. Laughter, shouts, and curses blistered the air.

Shane's stomach heaved. He staggered backward, tripped over his own feet, and fell hard. Rolling onto his hands and knees, he fought the urge to retch. These people didn't want his message of peace. He might as well face the truth. He had failed in his duty to them.

The door banged open, and Shane lifted his head from his hands. Moonlight reached him across the rough floor.

"What's this?" Con asked from the doorway. "Still here?" A match struck and flared as Con lit the lantern. "Why are you sitting in the dark, Cousin?"

"I couldn't seem to care."

Con flung himself into one of the chairs at the table. "I thought you planned to leave today."

"I thought so too, but circumstances changed my plans. Even I know not to travel alone at such a time. How many died today?"

Con ran a hand through his dark hair, leaving it rumpled. His face wore a haggard expression. "Three Indians, and the men who started the trouble almost went to the noose. We sent them packing instead. This was a hard day, and it's not quite done."

"How so?"

Con rubbed the bristles on his chin. "I don't suppose you prepared any food?"

"No, but I can make myself useful by cooking something for you." He heaved to his feet and started toward the rough board that served as a kitchen counter.

"It will have to be quick. Chrisman heard there's a wagon train camped on the Indians' side of the hill. A group of us will ride out tonight to escort them to town."

"Let's hope nothing goes amiss."

"Amen to that. You made a wise choice postponing your

journey. For the time being, you're better to remain in Bannack."

"Where it's safe?" Bitterness crept into Shane's tone.

"Where it's *safer*. You'd meant to stay longer, anyway."

"The sooner I leave, the better."

"Better for who? The sacred charges you're running out on or you?"

"I'm tired, Con." The words wrenched from his soul. "Maybe by the time I return I'll have figured out how to reach this town."

Con filled a tin cup from a jug of water on the table and drank it down in one gulp. He wiped his mouth with the back of his hand. "You won't come back."

"Is that so? Maybe I should ask you what I mean to do instead of trying to sort it out myself."

"No need to snap at me."

Shane reined in his temper. Con was in a foul mood, but he didn't have to respond in kind. "I'm sorry. My head aches."

"You said yourself that you're thinking of leaving the ministry."

"Not in so many words, but I'll admit I've come to question my calling. Why do you care so much what I do?"

Con's finger traced one of the scars in the table. "Maybe I wanted to see what you saw, to believe there could be something better." He looked up, his green eyes dark. "But I reckon you don't believe it yourself."

"That's unfair and untrue."

Con's gaze fell. "I'm sorry."

"My belief in God isn't about being a preacher, just so you know. There's so much more to faith than service. It's a quiet joy, a sense of peace, and the assurance that life won't destroy you, even when you don't know how to go on."

The strain in Con's face eased. "You almost make me think it's possible to leave the slum behind, after all."

CHAPTER THREE

WIND WHINED INTO THE CABIN, LIGHTNING flared, and rain
lashed the window. Even if Shane hadn't been wide awake, he
would have found it hard to sleep. He hauled himself out of
the small bed Con had rigged for him with rope and a mattress
tick along one wall. On his way to the table, his toe rammed
into something solid, and he yelped in pain. Fumbling for
matches, he knocked over the cup of water he hadn't finished
drinking the night before. The spreading spill missed the
matches, fortunately. He struck one and touched the burning
tip to the lantern wick. Light fell across his open Bible. He'd
read it until late in the night, seeking answers to the questions
that tormented him.

Words stood out on the page where he'd left off reading, an
account of the Apostle John's vision in the book of Revelation,
chapter twenty-one. "And I saw a new heaven and a new earth:
for the first heaven and the first earth were passed away; and
there was no more sea. And I, John, saw the holy city, New
Jerusalem, coming down from God out of heaven, prepared as
a bride adorned for her husband. And I heard a great voice out
of heaven saying, Behold, the tabernacle of God is with men,
and he will dwell with them, and they shall be his people, and
God himself shall be with them, and be their God. And God
shall wipe away all tears from their eyes; and there shall be no
more death, neither sorrow, nor crying, neither shall there be
any more pain: for the former things are passed away."

In the wake of what Shane had seen yesterday, it was hard
to picture a world without death, sorrow, weeping, or pain.
Bannack was closer to the place pictured a few Scriptures later:

"But the fearful, and unbelieving, and the abominable, and murderers, and whoremongers, and sorcerers, and idolaters, and all liars, shall have their part in the lake which burneth with fire and brimstone: which is the second death."

A gust shook the cabin, and Shane spared a thought for Con and the other men who had gone to help the wagon train. They'd known the storm was coming but had ridden out to alert the settlers to danger and lead them to safety. In this simple act of human compassion, he found his answer.

If he left the circuit, he'd be abandoning lost souls to their fate. He had to warn them about the second death and give them the hope of heaven. They might mock him, spit in his face, and bash him with their fists. He could even be killed. Ah, but violence at their hands held less fear for him than leaving his duty undone. He stared at the simple truth and accepted it as his fate.

"Watch out!" Amesly's panicked voice catapulted America from sleep. She sat up, straining to hear. Wind shook the wagon, making it creak and groan as if moving. America knew that for an illusion, for her wagon stood parked, its front wheels lashed to Addie's rear ones. Light flared across the bonnet. A rifle report cracked the air. Thunder rumbled and the wagon plunged back into darkness.

Several shouts went up at once outside the wagon. The sound of running feet thudded past.

Liberty started screaming.

Heart racing, America groped for her rifle. She crept to the rear of the wagon and peered out.

The heavens hid behind clouds, pierced here and there by moonbeams that lit the falling rain. The wind carried the sound of voices in snatches but obscured the words they spoke. From the edge of the wagon circle, a figure detached and floated toward her, appearing for all the world like a specter. The hair on the back of her neck lifted, and she cocked her rifle.

The shadow wore bloomers and clutched a shawl. "Psst! It's only me."

"Addie?" America let out her breath, easing her finger on the trigger.

"All's well." Addie closed the distance between them. "Amesly swears up and down that he heard Indians, but it was only a bear come to drink from the river."

"A bear?"

"Don't sound so scared. It's dead now. He took it for an Indian and shot it."

Liberty's wails penetrated the night, the louder for having been ignored.

"I have to get my baby. Come inside if you like."

"All right. I'll keep you company while you tend her."

America felt her way in the dark toward the rocking cradle. "Will you light a lamp?" she asked Addie over her shoulder.

The wagon creaked when Addie climbed aboard. A match scraped and sent up an acrid stench. America picked up her daughter and held her close.

"After all the excitement, I doubt I'll get back to sleep any time soon." Addie stretched to hang the lighted lantern on its hook. Her swaying shawl made shadows jump.

"My, yes." America raised her voice to be heard above Liberty's screams.

With a fresh diaper, a full stomach, and a tiny fist in her mouth, Liberty eventually quieted. Before long, her gentle gasps signaled that she slept, and America and Addie shared a smile. But when America tried to lower the baby into her cradle, Liberty startled awake and screamed once again.

America picked her up with a sigh. "This may be a long night."

"Here, let me take her." Addie held out her hands.

She gave Addie a doubtful look but placed Liberty in her arms.

Addie cradled the baby, and the piercing cries subsided into slumber.

"How did you do that?" America whispered in awe.

Addie smiled. "I have a way with babies."

"You certainly do."

"It comes in handy." She laid Liberty in her cradle.

America sat on the edge of the feather mattress leaving room for Addie. "Thanks for staying with me. Caring for a baby all alone in the middle of the night is lonely work."

Addie joined her on the tick. "I remember. Clyde helped me some, but husbands don't really understand a woman's burdens. Unless Travis was sick or teething, tending him in the small hours fell mostly on me."

A gust rocked the wagon as rain lashed the bonnet. The lantern swung on its hook, brightening then dimming as shadows raced in.

"Goodness!" America spared a thought for her oxen, out in such weather. The beasts would take rain in stride, but thunder and lightning unsettled them.

"I'll wait it out for a while before going back to my wagon if you don't mind."

"Of course not. I'm wide awake now."

Addie chuckled. "Maybe we should stay up and wait for morning. Bannack is only a short drive away, thankfully. We can rest there for a couple of days before setting up our cook tent."

"That sounds wonderful."

"If there's a vacancy at the hotel, I've a mind to rent us a room so we can clean up and get a good night's sleep. How does that sound?"

"That's kind of you." The idea of bathing sounded wonderful. A night under a proper roof where the pattering rain wouldn't keep a person awake wouldn't go amiss either.

"Addie? What do you think Bannack will be like?"

"From what I've heard, it sounds a fearsome place." The answer came out of the dark. "I'll admit that's not at all what I imagined."

Sleep tugged at America, and she closed her eyes to rest them a moment. "Why do you want to stay there then?"

"Where else would I go? At least in Bannack I can make enough money to provide for my son."

America couldn't leave it alone. "What do you hope for your future, though?"

Silence met her for so long she almost gave up on receiving an answer, but then Addie stirred. "I wanted, once, to have a simple life, to love my husband and be loved as we built our family together." She sighed. "Those days are gone forever. Now all I can think about is surviving. I would like Travis to know something better in his life, though."

"That's my wish for Liberty."

"Do you want nothing for yourself?"

She thought of Richard, buried in the shallow grave she'd made for him. "My life is over."

"That doesn't have to be." Addie's fingers twined about hers. "We'll make a way for ourselves somehow."

America squeezed her hand in silent agreement.

"Don't feel you have to stay on with me if you've a mind to go elsewhere." Addie gave her a gentle smile. "I'd love to have you, but I don't want to hold you back if you have other ideas."

"Where else would I go?" America echoed her earlier sentiment but with a feeling of unease. Owning a cook tent was Addie's dream, not hers. But how could she deny her friend help after everything she had done for her? Still, the day might come when she'd want to leave.

"I hope you don't feel obligated, that's all." Addie patted America's hand, yawned, and stood to her feet. "I'd better go back to my wagon now that the rain has let up. Morning will come early, I expect."

America saw Addie out of the wagon and doused the lantern. Then she sank into her feather mattress and fell at once into slumber.

Voices and thudding hooves dragged her awake before dawn had a chance to arrive. America moaned, rolled over, and pulled the quilt over her head. Whatever the trouble, she felt unable to face it after the fright she'd already suffered tonight. The sounds wouldn't go away, however, and grew more urgent.

She threw back her quilt and heaved herself out of bed.

A glance outside showed a group of men riding into the moonlit camp. The rain had let up while she slept, but puddles shone on the ground and wind still buffeted the wagons.

Her fingers fumbled with the buttons of the blue wool dress that, being her darkest garment, made do as mourning garb. Liberty didn't stir, despite the new sounds, and America bent to reassure herself that her baby still breathed.

"Ma'am?" a voice called from the rear of the wagon.

"One moment," she answered in a hushed voice.

Liberty stirred but settled back to sleep.

Grant Hadley stood below the wagon steps, his hat in his hands. "We're going to hitch up now."

"Why? And who are those men?"

"It's nothing to worry about, but there's trouble with the Indians at Bannack. The town sent an escort to see us to safety."

"In the middle of the night?"

"It's near morning. With the camp awake, we thought we should get a jump on the day. When it comes to Indians, it's better safe than sorry."

"I suppose that's true." She dragged out the words, not sure she believed that anymore. "I'll prepare."

Grant Hadley moved on.

America withdrew into her wagon and pulled on her high-topped walking boots. She bent to lace them, hoping Liberty would remain asleep long enough for her to hitch the team.

With the camp in an uproar, that seemed unlikely.

Light bloomed along one side of the wagon bonnet. "America?" Addie whispered.

"Just a moment." America met her at the bottom of the steps.

"Shall I stay with Liberty while you hitch your team?" Lantern light put shadows and hollows into Addie's face. "Travis will be over to help after he's seen to our oxen."

"Thank you."

"You don't sound happy about the idea."

"Oh, no. It's not that. I hate being so dependent on the kindness of others."

"That mindset landed you in a passel of trouble the other day. It's a mercy you weren't scalped. For Liberty's sake, if not for your own, let us help you."

Addie was right, although she knew Pete Amesly wouldn't see it that way. The notion stirred a memory. "I wonder if Amesly did hear Indians last night."

"Perish the thought."

"If he did, they meant us no harm."

"I doubt that. I hear tell the natives are up in arms. No, Amesly must have been mistaken."

America frowned but said no more. What if Amesly had heard Indians? That would mean they had gone by in peace, leaving them unmolested. The image of her captor smiling as he let her go returned to raise a question in her mind.

Could the Indians be different than any of them imagined?

By some miracle Liberty remained asleep, so Addie held the lantern while America roped her two lead oxen and tied them to the wagon. Richard had yoked the beasts with no trouble, but she couldn't heft the yoke like he could. She had to twist the first ox's head sideways and flip the oxbow that rested on its neck to attach it to the end of the yoke she'd left leaning against the wagon. Then she'd hurry to lift the other side of the yoke, thereby straightening the first ox's neck while pinning the second's bow to the yoke as well.

The whole business made her uneasy. She had to stand between the shifting beasts, and if she fumbled, injury could result.

As if sensing her hesitancy, the oxen always fidgeted, and today was no exception. She approached Babe, who gazed at her with a placid eye but backed a step. Taffy shifted sideways to avoid her.

She had to do this, but each time seemed harder than before. Either Babe or Taffy could shift and crush her at any moment. What then would happen to her baby without a mother to protect her? If only Richard were alive to take this chore from her.

"May I be of assistance, ma'am?" A big man astride a horse doffed his hat.

Liberty began crying inside the wagon, no doubt awakened by the man's deep voice.

He dismounted and nodded to America and Addie in turn. "If I may introduce myself, I'm Donald Dillingham, a deputy of Bannack."

"Good morning. I'd better see to your baby, America." Addie sounded weary.

"Thank you," America called to her softly.

"I'm happy to help." Addie set the lantern on top of the blocked wagon wheel and dutifully climbed the rear steps into the wagon.

America looked up at the stranger wearing dark clothes and a deputy's star. He handled his horse well and would have no problem managing a couple of willful oxen. "Morning," she answered civilly before turning to place the oxbows on the animals' necks by herself.

"Here, let me do that." He dismounted in an easy movement.

"Thank you for your offer, but I can manage." As she spoke,

one of the oxen tilted its head to look at her. She stepped out of the way of its swinging horn. Her heart pounded, but she schooled her features to hide the fear the episode had induced.

The deputy stood with his feet apart. "I hate to see a woman tending heavy chores, no disrespect to your husband."

"My husband is in the grave, sir."

"I apologize for my thoughtless remark. Please accept my condolences." He walked toward her, coming within the circle cast by the lantern. Light gleamed in his brown hair and thrust the planes of his face into relief. He was younger than he'd at first seemed. He smiled. "Perhaps you'll let me redeem myself by helping you."

"Truly, that's not necessary."

"It would comfort me to lend a hand. It goes against the grain to stand by while a lady struggles at a task I can easily manage."

"Well, all right, since you put it that way." She stepped out from between the oxen with more than a little relief. "I appreciate the kindness."

He rested his hat on the wagon box and, moving with deft skill, yoked the pair of oxen in minutes. "Are those yours as well?" He gestured toward the two dark shapes grazing in the wagon circle, barely visible beneath the lightening sky. The others must have already been yoked by their owners.

She caught herself gaping and shut her mouth. "They are."

"If I may?"

"Thank you." She disliked being beholden to someone she didn't know but hated holding up the wagon train even more.

Dillingham made short work of roping the oxen and led them to the wagon to be yoked.

"Thank you, Mr. Dillingham. That would have taken me far longer."

A slight figure hurried out of the shadows toward them. "Mrs. Reed, do you need any help?"

"Thanks for the offer, Travis." America cocked her head.

Liberty had stopped crying, but her hiccups carried through the canvas of the wagon bonnet. "I need to check my baby."

"Go ahead." Dillingham lifted the second yoke onto the oxen's shoulders. "This lad and I will have your team hitched and ready in no time."

The glow from the lantern on the wagon wheel penetrated the bonnet to cast soft light into the interior. Addie sat on the edge of the bed patting Liberty's back. Sucking her fist, she breathed in soft gasps.

America reached for her. "Thanks for minding the baby."

Addie smiled. "It's never a hardship. I'd best get back to my wagon, though."

Liberty snuggled against her neck, and America wrapped the soft blanket more securely around her, grateful for the luxury of holding her daughter while others hitched her team.

Outside the wagon, the lantern withdrew. She went to look out, and Travis met her at the rear of her wagon, offering a shy smile. "Ma has leftover johnnycake when you want it, and Deputy Dillingham said to tell you goodbye."

"Thanks again." She smiled at Travis with a nudge of guilt. He had enough to do without taking on her chores, but he didn't seem to mind that nearly so much as she did.

Travis raised the lantern, shedding more light as she climbed down the steps. In his other hand, he held a bullwhip. "We'll head out soon. Jimmy Baker and Ted Lewis have gone to walk ahead with lanterns." Did she detect a note of envy in his voice? Guiding the wagon train with lanterns by night must seem a rare privilege for a half-grown boy.

America's team, hitched and ready, stood before her wagon. She ran a hand over Taffy and patted Babe in forgiveness, then stepped back as the wagon train moved out.

"Get up! Haw!" Travis lashed the whip on the ground.

The oxen lumbered forward. America's wagon lurched and swung into place behind Addie's. They were lining up single file to follow the boys carrying lanterns on foot.

"I'll go and walk beside your ma for a bit," America shouted to Travis.

He nodded that he'd heard her. "Do you want the lantern?"

"You need it worse than I do."

"Careful of rattlers. They can come out at night, just so you know."

She held tightly to her baby while scanning the ground for snake holes. Catching up to Addie wouldn't take long. Liberty remained quiet, content to be held close to her mother's heart. The wind tugged at America's plaited hair, making her regret not putting on a bonnet. She didn't much like wearing them, so she went without one most of the time, but sometimes nothing else would do.

She slowed as she reached Addie. Her friend walked beside her team, clutching a bullwhip and a small bundle in one hand and a lantern in the other.

"It's leftover johnnycake from yesterday." Addie placed the cloth-wrapped bundle in America's hand. "I wish I could give you coffee to go with it."

"I'm thankful for this much." She could never repay Addie for all she'd done.

They walked in silence for a time while America ate the johnnycake, a cornmeal waybread that filled her belly. Dawn light spread across the sky, painting it in shades of red and gold.

An ox strayed. Addie flicked her whip and lashed the ground beside it to bring the beast into line. "Did I ever mention that I like your full name? America Liberty Reed. So patriotic. I've been meaning to ask how you came by it."

America swallowed a bite of johnnycake. "My father belonged to the Liberty Party."

"The Liberty Party?" Addie crinkled her brow in obvious puzzlement.

America stepped around a puddle left by the night's rains. "It didn't last long, but it stood against slavery."

Addie scowled. "I'll be glad when this horrible war between the states is over."

"I'm sorry to have reminded you of it." She filled her lungs with cool morning air scented by damp grass. "I'd hoped to hear at Fort Bridger of its end."

"I wish matters could have resolved so quickly." Addie glanced at her. "Were you so isolated on your homestead that you knew nothing of the war?"

America shook her head. "Who would bring me news?"

"Did no one visit you at all?" Amazement filled Addie's voice.

She kept her eyes on the path beneath her feet. "I was snowed in all winter."

"And birthed alone? I can't imagine."

"I survived." America let the simple statement speak for all the heartache, terror, and suffering she preferred not to recall. That time in her life had ended.

"How did you ever manage? I'm sure I wouldn't have."

"You would have done just fine." Addie had a resilient nature and would have survived in such circumstances, maybe even better than America had.

"The spring thaw must have relieved your mind considerably."

"It didn't, actually. I tried so hard to keep my home. I didn't want to give up everything Richard and I had built. I broke as much ground as I could, but I'm not the farmer my husband was. I planted too soon, and frost withered my seedlings. I had no choice but to leave. Liberty and I would have starved for sure."

"Leaving may have been for the best." Addie lashed her whip again. "I hate to think of you all alone on a homestead with a baby. You're so young to have suffered so. May the good Lord spare you further hardship."

America murmured polite thanks and kept her doubts to herself. Addie's good Lord had taken the two people who meant the most to her—first Gramma, and then Richard—right when she needed them most. She could only think that God meant to punish her. But then, for her sins, perhaps she deserved it.

CHAPTER FOUR

AMERICA STUMBLED ON HER SKIRTS, WHICH had grown heavy with mud as she walked alongside the oxen. Abandoning modesty in favor of practicality as some of the other women in the wagon train had already done, she tucked the hem of her skirts into the belt at her waist. This bared the lower part of her legs, but her thick boots encased that portion of her anatomy.

She'd left Liberty sleeping in the wagon, something she couldn't always allow. Sometimes the trail narrowed where the geography forced the wagons to follow one after the other. When that happened, ruts dug so deeply into the earth that traveling over them canted the wagons at angles too severe for comfort or safety. In places where they could fan out, the wagons made better progress, but she nonetheless had to contend with sagebrush, stinging nettles, and the barbs of prickly pear. These discomforts paled in contrast to the possibility of stepping on a rattlesnake, however.

Her wagon crested a hill behind Addie's and started down the other side. The way before them led to a town, its jumbled buildings sprawling in the sun beyond a grove of cottonwoods through which a creek wended. The grasses in the open spaces surrounding the town had a stubby appearance, cropped short by the herds of mules and oxen that must have foraged them in previous days.

The branches of the cottonwoods, budding with new life, closed above her. The wagons rolled to a stop in a clearing. Addie, wearing a calico bonnet as protection from the sun, walked back to her. "Nate—Mr. Whalen tells me we have to camp here at the edge of Yankee Flats. It's the part of Bannack where Union sympathizers live."

"What will we do? There's no forage." The small amount of feed she carried wouldn't sustain her oxen long.

"A ranch six miles away rents pasturage."

She wanted to weep at the thought of going on any farther. "Is taking them there safe? We had to have an escort into town."

"Probably no less risky than staying in Bannack itself. Thankfully, Nate offered to drive my oxen. Bill Baker will include yours with his own team if you like."

America blew out a breath. "I can't thank him enough for doing that. My feet ache, I'm half frozen, and all I want to do is catch up on the sleep I've missed." Pete's bear, the baby, and the men guiding the wagon train into Bannack had all contributed to her restless night.

Addie brightened. "We can rent a room at the hotel, clean up, and take a nap. What do you say? I promised to treat you."

"Thank you. That sounds heavenly." America welcomed the chance to change out of her wet clothing, wash in privacy, and sleep with a solid roof over her head.

The fringed dimity curtain dropped into place across the hotel window, shutting out the sight of rough buildings cupped by the sagebrush-dotted hillside folding down from the sky. America stifled a yawn. She'd slept soundly, and no wonder.

She couldn't have afforded to pay for lodging at the Merrick Hotel where Addie had splurged on a suite of rooms for a couple of nights. She registered just past noon and, after bathing, they'd lain down for a nap.

She checked Liberty in her rocking cradle beside the bed, lying motionless in slumber. Tuckered out from her crying jag the night before, followed by the journey, she probably wouldn't stir for some time. America smoothed the tan calico frock she'd changed into after bathing. While the light color didn't suit a widow in mourning, she couldn't wear her blue wool, which needed laundering and her trunk held nothing darker. When leaving St. Louis as Richard's bride, she'd never dreamed that within a year she would need widow's weeds.

Addie's rasping breaths, hovering on the edge of snoring, came from the brass bed they'd shared. After nights spent sleeping in a makeshift bed on a false floor above the supplies in her wagon, napping on a feather tick seemed incredibly luxurious. She hadn't wanted to get up, but the lingering excitement of so recently reaching their destination had summoned her from bed.

She should remove herself from the room so as not to wake Liberty or Addie, but showing herself downstairs unescorted wouldn't be proper. That left the balcony as her only option. She brushed the tangles from her hair in the standing mirror on top of the polished oak chest of drawers. Leaving her hair loose, she tiptoed to the balcony door. The knob rattled under her hand, and she glanced back at the two sleepers.

Neither stirred.

Open to the sky, the balcony extended over the front porch. America curled her fingers around the railing as the breeze lifted tendrils of hair from her neck. Scents wafted to her in the rain-washed air—the sweetness of lavender from the soap she'd used and a rich overtone of cedar her dress had picked up from the trunk lining. She hadn't felt this clean in a long while.

Muffled laughter carried from the lower floor of the hotel. Otherwise, the town seemed quiet. Although a couple of men walked down the boardwalk, the rutted mud of Main Street lay undisturbed. It had dried somewhat since their arrival but would still not be pleasant to travel.

A door creaked open below. Laughter, the chink of glass, and the stench of tobacco mingling with whiskey rose to her.

She'd glimpsed swinging doors that might lead to a bar when they'd first arrived, but it was early yet for partaking of spirits.

One voice in particular drew her notice as it rose and fell in conversation with another. She couldn't understand anything either one said, so listening to the sound of them didn't seem like eavesdropping. Gripping the balcony rail, she leaned out, the better to hear the intriguing cadences.

A door whined open and thudded shut. Boots thumped on the wooden porch boards. The footsteps stopped underneath America. She jerked upright, heat flaring in her cheeks. It wouldn't do to be caught hanging over the balcony rail like a hoyden.

"I'm not the one you should ask," a deep voice rumbled. "Sheriff Plummer's your man, and he's gone off to Sun River to get hitched."

"Are you not the owner of this hotel?"

About to steal toward the balcony door and escape, America paused, arrested by his accent. Now that she could hear it better, he must be Irish.

"Well, yes, but—"

"Tell me. Do you fear God, Atticus?"

"Of course I do, but I also fear the mischief this town might get into if we close the saloons and bars for an entire day."

"Do you really believe that?"

Silence followed, punctuated by a whinny from the stables.

"Ask Sheriff Plummer when he returns."

"And that's your whole mind on the matter?"

"It is."

"Very well."

At any moment, one or both of the men could step onto the boardwalk and find her out. America eyed the closed balcony door. She'd never reach it without her footsteps being heard. Even if she could, the handle might rattle. The door would probably creak on its hinges, betraying her. She'd left it too late to make her presence known without embarrassment and would have to brazen things out, and the sooner, the better. She drew breath to announce herself.

A single pair of boot steps crossed the porch. The door screeched open and slammed shut. The other man thumped across the porch, and the door opened and shut again.

America let out her breath, weak with relief. Both men had gone inside, but what in the world had they been talking about?

A commotion started. Did it have something to do with the conversation she'd overheard? Her curiosity overruled caution, and she crept forward to listen. Raised voices and laughter reached her and, could it be—

Surely not . . . *singing?*

Feet scuffled, the door burst open, and a man splatted into the muddy street.

America stifled her gasp.

A man wearing a black bowler edged into sight on the porch steps. "Stop pushing in where you're not invited." He rubbed his hands together. "Come to think of it, I should have blacked your other eye."

The man in the street lay still as if stunned. An urge to go to his aid took possession of America, but she didn't know enough about the situation and shouldn't take such a risk. She had her baby to consider.

He turned his head, scraped mud from his face, and sat up. His blue eyes, made more striking by the purple bruise ringing one of them, focused on her.

America stood transfixed, unable to speak. She felt as if they had somehow touched.

He collected his slouch hat, which had fallen near him. "All right, Atticus," he said in lilting Irish tones. "I won't sing anymore, but I *will* speak."

Atticus pushed his bowler back on his head, revealing hair the color of a fox's tail. His gray coat, black vest, and gray trousers matched the formality of his bowler hat. "Stay out of my hotel, Shane."

"He's as hardheaded as they come," a second man, out of America's sight, slurred. "Maybe we should get it over and done with." A gun bolt clicked.

"Gentlemen!" America spoke without thought, sounding far calmer than she felt.

Atticus tilted his head and looked upward.

She mustered the courage to speak. "I feel the need to inform you of my presence."

"Well, I'll be hanged!" A man sprang from the porch onto the boardwalk. He turned toward her while a fraying hat that might have once been tan flopped about his head. Gray threaded his faded brown beard and hair. He wore black suspenders, without which his trousers would have sloughed off his thin frame. "Where'd you come from?" He waved his gun hand in a way that made her wonder how much liquor he'd consumed.

America found her tongue again. "I must apologize. I meant only to take the air, but I seem to have intruded into a private matter."

Atticus gave a smooth smile. "Please don't take it to heart, ma'am. There's no harm done. I'm Atticus Merrick, owner of this establishment."

"Thank you for your assurances, Mr. Merrick, but I must ask that you release this unfortunate fellow. I heard talk of shooting him, but a gunshot would wake my baby."

"That was only the whiskey talking. Virgil, put that gun away. There's no need to shoot anyone today. Isn't that right, Shane?" Atticus addressed the man in the street, the silk of his voice hardening to steel.

Shane staggered to his feet. "It's never a good day to be shot."

"Then stay out of my hotel with your Sunday school hymns."

Hymns? Who was this Shane? With his black eye and

eviction from the hotel, America had taken him for a troublemaker. But why would he, or anyone, sing hymns in a bar?

Atticus glared at Shane, tipped his bowler to America, and spun on his heel.

After several attempts to holster his pistol, Virgil finally succeeded. He trailed after Atticus.

Shane gazed at America with eyes of vivid blue. A lock of black hair sprang across his forehead. He was altogether too handsome for her comfort. He wasn't dressed like the miners she'd seen but wore a string tie and frock coat. His lips quirked into a smile. "I suppose you are part of the wagon train that pulled into Yankee Flats today."

"Yes."

"I'm sorry your introduction to Bannack wasn't more civilized. I'm Reverend Hayes. May I be so forward as to ask your name?"

The man might be a preacher, but he didn't have a lick of sense. Why else would he risk his life to thrust his beliefs on those who didn't welcome him? She returned his smile anyway. "Reverend Hayes, life in a wagon train has taught me not to stand on manners where practicality will serve. I'm Mrs. America Reed." She gave him her first name rather than her husband's but then regretted letting him know in this manner that she was widowed.

His eyebrows arched upward. "Are you alone at so young an age then?"

Her gaze faltered. "That is true."

"Forgive me for speaking so plainly." His voice gentled. "I meant no disrespect. I'm sorry for your circumstances, especially since you mentioned a baby."

"I appreciate your sympathy, Reverend Hayes."

He climbed onto the boardwalk that connected the buildings along the street and held his hat against his chest. "Mrs. Reed, the Bible commands us to watch out for the widowed and fatherless. I consider it my utmost duty to assist you."

"That's very kind." The urgent desire to escape flooded America. If this man's profession hadn't already made her uneasy, his words certainly would have. From what she'd observed, he had a penchant for minding other people's business.

A movement behind him drew her attention, and she started.

Shane followed her gaze to where the dark shapes of Indians on horseback peppered the hills above town. "So, our neighbors have put on their best bonnets and come calling. Not surprising, considering."

She didn't ask what he meant. Something told her she didn't want to know.

One of the braves broke away from the rest and spurred his pony downhill.

Shouts rang out along the street.

A man emerged from the general store across the way and stood with feet apart on the boardwalk. She'd seen that posture before. Now, who did it remind her of?

Oh, yes. Dillingham had taken that stance while confronting her over yoking her oxen.

The hotel door screeched. "Looks like trouble!" a masculine voice cried in warning.

Men swarmed onto the boardwalk below the hotel. More gathered in front of the general store. The thudding of hooves grew louder.

The preacher looked back to her. "Go inside and bolt the door."

She wanted to follow his advice but instead clutched the railing.

Hooves drummed on wood as the rider crossed the bridge over Grasshopper Creek from near the wagon camp on Yankee Flats. The lone rider turned down the main street through town with eagle feathers streaming behind him. Black paint ringed the pony's eyes and marked horizontal lines across its forelegs.

America started. What was her rescuer from the plains doing in Bannack?

The pony slid to a stop in a spray of mud. The rider raised a fringed lance, and the many-colored beads on his buckskin shirt glinted. "My uncle's blood cries from the ground in this place, asking why those he called friends would strike him."

"I have no answers for your uncle." Dillingham called from the boardwalk. "I am asking the same question."

"I, Tendoy, now lead my people." He shook his lance. "If the people of Bannack want war, we will fight."

"We don't want war, I promise you."

Tendoy lowered his war lance. "You are a good man, Dillingham. I know you speak truth. But do you speak for all?"

Dillingham nodded, but the murmur that ran through the crowd sounded mixed. "A few bad men killed Chief Snag, but I and the rest of the people of this town regret your uncle's death. We grieve with you."

"These bad men. You will punish them?"

"They stood trial." Dillingham spoke quietly but with emphasis. "We sent them away from Bannack."

"That is all?" Tendoy circled his pony between the boardwalks. "My people are angry. The young men want to fight."

A hawk screeched overhead as if confirming his words, and the bird's shadow rippled across the balcony. Tendoy's gaze lifted toward the sound then stopped on America. His face softened in a look of recognition.

America caught her breath, once again flying on horseback across the prairie.

Tendoy turned back to Dillingham. "My uncle would not want war against friends. His father's sister, Sacajawea, who guided the ones named Lewis and Clark to the big waters, would not have wished it. I will tell my people all you say." He wheeled his pony and sent it back the way he'd come.

America's hands throbbed, and she eased her cramped fingers from the railing. An ache started at the back of her eyes. Sensing someone watching her, she glanced down into a pair of faded gray eyes. Virgil Henry raised his flop-brimmed hat to her.

She backed away from the edge on shaky legs.

"Why didn't you go inside?" Shane called up to her.

How dare he take charge of her? She was no untried girl, but a woman with a mind of her own. He was a man she had only just met. She straightened her spine. "That, Reverend Hayes, is my concern."

There was no need to tell him that fear had rendered her legs unable to carry her.

America put a hand to the pulse throbbing at her temple. The room seemed airless. She unbuttoned her dress and loosened her corset stays enough to take deep breaths and ward off the dizziness threatening to overtake her. When she felt better, she walked with trembling legs to the oak side table and poured water from a porcelain pitcher etched with blue flowers into a matching cup. She drank the tepid water down, gasping between swallows.

Addie stirred in the bed but then nestled into the covers and lay still.

Lying down might help her headache. As quietly as possible, America removed her high-topped shoes and crept toward the bed. Travis had carried the small rocking cradle her husband had built to the hotel, and Liberty's tiny form lay swaddled within its confines. America's lips curved as she gazed at her baby. Sleep smoothed Liberty's face and slackened her rosebud mouth. Nothing seemed able to wake her, not even the commotion in the street. It had been a hard journey, and hardest on Liberty. America puckered her brow and bent closer in sudden concern, but the tiny chest rose and fell in a steady rhythm.

She eased onto the feather tick, closed her eyes, and let out a sigh.

"What was all that ruckus outside?" Addie whispered.

"Trouble with the Indians." Hopefully, she wouldn't have to explain more until she'd had time to recover from the shock.

"Goodness! Is it serious?"

"Yes, but it blew over."

Addie sat up, her dark hair a riot of curls that made her look younger than her twenty-eight years. "Maybe we should have stayed in camp."

Laughter gusted through the building.

Addie widened her dark eyes. "What was that?"

"The bar is starting up early." America propped herself with a pillow against the brass headboard.

"I must apologize." Addie twisted the wedding ring on her finger. "To my knowledge, hotel bars aren't usually so wild back home in St. Louis."

"I'll confess that giving up such a comfortable bed doesn't seem appealing, but I'd rather spend a peaceful night."

Addie shook her head. "There's no guarantee the camp will be much quieter unless the wagon master can keep the men from going into town after whiskey."

"That doesn't seem likely." America frowned. "I noticed Pete Amesly and Hiram Slatter on the boardwalk earlier."

"There'll be no escaping the devil's merriment tonight wherever we go, but camp might be less rowdy." She looked across America to Liberty's cradle. "I hate to disturb the baby, though. Shall we send Travis to ask for an early supper to be sent up? That way Liberty can sleep longer and might wake on her own, poor darling."

"It's kind of you to think of that."

"Nonsense." Addie smiled. "I'd just as soon not have to prepare food when we arrive back in camp. There'll be enough else to do before dark." She smoothed the quilt. "This hotel is nice during daylight hours, but I'll feel safer in camp tonight."

Tendoy had ridden into town waving his war lance, but Addie would sleep better without knowing that.

CHAPTER FIVE

SHANE STOMPED THE MUD FROM HIS boots before going inside the cabin. Light filtered in through the windows and made patterns across the rough floorboards. Silence blanketed the rooms. With everything going on lately, his cousin's absence didn't surprise him.

He dropped into a chair and lowered his head to his arms folded on the table. Imposing himself on others was a hard way to win favor. But with so many lost souls in Bannack—a burden that pressed him constantly—he couldn't stop trying to reach them. At least he'd given part of his sermon before being jettisoned from the saloon. He'd done his duty, but it had taken a toll.

Shane could admit that he wanted to be liked as much as anyone else. Constant rejection brought discouragement, a thing that had come his way too often while growing up in the slums of Manhattan. At Five Points, the neighborhood named for the number of streets that intersected there, gangs excluded newcomers.

But even after Shane escaped the slums and its dangers, in some quarters his Irish brogue prevented his being counted part of humanity. He'd survived childhood by changing as many odds as possible in his favor. He'd done no less when he'd changed his first name from Sean to Shane. No matter what Con thought, he refused to feel badly about doing what he needed to in order to survive.

He dragged himself up from the chair, refusing to wallow in self-pity. He'd escaped Five Points into a new life, and he intended to make it count for something. His reflection in the mirror above the washstand in the corner made him wince. He could be grateful Atticus had refrained from blacking the other eye, at least.

Mud soon soiled the water in the basin. He replenished it several times before putting on the only change of clothes he had: denim trousers and a pullover shirt sewn from the same fabric.

Feeling much improved, he prepared a meal of beans and cornbread, cooking extra for Con to eat later. His cousin might want to talk when he came home, but he couldn't make himself wait for him. Restlessness hounded Shane, springing from his roiling thoughts. He'd been struck down in broad daylight as much by the sight of the angelic face above him as by Atticus's fists. She'd stared at him with the same look a doe gave when caught by surprise, but then with flattering interest.

Why should this happen when he could do nothing about his feelings but decently ignore them? He would not wed her or any other woman and expect her to endure the privations of a circuit rider's spouse.

He needed to walk, although he had no particular destination in mind. Anywhere would do to escape his thoughts. His steps took him down Main Street as if urging him to return to the woman he couldn't put out of his mind. He would walk past the hotel without going in.

"You take that back!" The cry came from behind the Merrick Hotel and was immediately followed by the sick thudding sound of a fist on flesh.

Shane halted in his tracks. After the battering he'd taken that morning, he was loath to get involved, but he couldn't ignore this. He turned down the side yard and peered around the corner of the building.

"You like her, don't you?" A gangly man with red hair held a boy in his early teens by the shirt collar. The length of his arm prevented the boy from striking but didn't stop him from trying.

"None of your business, Pete!" The boy's failure to deny the charge answered the question.

Pete grinned. "How do you know it's not? A widow gets a mite lonely, and I have strong arms."

The boy flailed at his opponent with fresh vigor. "America isn't like that."

The woman's name brought Shane to attention.

"You've got it bad." Pete shook his head in mock sympathy. "You need to grow up, son, before you take on a woman like that one."

The boy's face went scarlet. "I'm not your son!" He swung his arms in futile fury.

Pete pulled back a fist.

Moving quicker than thought, Shane caught the man from behind and jerked until his hold on the boy broke. He spun Pete about and drew back his fist in an automatic reflex.

Pete's eyes widened. A vein stood out on his neck. "Don't hurt me." His high-pitched voice sounded younger than he looked. For a moment, he seemed not much older than the boy he'd been tormenting.

Shane barely stopped his punch in time. A wave of nausea went through him. He'd come too close to returning to the ways of the street. He released the man and stepped away. "Go on. Clear out."

Pete lost no time in rounding the corner of the building.

Shane pulled himself together and went to the boy. "Are you all right?" He clapped a steadying arm around his shoulder. The question wasn't necessary. With a split lip and a black eye as impressive as Shane's own, his condition was apparent.

"I hate him." He glared in the direction Pete had disappeared.

"I understand the sentiment, but I hope you can find the grace to forgive."

The boy looked at him as if he'd grown a second head.

"Why would you say a fool thing like that?"

Shane couldn't help but smile. "The ways of our Lord are strange to us."

"I'm all right now." The boy pulled away from him to stand alone. "Say, are you some sort of preacher?"

"I am, and you are on my circuit. That makes you my responsibility. I'd be obliged if you'd let me see you to safety."

The boy dabbed a finger to his bleeding lip. "Thanks for helping me. I can make it back all right, though."

Shane held out a hand so they could shake man-to-man. "I'm Reverend Hayes."

"Travis Martin."

"Do you think you'll land in trouble for fighting?"

Travis frowned. "I don't know."

"Can I put in a good word for you?"

His forehead smoothed. "Would you do that?"

"Certainly. It's clear you were provoked. That's no excuse for fighting, mind you, but it is a reason." Painfully aware that he, himself, had neither, Shane fell into step beside the boy.

Addie looked up from lacing her boots. "I wonder what's keeping Travis."

"I expect he'll be along shortly." America tucked her hairbrush into her satchel and ran a hand over the cool metal of the footboard. Sleeping in the brass bed had served as a reminder of softer days in a life now gone forever. She glimpsed herself in the oval mirror perched on top of the chest of drawers and made a face at her seriousness.

Going back to the wagon camp made sense for a lot of reasons. After a single day at the hotel, she already wished for what might have been, but that only distracted her from accepting the realities of her life. Memories of the only man she had ever loved washed over her. She clenched her fists. Kyle had made his choices, and she had made hers. Nothing could ever change that.

Liberty woke with a cry. America hurried to pick her up, grateful for the distraction. Holding her daughter, she almost believed God could be merciful. Liberty was proof that He hadn't given up on her entirely. In her daughter, she had a way to make amends, to atone for the past. No matter what the cost, Liberty must have a good life. She would see to it.

She tended to her baby, tucking her in again when someone knocked on the door.

"That will be Travis." Addie had stopped packing in favor of perching like a nervous bird on the edge of the lyre-backed slipper chair. Now she hurried through the parlor and flung open the door. She gasped. "What happened?"

America craned beyond Addie to see Travis standing in the doorway with a reddened, swollen eye. Beside him and a little out of sight stood a man wearing denim and holding his hat. "Goodness!"

She'd forgotten Liberty when she spoke. Her baby, slipping back to sleep when the knock came at the door, startled awake. Her cries drowned out any answer to Addie's question, but it seemed obvious Travis had engaged in fisticuffs. America picked up the baby and turned back to find Addie putting her arms around her son. He stood stiffly, as if embarrassed by his mother's coddling.

Patting her baby's back, America approached the doorway. The man beside Travis came into view. "You!" she burst out. "What are you doing here?"

"Evening." Shane gave her a nod before giving his attention to Addie again.

America's face warmed. He'd shown up her rudeness with his politeness. Surprised to find him beside Travis, she'd spoken more plainly than she would have otherwise. But honestly, didn't he care that the owner had warned him away from the hotel or that Virgil itched to shoot him? Even if he didn't care, she did. The desire to send him away for his protection sprang within her. "Mrs. Martin, this is Reverend Hayes," she murmured. "I feel certain he needs to be elsewhere."

"On the contrary." Shane bestowed a smile on America. "There's nowhere else I'd rather be at the moment. I hope you won't go too hard on Travis, Mrs. Martin. That fellow Pete provoked him."

"Pete!" Addie and America chimed in unison.

"What is that troublemaker up to now?" Addie asked.

"He was taunting Travis about . . . certain things," Shane answered vaguely.

"He said I wasn't old enough to be a man," Travis protested. "How dare he? I'm more mature than him by a long shot."

America refrained from pointing out that at thirteen, Travis had some years to go before he could consider himself fully grown. On the other hand, Pete might call himself a man, but he certainly didn't deserve the description.

"Won't you come in, Reverend Hayes?" Addie invited.

That was the last thing America wanted to happen. Reverend Hayes needed to get away from the hotel, not while away time in the parlor of their suite.

The good reverend didn't seem to share her concern. He commandeered the rosewood settee and rested his hat on his knee, giving every appearance of a man with hours to kill. "Are you leaving?" He pointed to America's satchel, waiting beside the door. "At this hour?"

"We hoped to find a couple of nights' rest in this hotel, Reverend Hayes," Addie explained. "I'm afraid the clientele makes more noise than we care for."

"Please allow me to accompany you."

"It won't be night for a while yet," America couldn't resist pointing out. "We'll have plenty of opportunity to walk back to the wagon camp."

"Even a short walk in a place like Bannack can lead to unexpected adventures." Reverend Hayes addressed Addie, but his gaze followed America as she walked her baby about the room to soothe her.

"I can watch over the womenfolk." Travis would have been more convincing without an eye swollen shut, but America didn't have the heart to tell him so.

Reverend Hayes switched his attention to Travis. "I'm sure that's true, but it never hurts to have someone watch your back. Even a sheriff has his deputies."

Addie smiled. "Thank you for the kind offer, but we're not leaving right yet. Supper should arrive soon."

"Supper!" Travis slapped his forehead. "Sorry, Ma. I forgot to order it."

Addie sighed. "Looks like it will be camp cooking tonight, after all. We should head back. Travis, go bathe that eye and pack your things."

"I'll get dinner tonight," America assured her. "You love to cook, and I like to let you, but I'm capable of producing a meal on my own."

"I do appreciate that." Addie rewarded her with a smile before turning to Shane. "If you don't mind waiting a few minutes, we can accept your escort after all, Reverend."

"I'm at your service."

"Well then, I'd better finish packing." Addie took herself through the doorway to the bedroom.

Suddenly alone with Reverend Hayes, America found herself at a loss. She hardly knew what to say to a man who faintly alarmed her all the while making her feel safeguarded. Her reaction to the man was not entirely logical, a fact that didn't escape her. "Thank you for taking care of Travis," she offered as an olive branch.

He gave a nod. "I'm glad I happened along. He might have been seriously injured. How does Travis know this Pete fellow, may I ask?"

"Pete belongs to our wagon train."

"You might want to keep an eye on him."

"Are you suggesting he'll pick on Travis again?"

Shane shrugged. "It's possible. He strikes me as the sort to hold a grudge."

America could testify to that. Pete hadn't let up on her since she'd joined the wagon train against his wishes. "Thanks for the suggestion. I'll make sure to look out for Travis." She hesitated. "Speaking of grudges, what was Tendoy upset about earlier?"

He winced. "I don't like to speak of certain things in gentler company."

"I gathered that his uncle was murdered in Bannack." She opened the subject he hadn't mentioned.

"I'm sorry you had to hear that, but sadly, yes."

"What happened?"

"If you ask me, the drunkenness of others caused his death."

"How sad."

"Alcohol is the curse of the West, I'm afraid. Tanglefoot, Tarantula Juice, Coffin Varnish—the names say it all. To increase profits, an unscrupulous saloon owner might cut liquor with turpentine, ammonia, even gunpowder. Either way, you'll want to watch yourself. Men will do regrettable things under the influence of spirits."

That explained the raucousness of the hotel bar's patrons. "I'm beginning to wonder if I've made a mistake coming here."

"That's a thing to ask yourself." Reverend Hayes spoke in his Irish lilt as his gaze searched her face. "You're a beautiful woman, if I may say so, and likely to draw unwelcome attention among the miners. It may not be comfortable for you here, and I wouldn't call Bannack safe at all."

Warmth crept up America's neck. "I thank you for your concern, Reverend, but I am here now and must earn my keep. Addie and I plan to set up a cook tent and provide suppers for the miners. If they become unruly, well, I have my husband's gun and know how to use it. But I would prefer it never comes to that."

Reverend Hayes's brow creased. "I hope you will think twice before availing yourself of a gun. If you won't carry yourself off to somewhere more suitable, at least you'll have honest work to do. I hope it goes well for you both."

He was not above offering an olive branch of his own, apparently. "Thank you. And you, Reverend Hayes? Bannack seems a dangerous place for you. Why do you remain?"

"I don't live here or anywhere, really. This town is part of my preaching circuit. I am committed to reaching it with the gospel of peace."

She quirked a brow. "Is that what brought about your black eye?"

He smiled. "I can't say I've attained my goal as yet."

"Reverend Hayes, I don't mean to preach to the preacher, but shouldn't you look after yourself better? For example, I'm certain you shouldn't be in this hotel. If the owner discovers you—"

He glanced at her and then away. "Watching over young Travis seemed more important than my own welfare."

America couldn't meet his eyes. She had taken him for a fool, not a hero, but he'd shielded Travis in a moment of need and now disregarded his own safety to see them back to camp. She had no idea what to think of such a man. How could he expect to keep anyone else safe when he wouldn't even fight to save himself? He probably relied upon the same God who had taken Richard from her.

A stray thought intruded. This man wouldn't protect her if he knew her secret. She pushed it away, annoyed beyond reason. Neither the good reverend nor anyone else ever had to know about that.

CHAPTER SIX

"THANK YOU FOR SEEING US TO camp, Reverend Hayes." Addie started up her wagon steps, then turned back with a smile for the preacher. "Won't you stay to supper?"

"Thank you, Ma'am, but I have a matter to attend." Reverend Hayes tilted his head toward Travis. "I hope you'll stay away from Pete from here on out."

"Yes sir." Travis sent the preacher a wary look. "I'll do my best."

Liberty cooed in America's arms, and Reverend Hayes moved closer. "May the good Lord look after this sweet lamb and her mother also." He searched America's face with his blue gaze. "Should you have need of my help, you have only to ask."

"Thank you." America wouldn't call upon him, but it was nice to know she could. His presence on the path from town had given her a feeling of safety absent from her life since Richard left it. Almost, it made her yearn again for a man's protection.

Reverend Hayes strode off, taking the path farther into the wagon camp rather than back to town. She watched him go. What sort of business did he have in the wagon train? She pulled her attention from the preacher and gave it to Liberty, absorbing herself in making her daughter comfortable. With Liberty fed and snug in her arms, she joined Addie at her cooking fire. "Smells delicious."

Addie straightened from stirring the pot suspended above the fire on a tripod. "It's only bacon stew and johnnycake."

"I'm thankful for your cooking." America rewarded Addie

with a smile.

"I made Travis's favorite meal."

"Where is he, by the way?" America tried not to sound worried about the boy, but she couldn't help being concerned. Pete Amesly was a bully, as she had found out herself. She hoped Travis honored the preacher's wishes and kept well away from the man.

"Travis went to the creek for water. He should be back soon, although I can hardly blame him if he lingers." A gust of wind stirred the cottonwoods, and Addie glanced up with a sigh. "It's beautiful here. I hope the town folk will welcome a cook tent."

After what America had learned about the inhabitants of Bannack, she wasn't sure how she felt about living among them. She rubbed Liberty's back and said nothing.

Travis returned, carrying a bucket in each hand. He gave his mother one and emptied the other into the water barrel strapped to Addie's wagon. His swollen eye made America inwardly wince.

"Supper's ready." Addie dished the steaming stew onto a plate and passed it to Travis, who helped himself to a slice of johnnycake. Addie dished up another portion for America and took Liberty while she settled on an overturned crate. She handed the baby back and after a moment sat beside America. They bowed their heads, and Addie called upon Travis to say grace. He rumbled out the blessing in a deepening voice that squeaked at odd moments. "And please watch over Reverend Hayes," he tagged onto the end of his prayer.

America heartily agreed with Travis's request on behalf of Reverend Hayes. She had known the circuit preacher little more than a day, but he seemed to have an important need for the Almighty's oversight.

They made short work of supper. Travis took a turn holding Liberty while America washed dishes and Addie dried. Sunset glowed in the westward sky, and the breath of night sighed through the grass.

"Shall we join the gathering?" Addie asked.

"Why not?" As a widow, America would watch alongside Addie without taking part in the dancing. It was better than hiding in her wagon. Her days of frivolity seemed far removed from her. Had it been only two years ago that she had danced with Kyle at a ball? "You and Travis go on ahead. I'll join you after I've fed Liberty."

Addie looked hesitant. "Are you certain?"

"Of course. There's no need to wait for me." America ignored her own discomfort at the idea of remaining behind alone. The other wagons were near, although most everyone would go to the gathering.

Firelight flickered through the cottonwoods by the time America emerged from her wagon with her daughter nestled against her. Relief coursed through her as she walked toward the clearing where dancers sashayed. The western wilderness unnerved her sometimes. Nate's harmonica wailed against the seesawing of Bill's fiddle. The lyrics of the music sang through her mind. "Mid pleasures and palaces though we may roam, be it ever so humble, there's no place like home." As she neared, Bill nodded to her without skipping a beat.

America grinned at him. Since she'd joined the wagon train at Fort Union, Bill Baker and his apple-cheeked wife, Sarah, had shown her many kindnesses.

Addie waved from across the dancers. America picked her way toward her in the twilight, wary of the children romping underfoot. She had no intention of falling with Liberty in her arms.

Addie held out her arms with a dimpled smile, and America transferred Liberty into her friend's safekeeping. Leaning close, Addie spoke near her ear. "The wagon master passed whiskey around to the men earlier. His wife is fit to be tied. Mrs. Taylor doesn't condone the consumption of spirits."

Some of the men did seem to step a little higher than

warranted as they danced, and they swung their partners with more gusto than usual. "Why would the wagon master do such a thing? He's always been against consuming alcohol in camp."

"Nate thinks Mr. Taylor wanted to keep the men out of trouble in town by offering dancing and a bit of drink."

America scanned the crowd. Some of the men were missing. "I'm not sure that worked, and it seems a poor choice."

Addie nodded. "That's what Mrs. Taylor said, but in different words."

"I don't see her here."

"I expect you won't."

The music hit a lull, and the dancers broke apart, laughing.

America put the Taylors' difficulties out of her mind. "Where's Travis?"

"He's around here somewhere. He won't admit it, but he's taken a liking to Jenny Taylor."

America spotted Travis's tousled chestnut curls. He stood with the blonde, blue-eyed daughter of the wagon master. Jenny looked sweet in pale-blue calico. The admiring expression on Travis's face confirmed Addie's words, and Jenny's shy smile seemed to say that Travis's feelings were returned.

America's smile faltered. Watching the pair of them saddened her. Kyle had been her first love, and she'd hoped to make Richard her last. She'd admired her husband and wanted to love him, but she had never summoned the depth of emotion for him that she'd felt for Kyle.

The fiddle and harmonica struck up "Oh, Susanna." Some of the dancers moved back into the fray, but others made their way to the front of the Taylors' wagon, where vinegar lemonade and dippers of cool water from Grasshopper Creek could be had.

America went in search of cups for Addie and herself. She circled behind the knot of people watching the dancers while they drank the tart-but-sweet beverage made from apple cider vinegar, water, and sugar. As they clapped in time to the music, her head started throbbing. Hopefully, she was only tired and not sickening. She would drink some of the vinegar lemonade with Addie then take Liberty and retire to her wagon.

A hand grabbed America's arm and jerked her off balance. She would have fallen but for the arm that caught her against a masculine chest covered in a black cotton shirt. Heart thudding, she looked up into Pete Amesly's laughing face.

"Come and dance!"

The stench of whiskey and sweat made her stomach heave. "You're drunk." She shoved him aside in disgust.

"Playing hard to get?" He snaked a hand around her waist and pulled her closer.

"Stop it!" The music hid the sound of her slap, but the red mark it left on his cheek was unmistakable. Pete's hold slackened. She yanked herself out of his arms.

His face flamed almost as red as his hair.

Right then, Reverend Hayes stepped between her and Pete. "Leave her be."

Pete held up his hands. "I won't argue with a fightin' man." He walked away with an uneven gait.

America glared after him. Her head throbbed harder, and she put a hand to her temple.

"Are you ill?"

Tears scratched at her throat at the sympathy in his voice. She shook her head. "Only tired."

"May I assist you?"

She hesitated, but then nodded. "Thank you."

"Where were you going?"

"To my wagon after cups for the vinegar lemonade, but now I simply want to return to Addie."

"Where is she? Never mind, I've found her." He guided her through the crowd with a hand to her elbow.

Addie walked toward them, rubbing Liberty's back. She

welcomed the circuit preacher with a smile. "Reverend Hayes? I thought you'd gone home after escorting us from the hotel. You're always welcome, of course." She added the last part hastily, perhaps fearing she'd offended him. She turned to America. Raising her voice, she spoke above the music. "What's wrong?"

"Pete . . ." America trailed off as heat scorched her cheeks.

"Pete needs a lesson in manners." Reverend Hayes's jaw tightened as if he might relish teaching it.

Addie frowned. "Did he harm you?"

"Not really, but he didn't help my headache." She took Liberty from Addie. With her baby in her arms, she felt a little better.

"Can I get you anything? Perhaps some of that vinegar lemonade?" Reverend Hayes looked at her with such warmth she wanted to weep.

"Oh, yes, do have some." Addie rubbed her back as she had Liberty's. "I'm sure it will help your headache."

America yielded to their concern. "I suppose it might."

Addie retrieved cups from her wagon, and Shane went after the vinegar lemonade.

Pete stood watching the dancers and clapping to the lively song, "Kingdom Coming." He smiled at her as if nothing at all had happened between them.

Reverend Hayes returned with the lemonade.

America sipped the refreshing beverage before asking him the question uppermost in her mind. "Why are you here, anyway?"

"As it happens, I'm on a mission. I've offered to hold church on the Sabbath. The wagon master was elsewhere when I looked for him, but Mrs. Taylor thought he would want my services."

"You'll find him over there." America pointed toward Erasmus Taylor, who was watching the dancers beside Grant Hadley. Neither seemed steady on their feet.

The preacher gave the two men a long look. "This may take a while."

America turned over yet again. The bed in her wagon box wasn't nearly as comfortable as the brass one in the Merrick Hotel, but that wasn't why she couldn't sleep. The steady patter of rain on the wagon bonnet didn't have anything to do with it either.

The thought of sitting through Reverend Hayes's sermon on Sunday had her tossing and turning despite her weariness. More than anything, America wanted to think that the God he trusted cared for her too. But how could she believe that when everything that had happened pointed to the fact that God wanted to punish her?

An image of vibrant blue eyes rose unbidden in her mind as snarled emotions she didn't want to untangle gripped her. Kyle's eyes were the same color as Liberty's. A cold weight settled in her chest at the thought. Sometimes her baby looked so much like Kyle that it hurt to look at her. She swallowed against a thickening at the back of her throat. If Richard had lived to see the daughter he thought belonged to him, would he have guessed her secret shame?

What a fool she'd been to trust Kyle's declarations. She could admit it now. Flattered by his attention and frightened by her parents' crumbling marriage, she'd looked to him for love. She thought she'd found it too, for a time. Now she knew better. Kyle had never cared about her. Thank goodness Richard had. When she'd told him she was pregnant, Kyle couldn't abandon her fast enough. She hadn't even known he'd joined the Union army until she'd overheard an idle comment one of his friends had made at a party.

If Richard hadn't offered for her right then, she'd have been completely ruined. Marrying him hadn't been fair, which must have been why God had taken him from her.

She brushed away tears and changed her position.

An old memory stirred. Once again she was eight years old. Floorboards creaked while dust eddied in a sunbeam that fell through uneven panes across a lump lying in Gramma's bed.

"Gramma?" The word broke from her lips in little more than a whisper.

The lump twitched in answer.

She took another step.

Gramma's beloved face peered out from the quilts.

America rushed forward, but when Gramma's forehead wrinkled, she remembered to be quiet. She wasn't supposed to bother Gramma, who needed to rest. Gramma didn't mind her visits, though. Leastways, she didn't tell Mother about them.

Gramma needed a lot of sleep lately and seemed tired soon after waking. Her skin had thinned and yellowed, and pouches made shadows under her eyes. Doc came and went often now, and Mother had started acting funny. She snapped more than usual, and when America put her ear to the wall that separated their bedrooms, she heard crying on the other side.

Gramma reached out her long fingers and grasped America's hand. "Child." She smiled as sweetly as ever, but for too short a time.

With a sob, America flung herself into the arms that rose to take her in.

"There, there, Ammie. Don't cry."

"You can't leave me." Her breath hitched as she whispered her fear.

Gramma rubbed America's back the way she'd always done. "Aye, I'm going, Ammie, and there's nothing either of us can do about it."

How could Gramma do this to them. To her? "*Why* must you go?"

"Hush, now, lamb. I have no choice."

"Then take me with you."

Tears stood in Gramma's blue eyes. "Darling, that is not for me to decide."

"Tell me where you're going." She touched Gramma's cheek just as a silver droplet fell, and its warmth ran across the back of her hand.

Hooves beat in the street outside, and she glanced toward the window. If that was the doctor, she'd have to leave. She gripped Gramma's hand. "Tell me."

Tears followed one another down Gramma's cheeks, but her lips curved in a soft smile. "There is a place, child, a place of shining light. Few find their way there, and of those, many faint, for the path wends through hilly lands without rain. Ah, but it is worth the journey. At the top of the hills, springs of water never run dry, soft winds blow, and the trees shine like emeralds."

America tilted her head. "What's the name of this place?"

"It's called—" A spasm crossed Gramma's face but then smoothed. "*Nevermore.*"

"That's a funny name."

"It's called that, you see, because those who find their way there never more know crying or sickness or pain."

A tap came at the door, and it opened. A rustle of taffeta and the scent of French perfume entered with Mother.

"Remember *Nevermore*, Ammie." Those whispered words were the last America ever heard from Gramma's lips . . .

America shook her head to dispel the sad memory and return to the grown woman trying to fall asleep in a wagon. She blinked away tears. It always made her sad to think of Gramma's passing, but it comforted her to picture her walking the hills of Nevermore. If such a place as heaven truly existed, she had no doubt Gramma had found it.

"Has this entire town lost its mind? Slow down and tell me what's going on."

On his way to the livery to get his horse, Shane swiveled on the boardwalk. The saddlebags he carried across his shoulder swung as he worked to match his pace with Con's. Wagons vied for position all along Main Street. A team of mules veered to avoid trampling two men unwise enough to try and cross the road. The driver leaned out of his wagon and showed his fist. Curses singed the air.

Con didn't slow his pace. "Got no time, Cousin. When Lady Luck calls, only a fool keeps her waiting."

"Would you please speak sense?"

"*Gold!* Bill Fairweather and Henry Edgar went looking for a little tobacco money. Ha! They found plenty. Word's out, and the stampede to Alder Gulch is on. Think of it. Forty miles of the gulch cut by Alder Creek lined with gold for the taking."

"I . . . see. Do you plan to take part in this insanity?"

"I'm on my way to my cabin to pack."

"Just like that?" Shane asked the empty air. Con had broken into a run that left him behind. As he watched his cousin disappear, a body slammed into his back.

"Have a care, preacher." Jared Stone caught his arm, saving him a fall.

Shane opened his mouth to answer the lanky miner, but Jared had already melted into the surging crowd. Shane hurried after Con.

Foodstuffs, pots and pans, knives, and clothing littered the table in Con's cabin. Shane shut the door on the noise and confusion in the street and shifted his saddlebags to balance them on his shoulder. "Have you decided to give up your position as deputy?"

Con propped a bedroll against the cabin wall. "Why not, when I can find enough gold to make a start elsewhere?"

"Are you convinced of that?"

"A man has to take his chances."

"But you bellyached at me about leaving."

"That was different."

Shane crossed his arms. "How so?"

Con smirked. "I don't suffer from the same delusions of integrity as you." Shane opened his mouth to retort, but Con cut him off. "Don't get me wrong. I admire you. When we were kids, I wanted to be like you—always so responsible. Even when you fought, 'twas for a reason, not only because of the filthy slum we lived in."

"Con—"

"Let me finish. You escaped Manhattan to live for something. Don't turn your back on that because you're afraid you don't matter."

"I don't quit as easily as you think," Shane managed to say.

"I'm glad to hear it. You can stay in my cabin until they declare it abandoned and take it for a sheriff's sale."

"What about you?"

Con shrugged. "I'll get by."

"Is that all you want?"

Con hauled a trunk into the center of the room before answering. "Yes, well, I seem to bring the slum with me wherever I go."

"It doesn't have to be that way, you know."

Con stopped moving long enough to look at him. "Maybe I need you to *show me* that's true."

Shane chose his words carefully. "I'm not proud of wanting to quit."

"Ach! Ashamed of being human?"

Shane folded his arms. "What's that supposed to mean, exactly?"

Con hauled a sack of dry beans from a shelf and dropped it into the trunk. "You might reach a good sight more people, *Saint Preacher*, if your feet touched the ground now and then."

"Saint Preacher. Is that really how you see me?"

Sacks of flour, sugar, and coffee followed the beans. "'Tis a name the miners call you behind your back." Con latched the trunk, then straightened. "What are you made of, Sean? You used to know. Ever since that preacher came into the slum, you've turned yourself inside out trying to be like him. You even changed your name to take out the Irish."

Shane slung his saddlebags onto his rope bed. "I'll not have you say a word against the man who rescued me from a wretched life."

"And now you're trying to save the whole world single-handed, whether it will or no. Even your preacher never did that."

Shane opened his mouth to speak but couldn't come up with a reply.

Con waved a hand. "'Tis no one's business but your own, I suppose. It's just that you seem unhappy."

Shane closed his mouth. How could he deny the truth?

Con put a hand to the back of his neck. "I'm one to talk, anyways. Maybe I'll find happiness, but it won't be here. I need out of Bannack."

"I thought as much. But why?" Shane pressed his cousin.

"Don't repeat this, as I'm not entirely certain." Con shook his head. "Let's say that I doubt the honesty of some of my fellow deputies."

Shane frowned. "Do you have cause?"

Con tied the second bag with a jerk. "I think so, as does Dillingham."

"Dillingham seems an honest man."

"We both suspect some of the deputies are part of a group of road agents robbing stagecoaches. If that's true, I'm square in the middle of a pack of murderers and thieves."

"Here." Shane picked up the bedroll. "Let me help you."

With the cart loaded, Con clasped his shoulder. "Ride north with me?"

"I'd like to, but I've changed my mind about leaving right

away. There's something I almost forgot I promised to do."

"Then I guess this is goodbye."

"Not forever. I'll visit you in Alder Gulch, although I hate to see you join the gold madness."

Con's green eyes glinted. "Needs must when the devil drives."

CHAPTER SEVEN

SEATED ON A TRUNK IN THE CLEARING where the wagon dance had been held a few days ago, America folded her hands and waited for Shane's sermon to begin. Beside her, Liberty slept in her rocking cradle, which Travis had toted from her wagon.

Wearing his frock coat and string tie, Shane stood with his feet planted apart and an open Bible in his hands. The gentle light of morning fell over him like a blessing. Behind him, Grasshopper Creek flowed between its banks. "The Lord is my Shepherd, I shall not want. He maketh me—"

Bill Baker snorted in his sleep.

Shane paused, and a crease appeared between his brows.

Bill pulled himself upright on the crate where he'd plunked himself down. America had overheard the Bakers' conversation that morning. Bill's wife, Sarah, had urged him to go to bed after standing watch the night before, while Bill argued that he was awake enough to attend church.

America glanced sideways at Sarah. She sat beside her husband in the rocking chair they'd hauled all the way from Kentucky. She wore an attentive expression, but a red stain crept up her neck.

"He maketh me to lie down in green pastures. He leadeth me beside the still waters." Shane cleared his throat with vigor.

Bill stirred. "Amen."

Sarah's blush spread higher, and a laugh caught at the back of America's throat. She coughed discreetly to dislodge it.

"He restoreth my soul. He leadeth me in the paths of righteousness for His name's sake. Yea, though—"

"Amen."

As a group, they now seemed taken with coughing fits.

Sarah watched her husband like a hawk.

"Yea though I walk through the valley of the shadow of death, I will fear no evil, for thou . . ." Sarah shook her husband. He roused with a snort. ". . . art with me. Thy rod and thy staff they comfort me."

Shane's reading picked up in tempo and emphasis, but America had stopped paying attention. She didn't know Shane's merciful Savior. God had left her to walk alone through a valley shadowed by death, in a place far from her grandmother's hills of Nevermore. She wished she could hide away until the sermon ended.

Shane droned on. At times his gaze rested on America. When he gave the closing prayer, she stood with the others but didn't shut her eyes. Grasshopper Creek curved through the surrounding grasses like a snake. The clicking of its namesake insects mingled with the trill of meadowlarks to provide a backdrop to the rise and fall of Shane's voice. Even on the Sabbath, two miners crouched on the banks, leaning over the brown water with sifting pans.

"Have you recovered from your headache?" Shane asked at her elbow.

America jumped but managed to smile. Absorbed in watching the miners, she hadn't noticed time passing. The church attendees had carried the trunks and crates they'd sat on for the service back to their camps. "I'm none the worse, Reverend Hayes."

"Please call me Shane."

She shook her head. "It wouldn't be fitting." But she'd already started thinking of him by his given name after he saved her from Pete.

His smile stole her breath. "I hope you won't stand on formality."

Liberty's waking cry saved America from making a response. "If you'll excuse me . . ."

"Of course." Shane stepped aside.

America picked up her daughter and started back to the wagon to change her diaper.

"Would you like me to bring the cradle?" he called after her.

The idea of Shane carrying Liberty's cradle into her wagon or otherwise helping her with the baby was more than America could think about right now.

"Why don't you bring it over here?" Addie called. "That way America can put Liberty down while she eats her dinner."

Unable to resist a backward glance, America turned her head.

Addie smiled up at Shane. "You're welcome to stay for dinner, Reverend Hayes."

"I don't want to impose." Shane dragged the words out with obvious reluctance.

"Nonsense." Addie waved a hand. "There's always enough for you."

America waited before ducking into her wagon, but he lowered his voice, and she couldn't make out his reply. Hopefully, he had refused. His quiet air, rich voice, and eyes like Kyle's already set her on edge without his also delving into spiritual matters.

When she emerged with Liberty in her arms, the remaining trunks and the rocking cradle had been moved to Addie's camp and placed around the cookfire, where they would eat. Shane talked with Nate Whalen while Grant Hadley sat on a crate facing them.

Travis stood beside Grant, gesturing while he spoke. "He woke the whole camp, but his 'Injun' turned into a bear."

Grant laughed. "We call him Injun Pete now." He sobered. "Leastways, we *did*. He left for Alder Gulch yesterday."

America couldn't help feel gratitude over that bit of news. She wouldn't inquire too closely into Pete's reasons for leaving the train or if it had anything to do with Shane's long conversation with the wagon master.

Addie looked up from laying out food on a table improvised from a trunk with legs made from poles in brackets. "Travis, can't you talk about something more pleasant?"

Nate stood and clapped Travis on the back. "What do you say? Shall we see if your Ma needs any help?"

Travis pulled away from him.

"No need!" Addie called. "Dinner is ready. America, come on over and dish up while I hold Liberty."

Addie's cook fire would not be lit on Sunday, but her beans and bacon were always delicious, hot or cold. America added a helping of pickled vegetables and a wedge of cornbread to her plate. Several pies waited on the trunk to be cut into when dessert time arrived. She poured a dipper of water from a metal pail into a cup and carried her dinner out to the clearing. Once America settled on the trunk she'd occupied during the service, Addie positioned Liberty beside her in the cradle. The baby fussed but then found her fist.

"Help yourselves," Addie called. "I hope you don't mind plain fare, Reverend."

Shane smiled. "Not at all. I'm thankful for a good meal and pleasant companions. Shall we pray?" He bowed his head. "For health and food, for love and friends, for everything Thy goodness sends, Father in heaven, we thank Thee."

A lump formed in America's throat, and she felt like crying. She'd heard mealtime prayers before, but never spoken with such simple sincerity. Why did this preacher affect her so strongly? She put a hand to her stomach, which had twisted into knots. With her appetite gone, she tried her best to eat.

Addie carried her own plate over to sit beside her on the trunk. "Is something wrong?" she asked, low.

Shane looked across to America as if he'd caught Addie's question.

"My stomach isn't feeling so well," she answered.

Addie touched her forehead. "You're not fevered, anyway." She shuddered and glanced at Shane. "We lived in fear of cholera on the journey. It takes a person in such a short time. It's possible to wake whole and well but be in the grave by nightfall."

"I understand that all too well." Shane's expression grew distant. "I've held more than my share of funerals."

Addie's face softened. "I imagine your profession must prove trying at times."

"That's the way of it. I've ridden through dangerous territory alone, endured sickness with only God's angels to tend me, and slept many a night in the cold and rain. Yet, I count my own discomfort but a small cost if it saves even one soul from a life of sorrow."

"Is such a thing possible?" America spoke her thought aloud.

Shane's gaze shifted to her. "We live in a fallen world, Mrs. Reed. Where freedom reigns without rule, lost souls will commit dark deeds."

America glanced away, unwilling to let him see how his words affected her. Her parents' indifference had given her the freedom to rush into error.

"And yet our Savior gave his life to save even the worst of sinners," Shane concluded.

She stared at him, dumbfounded. It was almost as if he knew what went through her mind.

Nate gestured with his tin cup. "I grew up with that belief, but it's sure hard for a man to accept when he's the injured party."

With the sun behind Nate, Shane squinted in his direction. "Yes, it is. But none of us deserves God's mercy. It's a miracle that brings a different kind of freedom to all who receive it— the freedom to live a life of meaning."

"Do you live such a life, Reverend Hayes?" America asked on impulse.

His smile came a little too late. "I like to think so."

Nate's grin flitted across his face. "With all respect,

Reverend, I'm not sure it's possible to find a life of meaning in a mining camp."

Shane looked at him without speaking for a moment. "I won't mention in front of the ladies all I've seen, but your thought holds merit. While living a meaningful life depends more on the condition of the person than his surroundings, some places raise more temptations than others. A man can't take God's hand, for example, if he's clutching gold in both fists."

Grant scowled. "Ain't the streets of heaven paved with the stuff?"

"That's true." Shane nodded. "It's not gold itself but the love of it that spawns evil."

"Well then, I guess I'm safe." Nate smiled. "Gold is only a means to an end for me. My heart belongs elsewhere." He didn't elaborate, but his glance skittered toward Addie.

"There was this man who proposed to a widow at her husband's funeral," Travis growled. He set aside his cup and wiped his mouth with his sleeve. "She refused him due to his lack of proper feeling."

Nate's ears turned red.

Addie stood. "Anyone want another helping? There's plenty, so don't be shy."

Since they had barely begun eating, her remark seemed strange to America. Could there be something going on between her and Nate? Addie hadn't said anything to her about him, but that might explain Travis's animosity and the tension in the air.

Shane tilted his head, looking up at Travis. "How's that eye healing? Come over here and let me take a look at it."

Holding his jaw tight, Travis stared at Shane then moved around to stand beside him. "Yours is worse."

"Is that so?" Shane asked.

"I have to say, Mrs. Martin." Grant spoke with his mouth full. "These are the best beans I ever ate. What'd you put in them?"

Addie's face lit with a bright smile. "Oh, this and that. It's just something I threw together."

America smiled to herself. Addie certainly guarded her recipes. But then she hoped to make money from cooking them. She looked down at her daughter, who stared back at her with deep interest. Cooking for the miners was America's means to an end. If she earned enough gold, she could start over somewhere more suitable. And maybe, if she provided a good life for Liberty, she could convince God to forgive her for living a lie.

She lifted her head and caught Shane watching her. They both looked away.

Nate gave Addie a weak smile as she collected his plate. "Thanks for the home cooking."

The others murmured their agreement.

Nate pulled out his harmonica and played a sad melody. Across the wagon circle, several children started a game of tag. Erasmus Taylor and his wife joined their camp with a pan of bread pudding. Bill and Sarah Baker, carrying a spider frying pan filled with what looked like cobbler, crossed the grass toward them with their daughter, Jenny, trailing behind. Travis turned his head at her approach. Other dessert offerings soon crowded Addie's improvised table. The children pressed in eagerly and received sweet rewards.

Bill seemed more alert as he gave Sarah an affectionate smile. "I'll fetch your rocker, Mrs. Baker."

Sarah's face pinked, and she sat with obvious delight in the chair her husband brought over.

Liberty fussed in America's arms.

"Take my place," Sarah invited America. "Please, I insist."

America gave her a grateful smile and settled into the chair. "Thank you for your kindness."

Sarah beamed as she perched on a trunk beside her husband.

Addie, still seated on the trunk they'd shared, put her hands in her lap and sighed. "I can't say I'm looking forward to tomorrow's journey. It's been nice to stay put for a spell."

"Where are you going?" Shane asked.

"We're of a mind to go on to Alder Gulch," Erasmus answered him.

America felt the weight of Shane's gaze on her. "All of you?"

"Yes." Erasmus nodded. "We decided the matter yesterday."

Shane's eyes narrowed. "Are you sure you want to do that? The towns springing up along Alder Gulch could be rough places to take women and children."

Erasmus stroked his beard. "I reckon we'll find out about that when we get there."

"Let me light your path, Reverend." The lantern swinging in Nate's hand hissed. He caught up to Shane. "I'd hate for you to land in the creek or turn up scalped."

"Thank you for your lantern and the company, although the moon is bright tonight, and I doubt there's much danger of Indian attack."

The soft ground cushioned their footsteps. The cottonwoods closed in. A branch creaked and the breeze sighed through leaves.

"Why do you say that?" Nate asked.

"Tendoy promised to take the men who wanted to fight on a long buffalo hunt."

"Will he really do it?"

"Tendoy is a man of his word. He understands his people well and will work for peace. His aunt, Sacajawea, influenced his family and the Shoshone to think kindly of settlers."

The trees thinned when they reached the creek bank. The grasshoppers nearest them went silent, but farther along the characteristic rattling click they made lifted in a chorus. Nate raised the lantern higher. Shadows gathered under their feet then rushed to extinguish the moonlight that glazed the water sliding beneath the footbridge.

Shane hunkered into his coat. His boots thumped on the bridge's rough planks. Even in late spring with the days warming, the temperature remained chill. "Thank you for seeing me home. I'd have left before dark but for the pleasant company." He didn't want to admit that he'd lingered in the presence of a certain amber-eyed widow. No doubt about it, Mrs. America Reed intrigued him.

He reminded himself that a circuit preacher had no time for tending anything but his flock. They turned onto Main Street, where a burst of music and laughter met them.

Nate pivoted at the edge of the boardwalk to light Shane's way. "The town is busy tonight."

"Mind yourself on the way back. I'd hate for you to come across any trouble."

Light fell from open doors and windows onto the boardwalk. After the gentle gathering they'd left, this music sounded feverish, and the laughter frenzied. They rounded another corner into a quieter section of town. When they reached the place where Con's cabin backed to a stand of trees, Shane breathed easier.

Nate stopped at the door. "Shall I come inside?"

"Don't bother. It's a full moon, and I have only to strike a match and touch it to my lantern's wick."

"It's no trouble."

"I can find my way around this cabin blindfolded."

"I'll say goodnight and goodbye then."

"You'll see me, the Lord willing. Alder Gulch lies within my circuit."

"Safe journeys, and I'll look forward to meeting you again."

Nate strode down the boardwalk, the light fading as he strode away.

Shadows moved in on Shane, making him wish for Nate's lantern, after all. A sulfur match would have to do. He groped for the box in his pocket, his thoughts going back over the day. What had caused the sorrow he'd glimpsed on America's face when she'd looked at her daughter? Did she miss her husband? She couldn't have been a widow for very long.

An owl's hooting interrupted his thoughts, and the rustle of wings rode the night wind. He tipped his head to search for the bird. Starlight shone from the sky, and he breathed in a lungful of sagebrush-scented air.

A darker shape detached from the shadows nearby. He dropped into a defensive posture. "Who's there?"

The figure moved into the moonlight, and Shane straightened. "Dillingham! It's an odd hour for a visit. What are you doing here?"

"I'll explain inside, if it's all the same to you."

Did this have to do with Con's leaving? Shane entered the cabin and struck a match. The stench of sulfur tickled his nostrils.

Dillingham shut the door behind them.

Shane struck several more matches before lighting the lantern. A circle of light spread across the scarred table. He shook the last match out and gestured toward a chair. "Have a seat."

Dillingham remained in the shadows. "Thank you, but I'd rather stand. It's best if I say my piece and leave."

Shane waited. Whatever brought a caller at this hour had to be serious. After what Con had told him about the suspicions he shared with Dillingham, Shane suspected what the matter might be.

"Tonight I overheard several deputies planning to rob Wash Stapleton and two others on their way to Alder Gulch." Dillingham talked and paced. "The store was closed, and I'd come in by the back door when I saw light in the sheriff's office. They didn't know I was there, and I don't think they heard me leave."

Shane let out his breath. "Lord, have mercy!"

Dillingham's pacing picked up speed. "I wrestled with my conscience for a spell. It meant taking my life in my hands, but A man has to live with himself. I warned the three men they planned to ambush."

"You did the right thing."

Dillingham halted. "I told Sheriff Plummer, but I wanted you to know too, in case something happens to me. You're one of the few people I trust in this godforsaken place. I'm leaving for Alder Gulch in the morning. I hope to arrive in one piece, but I have no guarantee that will happen."

"I can ride part of the way with you. I plan to leave for Deer Lodge in the morning."

"Then I'd have two people to keep alive. Thanks just the same, but that's not a good idea."

Shane thought of the Colt Paterson revolver in his saddlebag. He'd drawn it on game to provide a meal in the wild but never on a man.

You've gone soft. Con's accusation returned to his mind.

He loosened the string tie about his neck, which all at once seemed tight. "What you mean, of course, is that I'd be useless in a fight."

Dillingham's silence answered him.

Shane couldn't leave it alone. "Do you believe that God looks after us?"

The tension left Dillingham's shoulders. "Of course, I do, preacher, but that doesn't mean—"

"What doesn't it mean?"

The deputy started pacing again. "That a man can't defend himself when called upon to do so."

"God asks us, when struck, to turn the other cheek."

"I doubt you'd live long in Bannack doing that." Dillingham

came to rest in front of him. "The Bible also mentions that there's a time for war and a time for peace. Confusing the two leads to problems, I reckon."

"You know the Bible," Shane conceded. He'd raised an interesting point Shane would have to think about.

"My ma made sure of that." Dillingham nodded, the lantern light gleaming in his hair. "Look, I do appreciate the offer of help. No offense intended, but I travel better on my own."

CHAPTER EIGHT

A STRAY WISP OF HAIR, DANCING in the breeze that followed the creek, whipped across Addie's eyes. She tucked it behind her ear and pulled her shawl closer around her shoulders. The Bakers, Taylors, and others who had brought and shared dessert had gone. The preacher had left for home, America had taken her baby back to her wagon, and Travis was bedded down for the night. Beyond the circle of light shed by her lantern, the wagons hunched in darkness, with trees behind and the heavens above.

Tomorrow would be a trying day. She really should go to bed.

Music and the babble of voices drifted to her from town. The saloon doors must be propped open, spilling wayward sounds into the night. Addie had only a hazy idea of what went on in such establishments, but from the little her husband had told her, she wished Nate didn't have to walk by them alone on his way back to camp.

He was a grown man who could take care of himself, but she would wait up for him all the same.

In the hills beyond camp, coyotes yipped and wailed, their uncanny cries sending shivers down Addie's spine. She'd heard wolves howl aplenty on the journey from St. Louis, but the caterwauling of coyotes set her nerves more on edge. The creatures usually avoided the wagon camp, but if they approached, the guard would shoot them.

Lantern light walked up the trees along the path from town. Addie's stomach churned, and her breath caught. Why should she feel like this at Nate's approach, for heaven's sake?

He reached the camp and turned aside from the path. His long strides carried him to her. "Evening." He took off his hat and tucked it under his arm. "You're up late."

"I wasn't sleepy." She stifled a yawn.

Nate chuckled. "That seems to have changed."

"I should turn in now, I guess." Her tone betrayed her reluctance.

He set his lantern on the trunk beside hers. "Come look at the stars with me."

"All right." Ignoring the inner voice that warned her to be careful, she fell into step beside him.

"We'll go down to the water but stay where the night guard can see us. I don't want to get far from camp."

He didn't explain why, but Addie knew many reasons why it wouldn't be a good idea. They stood on the banks of the creek in the moonlight. The coyotes had left off wailing, but Grasshopper Creek's namesake creatures still rattled as they called for their mates.

Pinpoints of light shone from the sky, some brightly, while others clustered so thickly they resembled milk. Nate pointed out the North Star and the two Bears. "Do you know the story of the Great and Little Bears?"

She thought back to her childhood, when such things had been important to her. "I don't think I do."

"It originated in Greek mythology. You see, Zeus desired a woman other than the one he married. While walking in the forest with Callisto, the object of his affections, he noticed Hera, his wife, walking toward them. Thinking on his feet, Zeus turned Callisto into a bear and walked Hera home. He hoped to return and change Callisto back into a woman. Unfortunately, Callisto's son went hunting that day and shot an arrow through a bear's heart. Imagine the young man's surprise when the dying bear turned into his mother. Zeus heard him weeping and—to prevent Hera from learning what had happened— transformed Callisto's son into a bear also. He hung them both in the sky as constellations. Callisto is the Great Bear, and Arcas, her son, became the Little Bear."

"What a sad story."

"It's a cautionary tale. The moral is to be faithful to your spouse or suffer the consequences."

But what if your spouse is dead?

The question pressed Addie, but she kept it to herself. It didn't need an answer. She couldn't imagine anyone taking Clyde's place at her side. She'd only recently lost him at the Laramie crossing, and grief left her confused. She filled her lungs with cool air. "We should head back. Tomorrow will come early."

"That it will, but stay a moment longer. There's something I want to talk to you about."

She hesitated, not sure she wanted to hear what he had to say. He sounded so serious. "What is it?" she finally asked.

"The preacher started me thinking. I'm not sure that you going to Alder Gulch is such a good idea."

"Most of the miners I mean to cook for are there."

"You could settle in Idaho City instead."

"But in Alder Gulch I'll earn enough to open my own restaurant in no time."

"I hate to think of you slaving away like that." Regret laced his voice.

"I'm willing to do it."

"The men may give you trouble, being as how you're so beautiful."

"I believe you flatter me." Her face warmed at the compliment. "However, I will deal with that if it happens, but I need to survive. That's not easy when you're a widow. Going to Alder Gulch where the gold is flowing will help me establish a restaurant of my own. If I went somewhere more settled, I'd wind up a servant all my days."

"It's a man's job to provide for a woman."

"My husband can no longer do that." She stated the bald

fact in a flat voice.

"You're young and beautiful. Someone else will step in if you let him. Maybe a miner who could earn enough for your care." He moved closer. "Addie, I—"

"You forget yourself, Mr. Whalen." Her heart pounded.

He took a backward step. "Forgive me. It's just that I care about—"

"Please, don't!" The cry broke from her on a wave of grief. "I can't hear this right now."

Nate stood with the moonlight at his back and his face in shadow while in the creek behind him, grasshoppers called for their mates. "I apologize. I didn't mean to upset you."

Addie wrestled with herself until she could speak softly. "Don't give it another thought. I know you meant well."

"Sleep on it, will you? Perhaps you'll see the merit in going to Idaho City."

She held onto her patience. "I've made up my mind. I'm going to Alder Gulch."

Nate flung himself down and crawled into his bedroll, turning onto his back and raising his arm over his head. The same stars he'd watched with Addie shone down on him now, ever bright. It almost seemed he might reach out and catch one in his hand, but that was an illusion. Something as precious as a star or a woman's heart could not become his simply for the taking. He'd forgotten that tonight.

Addie had waited up for him and seemed to give him every encouragement to speak his mind, or so he'd persuaded himself. He'd lost his head and allowed his desires to get the better of him. Being in Addie's presence seemed to have that effect on him. At any rate, he'd made a mess of things and would have to mend his fences with her. They both needed a little time before he tried to talk to her again, but they only had a couple of days before reaching Alder Gulch. He tried not to take her rejection to heart. She hadn't been bereaved for very long, and he should have respected that.

Nate hadn't wished for this heartache, but he couldn't get Addie out of his mind. He'd liked Clyde Martin when he'd met him as a member of the wagon train. At the time, Addie had been one of the wives. It was only after her husband's death that he'd noticed her as a woman. He wished it could have happened after she'd been widowed longer. It would have made things easier for them both . . . and probably for that son of hers, as well.

The Great Bear and the Little Bear shone in the night sky, their story reminding him to tread lightly with Travis. Coming between a mother and her child would bring nothing but sorrow to anyone. But Nate wasn't about to give up and let himself be driven away from the woman he loved.

Everything had changed for him since he'd fallen in love with Addie. It had happened so quickly. She'd given him a soft look and a smile. That had been enough to claim his attention. Observing her over time had only caused his admiration for her to grow. Her gentle ways and quiet conversation bound his heart to hers. Dark-haired and with warm brown eyes, she wasn't hard to look at either.

Nate had mostly drifted during his life. Now he wanted nothing more than to settle down and make a home for Addie and her son. He longed to ease her life, provide for her, and smooth the creases from her forehead. He would do that with a thousand kisses if only she would give him the right. Hopefully, time would heal her wounds and allow him the chance to love and cherish her.

However long that took, he would wait.

Archibald's hooves clopped along, and Shane's saddle creaked in rhythm. The trail cut through rolling grasslands dotted by the dark shapes of buffalo. In the distance, mountains lifted snowy shoulders against a blue sky. Traveling the open road always restored his soul. The Lord Himself had taken time away from His flock when He needed it. Who was he to spurn such wisdom?

Time spent alone seemed especially important right now in order to sort himself out. No point dragging others into his confusion. Right when he'd decided to continue in service to the Lord, America had entered his life. Now, thoughts of her occupied him, distracting him from his mission. Watching her tenderness toward her baby was almost his undoing. The sight filled him with an urgent desire to protect them both.

What was a woman like America doing in the gold camps, anyway? He pictured her in a drawing room or on the arm of a fine gentleman—*not* cooking for miners in a gold camp. He'd encountered enough widows to know their lot was not always an easy one, however. That was why they often remarried quickly. America would probably do the same.

That thought didn't sit well with him.

Perhaps he should help America find a proper husband. Favoring that idea even less, Shane put the whole matter out of his mind. He ought to be dwelling on more important concerns. If Chief Snag's murderers had gone to Deer Lodge, he had only a few days to prepare his heart to speak to them.

Those who lived by violence would also die by it, as the Bible made clear. The murderers had probably not considered that truth from the Good Book, if they knew it at all. They seemed to live from day to day, satisfying the needs of the flesh without considering eternity. Shane didn't understand that mindset, having lived with the idea of mortality from an early age. He'd left his mother and father in the grave and come to America during the famine by casting himself upon his Uncle

Seamus's dubious mercies.

God had spared Shane when the potatoes went bad, and He'd delivered him again from Uncle Seamus's drunkenness. He'd been too angry to believe that then. Understanding came later, after David Masters arrived in Five Points. The man of God had endured the hunger, sickness, and gang violence Shane suffered for no other reason than because he'd cared.

That act of mercy had introduced Shane to a man with a heart that hurt for the injustices others withstood. It caused him to question his own view of the world as something to be fought in order to survive. The gentleness God had shown him through David Masters overwhelmed the anger that drove Shane, and he'd given up fighting forever.

At least, that's what he'd meant to do. Circumstances had tested his resolve of late, but he needed to conquer this weakness. How could he lead others away from violence if he failed to master it in himself?

The short layover in Bannack had been enough to throw America off her stride. Even before that, when traveling with the wagon train, she'd barely managed to tend her oxen and care for her baby, let alone keep body and soul together. She unhitched her oxen and turned them out to graze in the wagon circle with a feeling of relief. They hadn't traveled far from Bannack on this first day out, but she would welcome her bed tonight.

Travis came up from the Beaverhead River with a pail of water in each hand. With the wagons close by the banks, they could haul water in relative safety. Guards watched over the camp all day and night now that they'd left the protection of Bannack behind.

Addie would start supper soon. She should lend a hand.

Liberty cooed from her rocking cradle where it rested in the shade of the wagon. America's heart melted. Her daughter would need to be changed and fed before it would be possible to help Addie.

What was Shane doing right now? The thought appeared out of the blue. Did he think about her as much as she did him? Maybe now that they were apart she could be free of him. Somehow, the idea didn't fill her with joy.

Taking care of Liberty took her mind off Shane . . . at least for a while. Later, she brought her daughter along to the cook fire. Addie bent over a pot hung from a tripod above the flames. Her hair, neatly pinned at her nape this morning, had come partway down, and her smile didn't seem as bright as usual. America had to repeat her offer to help. Something had made Addie flustered and distracted. Reading her hesitancy to talk from her quick glances and pressed lips, America refrained from asking what was wrong. She simply took the spoon from her hand. "You're tired. Go sit down while I finish up."

Addie opened her mouth to protest but then nodded in quick agreement. "I'll hold the baby." She sat on the wagon tongue where she cooed at Liberty. America stole glances at her, smiling at the faces she made while talking to the baby, happy to see the furrow between her brows smooth over.

The wind kicked up, so America made sure to stir the pot from downwind of the fire, even though that meant dodging smoke. More than one woman had lost her life while cooking in a wagon camp when her skirt blew into the flames. She'd heard that in some wagon trains the women had taken to wearing bloomers instead of skirts as a precaution, but America couldn't imagine doing that. She bent over the pot and stirred what looked like a stew made from jerked beef, potatoes, carrots, and possibly parsnips. It smelled wonderful, and her stomach growled in anticipation. How Addie could dress up even the plainest fare never ceased to amaze her.

She pointed to a large porcelain bowl on the top of the trunk

Addie used as a table. "What is the dough?"

Addie looked up from kissing Liberty's fingers. "It's hoe cake. Travis, bring the skillet for America, please."

America heated bacon grease and shaped the cornmeal dough into small cakes for frying. The familiar chores took her mind off her aches. Addie's visit with Liberty did them both a world of good, and it was nice to work without having to stop every few moments and comfort a fussing baby.

Later, she ate two helpings of stew, ravenous from the day's exertions.

Addie washed the dishes, and America picked up a dishtowel to dry, but then Liberty woke and began talking to herself. Travis stepped in to walk the baby around camp as he talked to her in the singsong voice she seemed to love.

America picked a tin cup out of the rinse water and wrapped the cotton cloth around it. With her stomach filled, Nate's harmonica whining, and chores nearly done for the day, tension sloughed from her. The fading sun slipped below the horizon, taking the day's heat with it. All through the camp, soft laughter mingled with the murmur of voices.

Addie finished washing the dishes and stretched with a hand to her lower back. "I sure hope tomorrow will be easier. Thanks for helping out today. It meant a lot."

America smiled. "I'm glad to lend a hand."

Addie frowned. She'd been serious all through supper, but not like this. "Can I ask you something?"

"Sure."

"I wonder if having you help me cook for the miners is fair to you."

America glanced sideways at her. "Why wouldn't it be?"

"I'm thinking of the baby, mostly. Living in a mining camp is rough, and building a home for us will take time. Maybe you should go on to Idaho City, where you and Liberty can be more comfortable."

America tamped down a rush of panic. "What would I do

there? No one would know me. I might not find a job."

"I'm sure someone would give you one, but if not, you could always call upon a church to help you."

America shook her head and dried the last plate. "I don't want to be a burden. Besides, you need my help."

"I do, but I don't want you deciding your future on my account. Do you really want to come along to Alder Gulch?"

America laid the wet towel across the top of the trunk to dry, taking more care than she normally would. She straightened and turned to Addie. "The journey from Fort Bridger was hard, but it would have been much worse without your assistance. You fed me, helped me with my baby, loaned your son to tend my oxen, and welcomed me at your fireside. That means so much to me. Helping you in exchange is the least I can do."

"But is it what you want for yourself?"

"Yes, of course. I meant what I said. Earning enough to set myself and Liberty up for a better life is worth a little hardship. I can always move to Idaho City later." She laughed. "It's your fault for promising to pay so well."

Addie smiled. "You're worth every penny, but I'm worried that earning your keep may prove a hardship in such a place."

"I promise to see you through, no matter what."

CHAPTER NINE

SHANE WALKED INTO THE RECEPTION AREA of Bishop David Masters's office in Idaho City. David's secretary, Emma Bradley, looked up from her desk. "You've just missed him, I'm afraid. He's gone for the day." Her eyes took on a bemused look while her gaze wandered over his face.

Not for the first time, Shane wondered about her reaction to him. The way she softened her voice while gazing at him with calf's eyes could only lead to one conclusion. He found her attention distracting. However, he could avoid her most of the time when his circuit took him to other locations. Considering Miss Bradley's spinster status, how could he determine whether she admired him for himself or as a potential husband?

She wasn't bad to look at for someone who admired curvaceous women with ruddy skin and flaming hair. Even if Shane *had* been interested in romance a certain blonde widow with the ability to tie him in knots with one glance from her amber eyes had already snared him. If he ever forgot his intention to live a single life, America Reed would be to blame.

Not that I have any expectation of doing anything of the sort, he hastened to assure himself. A circuit preacher's wife faced loneliness as a matter of course. He'd seen how a man could break a woman's spirit by leaving her alone and starved of affection. It had destroyed his sister, and although he'd searched for a way to save her, he had found none.

Shane left a message letting David know he was in town, took his leave from the spinster Bradley, and made his way to one of the local watering holes to begin his search for Chief

Snag's murderers. He strode through the tall glassed doors into the gentlemen's club. The bartender looked up, his face taking on a familiar wariness. Shane didn't mind it so much in Idaho City, where fists battered him less often than words. The man turned his shoulder without offering a greeting.

"Good evening to you, Cyrus," Shane corrected the omission. "How have you been since last I saw you?" He tried to keep the Irish from his voice for the sake of his errand, since it had annoyed the man on a previous occasion. Cyrus had nicknamed him Shant after the shanties the poor Irish lived in. Hopefully, he would have forgotten to use the slur.

"Can I get you anything, Shant? Maybe a shot of whiskey, or do you favor brandy perhaps?" Cyrus smirked.

"I want neither, as well you know." Shane returned his smile in a cheerful manner. "I have business with Buck Stinson. Have you seen him in town of late?" If he asked for every man involved in Chief Snag's killing, the bartender might guess his reason. Buck Stinson seemed to have the stronger personality, so Shane would probably find them all once he located him.

"Why should I tell you something like that?" Cyrus leaned on the counter as if he had all the time in the world to harass Shane, which was possibly true. Outside, the curtain of night drew across the day, but few customers patronized the bar.

"Have you a reason not to?" Shane shot back.

Cyrus's face went red, and Shane realized his mistake. He shouldn't have challenged the man on his turf. Whether in the slums or outside them, some things never changed.

"You'll receive no help from me," Cyrus growled. "I doubt anyone else in town will do anything for you, either."

"Thank you for your time all the same." Shane started for the door.

"Stay away from now on, Shant."

He pushed his way out the door and into the street. With Cyrus's filthy insults clinging to him, he felt unclean. He tried not to let them bother him, but truth be told, they hurt more than he cared to admit.

The bartender at his next stop gave him a lukewarm welcome. Grady knew nothing about Buck's whereabouts. Shane thanked him and stepped out onto the boardwalk.

"Hey, Reverend!" a feminine voice called from the balcony over the saloon. The light from a cigarette glowed as an unseen hand carried it in an arc. Tobacco smoke wafted on the night air. "You looking for Buck?"

He peered upward but couldn't make out who the voice belonged to. "I am."

"You won't find him here. There's no reason Grady couldn't tell you that. Buck left town a couple of days ago."

"Do you have any idea where he went?"

"What do you want with him?" Caution entered the woman's voice.

"Just to talk. He didn't ride toward Alder Gulch, did he?"

"I couldn't say."

"Thanks for the information. You saved me the time I would have spent looking for a man who isn't here."

Silence answered him. He glanced up at the balcony. The light from the cigarette had vanished.

America held Liberty close and walked beside Addie, who drove the oxen hitched to her wagon from the side. Travis brought America's own team and wagon along behind them. America's feet ached, but her spirit soared as the wagon train rolled through the Ruby Valley beneath a sky that went on forever. Sagebrush and grasses spread across the wide valley to the feet of lofty mountain ranges with names like Tobacco Root, Highlands, and Snowcrest.

They rolled past Beaverhead Rock, a large rock formation the Shoshone tribe had named for its resemblance to a beaver's head. Addie told her that while guiding Meriwether Lewis and William Clark during their explorations, Sacajawea saw the distinctive formation in the distance and knew they neared her people's encampment.

They turned southeast at a crossroads where four ancient trails intersected near three rivers that flowed into one another. The trampled grasses showed where wagons had recently camped. Miles later, they neared a roadhouse brooding beneath the shadows of cottonwood trees. The two-story building sat well back from the road.

America glanced at Addie. "I don't like this place at all."

"It must be Robbers Roost," Addie informed her. "Grant told me that road agents watch for travelers from the balcony and ride out to relieve those who pass of their valuables."

The balcony sat empty today, and as they crept by, the windows stared blankly. A wagon train of their size might present too much of a challenge for a gang of road agents who preferred easy pickings. Still, they traveled well away from the notorious hideout before stopping for the night. For their camp, Grant chose a spot along the banks of the Ruby River, named for the garnets found in its bed by early settlers who mistook them for rubies.

Standing with the wind blowing her unbound hair, America gazed out across water stained red by the sun dipping toward the mountains. Liberty cooed in her arms, and she smiled down at her. With the wagons nearby and the guards on duty, America could take a moment before going to bed to breathe in the cool evening air without worry. In a smaller train, she wouldn't have dared to leave her wagon.

"There you are." Addie came up from behind and joined her on the grassy river bank. "Are you feeling any better tonight?"

"Some, although my feet know I've walked on them." She glanced sideways at Addie. "How about you?"

"Same here. If we must walk ourselves into the ground, at least we can do it in the midst of beauty, however. Just look at that sunset."

"At times like these, I'm glad I joined the wagon train." America laughed. "I'm not so fond of it when my oxen give me trouble, though."

"We pushed them too hard today and camped later than usual."

"That will make tomorrow's drive all the shorter."

"Your hair is flying everywhere. You'll have tangles." Addie pulled America's hair back and began plaiting it.

America squinted, having looked too long at the sun. "I wonder what tomorrow will bring."

"I'll confess to being a little nervous about finding a location for my cook tent. So many wagons, carts, and riders on horseback have passed us these couple of days that I'm beginning to wonder if there will be a place for us when we arrive."

Addie tugged her hair, and America winced. "Those were miners. There will always be room for anyone willing to feed them."

Addie sighed. "You're right. Guess I'm thinking too hard."

"That's easy with something so important."

"I don't know what we'll do if it doesn't work out." Addie gave a shaky laugh. "There I go, worrying again."

America smiled. "We can always move in with the Bakers if it comes to that."

Addie's lips curved into a gentle smile. "They are kindness itself, but they might not have the means to provide for us and themselves too. No, I wouldn't want to expect it."

"Have you any family who could take you and Travis in?"

"Not living." Addie pulled a short piece of ribbon from her pocket and tied off the braid. "What about you? You never mention having family."

"No, there's no one." That wasn't strictly true, not if you counted a father who ignored you and a mother who spent her time traveling Europe in the company of her friends. Since their rather scandalous divorce, neither had made time for their daughter. "Maybe I'll take the good reverend's advice and find somewhere more suitable to live."

"He suggested you do that?"

"Why do you sound surprised?"

"No reason, really. I would have thought he'd want to keep you around."

"Why would you say that?"

"Haven't you noticed the way he watches you?"

She had, but she'd put that down to irritation when she annoyed him. Well, mostly. There had been a few heart-stopping glances from his gorgeous eyes. She brought herself up short. The last thing she needed in her life was a man, and especially not one on intimate terms with the Almighty. Losing Kyle and then Richard had taught her that steering clear of romantic love was the only way to avoid heartache, and she intended to do exactly that. Except now that Addie had mentioned Shane's interest in her, she couldn't seem to stop thinking about him.

She told herself it was only natural to be flattered by a handsome man's attention, but her reaction felt like a whole lot more than vanity.

Shane crossed the gray carpet woven with lighter fan shapes, walking toward the table in the hotel restaurant where David Masters waited for him. Dressed in a black jacket, white shirt, and string tie, the bishop kept his hair cropped short and his face clear of whiskers. He looked little older than when Shane had first met him four years ago in Five Points.

The bishop stood and extended his hand in greeting. "Shane! You're a sight for sore eyes, I must say. How have you been?"

Shane shook his hand. "I'm faring well for the most part, but I find the circuit difficult at times."

David sat down, and Shane pulled out a rosewood chair across from him.

From behind his spectacles, David's brown eyes shone with warmth. "What troubles you?"

"My inability to influence my charges with the gospel of peace." When the confession left his lips, Shane's tension eased.

David nodded in quick understanding. "You tend toward impatience as I recall."

"I'm guilty of that, I suppose."

"You've only ridden a circuit for half a year now. That's not much time to develop as a preacher. Give it a chance. I suspect you'll find it easier in time."

"I hope I won't disappoint you."

"I have no doubt about your success."

"I wish I had your faith."

David smiled. "That too comes with time."

Shane gave his order to the waiter then returned his attention to David. "Thank you for supper."

"I'm happy to provide it. I don't imagine you've eaten all that well this past month. Miss Bradley mentioned you looked in need of a good meal."

Shane lifted a brow. "Did she?"

David unfolded his napkin and laid it on his lap in an elegant gesture. "She thinks highly of you, in case you wondered."

Shane shook out his own napkin while hiding his amusement at David's attempt at matchmaking. "I'm honored." He kept his voice neutral.

"She'll be in church on Sunday and would welcome your company at her side."

Shane couldn't hold back his grin at the obvious ploy. An unfortunate lapse, for David would surely give it the wrong interpretation. "I wouldn't want to mislead such a nice woman about my intentions," he said hurriedly.

"What would those intentions be, if I may ask?"

"To stay away from romance."

"That's a worthy ambition if you can manage it." David laughed. "But it can happen that romance won't stay away from you."

The image of America peering at him from the balcony of the Merrick Hotel arose in his mind. He pushed the memory away with a grimace. "I'll do my best to avoid attachments, regardless."

"Why would you want to do that?"

"For the sake of my calling."

David sipped from his water glass and set it down before speaking. "Some people live rewarding single lives, but most of us do better to marry. Either way, your service as a preacher should have no bearing on your decision. Are you certain you're not hiding behind your ministry?"

Liberty slept through the night, a rare treat from a baby in her fourth month, and America woke stronger in body. Excitement charged through the camp in anticipation of their imminent arrival at their destination, and they made an eager start.

Riders and wagons had overtaken the train all along the way, but America hadn't expected anything like what she saw when they entered Alder Gulch. Settlement after settlement unfolded for miles along the creek. Numerous wagons, tents, dugouts, and brush wickiups littered the banks of the creek. Men in rough garb with sluice boxes and gold pans bent over the water, hoping to become rich.

"Where do they all come from?" America asked.

Addie lashed her whip on the ground beside her lead oxen, and the beasts turned in response. She glanced at America.

"Some take a steamboat to Fort Benton. Others bring wagons like we have. Then there are those who ride."

"It's amazing how quickly they've arrived."

"But not surprising." Addie's voice took on a wry note. "Where gold can be had for the taking, men are bound to follow."

America thought about that idea. She could understand accepting a risk that could lead to wealth . . . or poverty. That's what she and Addie were doing, but in a different way.

Wagons peeled off from the train. Those who had joined their lives for months now bid one another goodbye. Several families drove away to seek their fortunes together.

Nate rode up and reined in his horse to walk beside them. He tipped his hat. "Grant tells me there are a couple of towns starting up a little farther along. Might be good for finding hungry miners with money to spend."

Addie nodded. "Thanks for the information." She looked at America. "What do you think?"

America shrugged. "Whatever seems best to you is fine by me."

"It sounds like a possibility." Addie lashed her whip again. "Why don't we take a look?"

Nate squinted against the brightening sun. "Mind if I come along? I'd feel better if I saw you settled."

"I'd appreciate that." Addie spoke in reserved tones.

Nate's smile laid his heart bare.

America stole a glance at her friend. How was Addie faring against Nate's attentions, with her husband only a few months buried? Spots of color stood out in her cheeks, but she seemed otherwise composed.

"Thank you." Nate tipped his hat again. "I'm obliged."

The company stopped at noon outside a town going by the name of Nevada City, one of a string of towns starting up in Alder Gulch. They ate leftover bread and jerky and drank the clear, cold water. America rested her feet while sitting on a crate and playing with Liberty. Her baby's laughter set off her own and started Addie and Travis giggling as well.

Bill Baker, with his wife next to him, cleared his throat from beside America's wagon. "Just thought we'd say goodbye. We're heading off now."

America stood. "So soon?" She'd known they would separate at some point, but now that the time had arrived, she didn't like it one bit.

"You'll have to come by and see us," Sarah invited. "Bring that sweet baby for me to hold." Her voice choked off, and she dabbed at the moisture glistening on her cheeks.

Bill shifted from one foot to the other and looked at his wife as if she might explode any minute.

"Thank you, and you must do the same." Blinking to keep her own tears at bay, America went to her. "Would you like to hold Liberty now?"

"I'll say!" Sarah's smile broke out.

America transferred her baby into Sarah's willing arms and stood back to admire the sight they made. "You've been such a help to me. You made a hard journey easier, and I thank you both."

"I thought I heard your voices." Addie walked over from her own wagon. "Did you say you were leaving the train now?"

"That's right." Bill answered in his gruff voice. "We wanted to tell you two ladies that if your plans don't work out, well . . ." He cleared his throat again. "You can come to Nevada City and stay with us."

"Thank you so much." Tears rose in Addie's eyes. "That means more to me than I can say. I'd settle here but I want to set up my cook tent in Verona. Grant told me there are more miners there."

Bill patted her back, looking uncomfortable at the possibility of Addie weeping. "Don't you worry none. Are you ready, Mrs. Baker?"

"Goodbye, little darling." Sarah kissed the baby's head and gave her back to America. She waved a final time, and their wagon moved off.

America swallowed against a lump in her throat. Having caught something of Addie's vision, she didn't expect to call upon the Baker's charity. Still, in a time and place riddled with uncertainty, it was nice to know friends were near. "Nevada City seems like a nice place to live," she said wistfully.

"Let's go on a little farther," Addie urged at her elbow. "Nate suggested Verona. I want to see what it's like."

Verona was a misspelling of Varina, the name of Jefferson Davis's wife, the first lady the Confederacy. As Grant had remarked with ill-concealed scorn, "If the founders want to name their town after a beautiful woman, they ought to make sure they have the spelling right."

They drove their wagons the four miles to Verona. Addie chose for her cook tent a location a little distance from where a mercantile bakery was under construction.

They stopped for the night, and Nate rolled out his bedroll a short distance away.

His proximity comforted America. In a new place, she lay awake and found herself party to an argument that sprang up between two miners. If she'd fallen asleep, they would have roused her, for they obviously felt no need to keep their voices down. Their slurred words and blustering challenges announced their inebriated state.

With the two shouting at one another not far from the wagon, Liberty woke with a wail. America pulled her baby close to comfort her, wondering if she had made the right decision in coming here after all.

CHAPTER TEN

SHANE MADE SURE HE ARRIVED EARLY to church on Sunday for the sake of prayer, but also to avoid Emma Bradley. She'd greeted him at the door on more than one occasion in the past, and he found it disorienting. It took a strong mind to resist a female determined to attach herself to him. Gifted in administrative skills, she would succumb to her natural tendencies and attempt to lead him about after the service.

Finding David already in the small prayer room off the main sanctuary, Shane knelt on a padded kneeler nearby and bowed his head. He prayed for the souls of those who would attend the service that morning and also for those who would not.

He remembered the saloon girl who had helped him and said a special prayer for her deliverance. Lifting up the three men involved in Chief Snag's murder came harder. He also prayed for the two widows who had gone to Alder Gulch. Their drive toward self-sufficiency could possibly lead them into harm's way.

Shane heard David rise and go through the door into the sanctuary but lingered a little longer to ask God to relieve his own confusion. He couldn't get the last question David had asked at supper out of his mind. Could he be using his calling to hide from his feelings for America? And if so, why? Drawing a blank, he put the question from his mind and focused on other matters.

He prayed on David's behalf, that as God's instrument he would deliver a sermon that fed the gathered flock. Some traveled many miles to attend church. They came to socialize, but also to receive morsels of hope. During Shane's visits, he had seen the weight of death crush a family, the disappointment of a marriage gone bad, and the sorrows a wayward child brought a parent. Heartaches came in with the congregation, but God met them all.

Shane left the prayer room with a lighter heart.

Emma entered at the back of the church, flushed and breathless, as if she'd rushed to arrive. He had to admit she looked especially pretty in a deep blue dress that complemented her skin. Her hair cascaded in bright ringlets that bounced when she walked, color flushed her cheeks, and her eyes shone as she looked at him.

She navigated to his side at the front of the sanctuary. "Good morning, Reverend Hayes." Speaking in a throaty voice, she laid a gloved hand on his arm.

He smiled down at her. "Hello, Miss Bradley." He said nothing further. She might take his conversation as an invitation to attach herself to him.

"It's nice to see you looking so well this morning. You must have spent a restful night."

She refused to afford him the luxury of remaining silent, apparently. "Yes, thank you." He gave a curt nod in answer to her too-personal question.

Emma smiled, displaying even, white teeth. "I hope Bishop Masters found you for supper on Friday."

"Yes, he did. Thank you." Shane spoke brusquely but when her smile faltered, repented for being short with her. He had never inquired into the circumstances of her life, but loneliness might be the driving force behind her behavior.

The next smile he gave her came from the heart. "Perhaps you will do me the honor of joining me for service." He regretted his words at once, but enough compassion remained to endure her company despite her efforts to commandeer him.

Heat crept up Addie's neck. She stopped stirring the bacon stew in the Dutch oven and stepped back from the potbelly stove in the center of the tent. Its chimney ran to a stove jack in the makeshift canopy Nate and Travis had rigged. Three additional tarps formed walls to block the wind, while the side facing the street stood open.

"Begging your pardon, ma'am." The miner dipped his head, which set his frayed hat swaying. "I forgot there was a lady within earshot."

Addie frowned. "I prefer you leave curse words outside my tent." But Virgil Henry looked suitably chastened, so she gave him a forgiving smile. "More stew?"

He smiled as if she'd just offered him a placer claim. "Don't mind if I do."

She ladled his plate full at the stove and carried it to him, where he sat at a table Nate had built from sawhorses and planks. She plunked his second helping down in front of him.

Three more miners came in. Addie called a greeting and hurried to serve the new arrivals. She fetched biscuits and stew for them. When she thought no one was looking, she rubbed the ache in the small of her back and peered outside the tent. *What is keeping America, anyway?*

"Working too hard, Widow Martin?" Virgil asked. "Never mind. When I make my strike, I'll marry you and take you away from all this." He laughed, but his eyes looked halfway serious.

America rushed in, and Virgil's attention diverted to her. Addie hid a smile, grateful to lose her unwanted admirer.

Flushed, breathless, and with her blonde hair slipping from its pins, America looked fresh and beautiful in a tan calico dress. "Sorry I'm late," she murmured.

Addie smiled to ease the worried pucker between America's

brows. "How's Liberty?"

"Her colic is better for now. I left her sleeping in Travis's arms." She glanced toward Virgil. "I've met that man before."

"Where?"

"While I was on the balcony at the Merrick Hotel. He wanted to shoot Shane."

"Goodness, I thought he was a harmless old man."

"Not when he's drinking."

Addie blew out a breath. "He seems sober today, anyway."

America slipped past Virgil to clear a vacated table.

Virgil watched America in a way Addie decided was not seemly. Her protective instincts rose full force. "America, go outside and do the dishes, please."

America looked at her with gratitude and hurried out to the washing station behind her wagon.

Virgil lurched to his feet. "Thank you for that meal, Widow Martin." He tipped his hat, making it flop about like a chicken, and strode from the tent.

Addie watched him out of sight down the street before releasing her breath.

Another customer entered, and she smiled. "Mr. Whalen, won't you sit down?"

Nate had gone off to establish a claim shortly after helping Addie put the cook tent together, and she hadn't seen him since. Questions burst in her mind, but she restrained her curiosity for the time being. She would let the man fill his stomach before asking him the most urgent question—the location of his claim. Her reaction to Nate's absence had taught her that she didn't want to lose touch with him. She refused to try to figure out what that meant. Maybe she would later, but not now.

"Thank you, Mrs. Martin." Nate's brown eyes warmed. "You're a welcome sight to a starving man."

She lost her train of thought entirely. "Will you take stew?"

"If that's what smells so wonderful, then yes, please."

Chiding herself for letting Nate's inviting smile and flattering words turn her head, she slapped a plate of food in front of him. He fell on it like a starving man.

How long had it been since he'd had a proper meal? Remembering his sparse camp food, she felt a twinge of guilt. She could have served him with more care. It wasn't his fault he disturbed feelings she preferred to keep buried.

Addie served second helpings to the other three miners in the tent. When she walked away from their table, they broke into laughter. She hadn't heard whatever had set them off. Maybe that was best.

"Now just relax y'self, Marcus. Widow Martin wants a real man, like *me*." Will Brody thumped his chest.

In the three weeks since she and America had arrived in town, Addie had lost track of the proposals she'd had to fend off from lonely miners. Most she could take in stride, but the nature of this particular laughter set her teeth on edge. She carried a vinegar pie to the men's table. "Gentlemen, would you like to eat this pie or wear it?"

Silence followed her question. The three men's eyes widened in recognition of their peril.

"Well, I guess that tells me." Will Brody chortled. His companions followed suit, this time with better humor.

"Well done." The quiet words reached her, and she turned her head. Nate leaned back in his chair with a look of approval on his face.

She couldn't help but smile as she refilled his plate and walked back to him.

Nate watched her. "Keeping rough men in line can be tough, but you seem equal to the job."

"Thank you." She turned away to fetch coffee from the stove top.

Strange popping sounds punched the air.

A strong arm caught her waist. "Get down."

She let Nate pull her with him beneath his table. Chairs

scraped and dishes crashed onto the floor as the other guests turned their table on its side.

"What was that?" Addie asked. The answer rushed in on her. "Gunshots!"

Nate held a gun in his hand, his muscles tense. The eerie quiet stretched to its snapping point.

Addie sent up a silent prayer for the safety of Travis and Liberty. She could only hope they were safely tucked away, nowhere near the line of fire.

Why hadn't she gone to Idaho City when she'd had the chance? She knew the reason but hated to admit it. As surely as any miner, she'd come down with a case of gold fever. But earning quick money wasn't worth putting her life and her son's life in danger. Nor should she have invited America to come along with her baby. A thought occurred to her, and, she broke out in a cold sweat.

She'd sent America outside to wash the dishes.

America pushed the hair out of her eyes with the back of one soapy hand. Humming to herself, she swished the dishcloth across a blue willow plate Addie had carted all the way from St. Louis in her wagon. America spent a lot of time doing dishes at the wash station rigged from a wide board across saw horses, but that was all right with her. This simple chore kept her away from the lustful glances some of the miners gave her, and it only seemed fair to take over this duty since Addie did most of the cooking.

America had been glad to leave the cook tent. Seeing Virgil Henry again had brought back in vivid detail the sight of Shane lying in the mud, the sound of the rifle being cocked when Virgil took aim, and the taste of fear. Even now, her heart rate quickened at the memory of what it felt like to anticipate a man being killed in front of her.

The other reason was personal. Virgil Henry gave her the willies whenever he looked at her. She had been married and could recognize a man's interest, but what she read in Virgil's eyes was something that made her feel sick inside.

A small bird darted about the brush behind the cook tent. She smiled at it and washed another plate, her hands lingering in the warmth of the water. Virgil would be gone by the time she went back inside, and hopefully their paths would never cross again.

"You take back those lies!" someone shouted in the street directly behind her.

Gunshots split the air. "Don't shoot! Don't shoot!" another voice cried out.

America spun around, dropping the dishcloth.

Three men with guns drawn, all wearing badges, stared down at a figure who lay groaning at their feet.

She stared at the deputies, confused. How had they arrived so quickly to investigate? Why weren't they helping the person with blood pouring from his chest and a gash in his thigh? They stood over him doing nothing, almost as if they were letting him bleed to death on purpose.

Another lawman dashed into the street. "Gentlemen, surrender your weapons." His voice throbbed above the murmur of the gathering crowd.

They turned over their guns to him. He opened the chambers and reloaded them.

America frowned. *Why would he hide that the guns had been fired?* Her pulse fluttered like a frightened bird, and she put a hand to her throat. None of what she'd seen made sense.

A man in a frock coat came out of a wickiup across from where America stood. He bent over the bloodied individual and felt for his pulse. "He's alive." He looked up at the lawman who had taken the guns. "What are you doing just standing there, Gallagher? Arrest them at once!"

"I'm commencing to do that, Doc Steele." Gallagher leveled his pistol at the three lawmen. "Let's go," he barked. They walked off together.

Doc Steele called over his shoulder to someone inside the wickiup. "Come out and help me, Jones." A man wearing a red bib shirt appeared, and together they lifted the victim.

Agonized screams throbbed through the air.

America turned away with a sob. She wanted to leave this nightmare behind. Panting as if she'd run a race, and with nausea gripping her, she hurried toward the cook tent. Dizziness crashed over her in waves, so strong she stopped and held onto the wagon beside her. She bent with hands on knees and pulled deep breaths of air into her lungs.

"Lay him here." Doc Steele's voice emerged from the wickiup. No one had shut the door, and she could hear everything they said inside.

Her knees gave way, and she slumped against a wagon wheel. Tears squeezed from her eyes, ran down her face, and splashed the back of her hands.

"Will he live?" Jones asked.

America held her breath and waited for the answer she feared would come.

"Not likely, I'm afraid." Doc Steele's voice held regret.

She wanted to shake the doctor, urge him not to quit, tell him he had to make this right. Surely, something could be done for a good man who helped others. She rocked where she sat, weeping.

"Sad news," Jones said. "Poor Dillingham."

CHAPTER ELEVEN

AMERICA STOOD IN THE CROWD GATHERED at the foot of Wallace Street, the main thoroughfare through Verona. A large wagon with Alder Creek as a backdrop provided seating for Doc Steele and the other men judging the miners' trial for two of the deputies accused of shooting Dillingham. In a second wagon, deputies Buck Stinson and Haze Lyons sat in the company of friends. She'd last seen them when Deputy Gallagher marched them off.

The previous day, the other deputy arrested in the crime had gone free. Witnesses said that Charley Forbes had shouted at his companions not to shoot Dillingham. Others swore Forbes discharged his pistol as he shouted, and that his bullet was the one that had struck Dillingham's chest, ending his life.

America would have known the truth if she had turned around sooner. That she hadn't seen the actual murder might have been for the best. Sleep had not courted her well since then. Seeing a man gunned down in cold blood might have sent it away from her door entirely. Even if she had seen the whole crime, hers would have been only one voice among many witnesses anyway.

The trial had gone on until dark, resumed the next morning, and dragged until noon. America hadn't been able to spend much time watching the proceedings, but she'd gone to watch when she could. Right now, Travis was watching Liberty.

The attorneys had each rested their cases, and the time for a decision had arrived.

"Guilty or not guilty?" Doc Steele posed the question.

The miners returned a single verdict with barely a

dissenting voice. "Guilty."

America released the breath she'd been holding. Dillingham would receive justice.

"Guilty it shall be," Doc Steele proclaimed in ringing tones. "What punishment should they have?"

"Hang them!" the crowd shouted.

America did not join in. She couldn't willingly wish men to perdition, where they surely must go for such a heinous act.

Haze Lyons, one of the convicted men, began to cry. "Have mercy, I beg of you."

Someone in the crowd joined him in weeping. "Please. Spare their lives," a female voice begged.

"They're so young." One of the miner's wives protested. "They still have time to reform and live better lives."

"Now that they've been exposed as killers, they'll probably never do it again," a dance hall girl with wavy chestnut locks called out.

America read indecision on the faces around her. Right or wrong, the objections had swayed minds toward mercy.

"Excuse me, judge." One of the deputy's friends in the wagon waved a piece of paper. "If you'll read this letter Deputy Lyons wrote to his mother, I think you will know the heart of the man."

"Read the letter," the miner's wife demanded,

"Yes, the letter." Another woman took up the cause. Others joined in.

America wanted to stamp her foot. What did a letter between a man and his mother have to do with just punishment for murder?

"Put him on a horse and send him to his mother," a man in a pleated cravat and bowler hat said in a sardonic voice. Laughter and shouts of approval went up.

"Give me the letter," Doc Steele requested. After receiving it, he cleared his voice and read, "Dear Ma, I wish I could be home with you right now. The mountains are so lonely, and I miss your cooking." Doc looked out at the crowd a moment, then continued. The letter spoke of Haze Lyons's wish to bring home enough money to ease his mother's life. It even contained a bit of poetry.

America balled her hands into fists and waited for Doc Steele to finish reading. After he did, a hush fell.

The cry went up. "Take another vote!"

America held her breath while Doc Steele and the other judges considered the matter. Finally, Doc held up his hands for silence. "Those in favor of mercy say 'aye.'"

Some of the miners called, "Aye."

"Those in favor of hanging say 'nay.'"

"Nay." The reply resounded through those gathered.

"We won!" one of the miners who had voted for mercy proclaimed.

"No, you didn't. We won," someone corrected him.

An argument ensued, with each side claiming victory.

America scanned the area nearest her, searching for an escape route in case she needed to flee a brawl.

"Vote again." Someone in the crowd yelled.

Doc Steele held up his hands, but this time he had to call for silence. He glared at the crowd before giving instructions. "Those in favor of hanging, walk uphill. Those who want mercy, go downhill."

The miners divided into two equal groups and proceeded to shout one another down. America never thought she would see grown men acting like children in the name of law and order.

The next vote involved walking between pairs of men called upon to tally the count. This method faltered however, when some voting for mercy went through twice. Shouting and arguments broke out.

Good grief. America had never seen anything so ridiculous as this miners' court.

Hooves thudded in the street behind her, and she jumped out of the way in time to avoid being run over by a buckskin horse ridden by Deputy Jack Gallagher. Another woman shoved past her screaming. Jostling people boxed America in so tightly she could barely yield.

Deputy Gallagher brandished a pistol at the crowd. "They're cleared. Let them go."

America's throat went dry. If he shot that gun, she didn't want to be in the way of a stray bullet.

In the confusion, the two convicted men climbed out of the wagon and piled on a spotted pony. The Indian saddle on its back explained why they'd chosen this particular mount. It would be a crime worthy of hanging to steal a horse from a white man, but an Indian'swas fair game. Whipping the stolen pony into a gallop, they rode out of town.

America gaped after the retreating deputies in disbelief. She could barely credit a miscarriage of justice so outrageous that it could only be called a scandal. The crowd went wild around her. Some people cheered, others yelled. A fistfight broke out. The judges stood on their wagon box, gesturing and shouting for quiet.

America wanted to scream that she had seen the men who had gone free standing over Dillingham and watching the lifeblood drain from his body. Haze Lyons had a mother, but so had Dillingham—a mother who would never see her son again. But with the crowd riled and on the verge of becoming a mob, she didn't dare speak her mind. Instead, she wove her way out of the suffocating throng and started toward her wagon, turning her back on it all.

Morning mists danced above the waters of the Clark Fork River as Archibald galloped along the trail. Shane made an early start and expected to reach Alder Gulch in time for supper. His treacherous emotions leaped at the prospect of seeing America again. He sighed, having hoped time apart would free him from thoughts of her. Nothing could come of this foolish infatuation. While circuit preachers sometimes married, their families always suffered. He couldn't expect a woman like America to endure such a life. She'd suffered enough already.

A jackrabbit darted across the trail, and Archibald skidded sideways. Shane reined in both his horse and his thoughts. He needed to remain vigilant. Besides the risk of an accident, the Shoshone might not take kindly to the news that Chief Snag's murderers had ignored their banishment and drifted back to Bannack from Deer Lodge.

He turned southwest at the ancient crossroads to follow the Big Hole River. The sun shone, birds sang, and wildflowers bloomed, but he didn't linger. Shane had become used to long hours of travel, and so had Archibald. The trail forked again, and he followed the Ruby River southeast.

The sun rode high in the sky as a cloud of dust moved toward him. A wagon drew near, carrying two miners he recognized from Bannack. He guided Archibald off the trail to let them pass.

"Whoa." George Dalton called. The team of mules stomped to a halt with harnesses jingling. The big man shifted the plug of tobacco in his cheek. "Afternoon, preacher."

"Gentlemen." Shane smiled a greeting. "Headed back to Bannack, are you?"

George shook his head. "Naw. We're making a supply run to Deer Lodge."

Jared Stone took off the Stetson hat he wore and swiped a cravat across his brow. "Reverend Hayes, they could have used your services in Verona a few days ago."

Shane didn't like the sound of *that*. "Why do you say so?"

George turned his head and spat. "It's a fact. They had no one but the judge to pray at the burial."

Jared put his Stetson back on and adjusted the brim to shade his eyes. "Be still now, Dalton. He won't have heard the news yet."

Shane's mind came to attention. "News?"

George squinted one eye. "Dillingham has taken up residence in Boot Hill."

Shane stared at the man, not wanting to believe his ears. *"What* did you say?"

"Aw." Jared shook his head at his companion. "Why'd you go and tell him like that for? Can't you see he's taken it to heart?"

"What happened?" Shane enunciated each word.

Jared opened his mouth, but Dalton spoke first. "Three agin one, that's what. Each popped off a shot and dropped him where he stood."

A pulse thrummed in Shane's ears. "Three against one?"

"Yes, sir." Jared shifted in the saddle. "They called him a liar afore they shot him."

Shane looked Jared square in the eye. "Who did this?"

"Haze Lyons, Buck Stinson, and Charley Forbes are the names you want. They met up with Donald Dillingham, and afore anyone knew what they were about, they shot him. Deputy Gallagher arrested them, and they got a trial in the miners' court. Haze and Buck came off guilty, but not pretty Charley."

"The miners were all set to lynch 'em when the ladies objected." George snickered. "They had to vote again."

George snorted. "Heck, they voted three or four times, but they couldn't make up their minds what to do with 'em. Gallagher rode in and decided it was time to let 'em all go."

"What? He did this in front of the judges?" Shane could barely comprehend such an act of lunacy.

"That's a fact." Jared nodded. "'Course, Gallagher was waving a gun."

Shane closed his eyes. "May God have mercy."

"I'm sorry to bring you such news." Jared's voice came from a long way away.

"Are you all right, Reverend?" George's face swam into

view.

"Just taking it in." Shane straightened in the saddle. "Thank you for the information."

They parted, and Shane rode on with a heavy heart. Did the law mean nothing in Idaho Territory? How could men convicted of such a despicable act go free? He gripped the reins until his knuckles showed white and Archibald tossed his head in protest.

He eased off on the reins, but rage still coiled like a snake within him. He couldn't deny that he wanted Dillingham's murderers to suffer, but how could he call himself a man of the cloth if he longed for revenge? Didn't the Good Book teach that even murderers could repent and count upon God's mercy? As a preacher, he taught others about the miracle of God's forgiveness for sinners, but in this case, he didn't like the idea. Not one bit.

Archibald stumbled.

"Sorry, boy." Shane patted his horse's steaming neck. "I've neglected you."

He turned aside toward the river and dismounted in the shade of a clump of willows. Archibald lowered his head to the river and lipped water while Shane crouched to drink from cupped hands.

About to stand, he paused at the sight of his reflection in the glossy surface. What kind of man regarded his duty as more important than protecting a friend? While he'd gone about his appointed rounds, Dillingham had faced death with no one to watch his back. If Shane had wanted proof of his powerlessness, this man's death more than provided it. The truth stared him down, tangible as the image wavering before him on the water.

He had no power to save anyone.

A breath of wind pulled strands of America's hair from their pins and whipped them into her face. Petals of sweet William, beardtongue, and Jacob's ladder sifted through her fingers. The wind swept them away as they fell, onto the newly-turned ground overshadowed by a simple wooden cross at her feet. She strewed them, regardless.

Clouds eclipsed the sun briefly as they scattered across the sky, driven by a strong wind. Silence throbbed on Boot Hill, aching as she ached, mourning for a life cut short. She hadn't really known Dillingham, but she grieved for him. How unthinkable that the vibrant man who had yoked her oxen in her moment of need now lay beneath the sod. He'd seemed a decent man, young enough to have a mother and father living. Did any brothers and sisters wonder how he fared? Who would tell them of his murder?

This hilltop seemed lonely . . . and a little dangerous. She shouldn't have come alone, but she'd tucked Richard's gun into her basket. The image of Dillingham lying stricken and bleeding returned to haunt her. She could have done nothing to save him, but having witnessed his final moments, she needed to mark his passing.

Any remaining innocence left to America had died a painful death alongside this man. Dillingham's murder had taught her that nowhere was safe. She had seen enough to know that law and order as she'd once understood it didn't exist in the West. Those charged with protecting life took it instead. Justice could be silenced at the end of a gun. The innocent died, while the guilty went free. As long as gold and greed were the coin laid at the altar of addiction and lust, this would never change.

The last petals swirled from her fingers. Clasping her arms about herself, she gazed at the grave through a shimmering veil. She brushed her tears away with the scent of wildflowers heavy on her fingers, but more fell to wet her cheeks. The last time she'd given flowers to a dead man had been at Richard's grave.

Living on her homestead alone would have crushed the life from her, so she'd turned her back and left it behind. Maybe she should leave Verona as well, once Addie didn't need her quite so much.

Movement caught her eye. A man on a roan horse started up the hill. She recognized Shane from the way he sat in the saddle. A thrill of anticipation went through her, despite all her reservations about him.

He pulled up, dismounted, and hung his slouch hat over the pommel of his saddle. His horse moved off to pull at the grass while Shane turned to her. "Travis told me where to find you."

America didn't trust her voice. It was all she could do to meet his gaze. She felt vulnerable to be approached while crying.

Shane's face changed. He smoothed the moisture from her damp cheek with a hand that smelled of leather. "I'm so sorry."

She couldn't tell whether he meant the words for her or if he had spoken them about Dillingham, but she nodded. His sympathy unleashed her tears to fall in earnest.

With a groan, Shane pulled her into his arms. She buried her face in the wool of his coat. His fingers tangled in her hair, pulling it out of its pins. She wanted to be nowhere else but in his arms, but as the storm of weeping passed, she pushed away from him with the gentle pressure of her hand on his chest.

He released her at once and stood apart, his breathing not quite even. "That was . . ."

She put her hands to her burning cheeks. "Foolhardy?"

He pushed a hand through his hair and sent her a harried look. "Unplanned." He pointed to the lone grave. "Dillingham?"

She nodded.

He stood looking down, the wind tearing at his clothing. Then he knelt beside the wooden cross and bowed his head.

If he'd done anything else, America might have withstood it, but his constant reliance on God reminded her of how far away she had moved from her Maker. She waited for him to finish his prayer and rise to his feet before speaking.

"I have to go." She backed away, pivoted, and left him there.

"Wait!" His voice followed her.

She looked over her shoulder but held herself poised to flee. "I should relieve Travis from watching over Liberty and help Addie with the supper rush."

He held her with his blue gaze. "Why are you really leaving?"

America stared at Shane, unbalanced by the question. What could she tell him that would leave her with even a scrap of dignity? Everything, all of it, rose to choke her. She couldn't speak.

He walked to her and touched her arm. "Tell me."

She searched for words. The facts condemned her, as she feared his God did too. Her chin wobbled despite her efforts to control it, and she turned away from him to hide her shame. "It's just that . . . everyone dies."

He came up behind her, circled her arms with his hands, and leaned her against him. "I wish that weren't true, but it is. We think we own our lives, but they are only borrowed from the hand of God for a little while."

She pulled in a breath on a sob. "It's too hard to bear."

"It can be for those without hope." His breath stirred her hair. "But our Lord drank death's sorrow to remove its sting. Have you asked His forgiveness for your sins and given your soul into His care?"

She nodded. "After Gramma died I did. But I sinned so much more afterward. I must have worn out my welcome."

"You'll be glad to know that isn't one bit true." He spoke in his lilting Irish tones while turning her to face him. "The greater the sin, the more love is needed to cover it, and God is love."

CHAPTER TWELVE

SHANE STOOD ON THE HILLSIDE AND watched America hurry
away. Hopefully, he had eased her mind on the nature of God's
love. That had been hard for him to grasp as well. Although
Shane understood her confusion, he sensed that something else
troubled her also, a secret pain she guarded.

That too he understood.

His sister Ailish's screams sometimes woke him in the night.
When he closed his eyes, he could still see her battered face as
if it were yesterday. He'd been in his teens, but living with
Uncle Seamus had given him an education that made him
older than his years. The streets were another teacher. When
Ailish ran home crying one day, he already knew how love
strayed and passion turned to hate.

Rory O'Leary had seemed different, not one to turn his back
on the unwed mother of his child. Shane had been wrong about
that, as it turned out, and so had Ailish. The night she told
Uncle Seamus she carried Rory's child—and another mouth to
feed— he turned on her with his fists.

When Shane tried to stop the beating, Uncle Seamus sent
him flying, and he smacked his head into the wall. By the time
he came to, Ailish had lost the baby and lay near death.

Shane went looking for Rory.

Needing someone he could trust to back him up, in case
Rory had someone watching over him, too, he made a stop.
Con had been more than willing to come along.

Pulling his thoughts from their course, Shane turned back to
pray at the grave. He'd resorted to the old ways when offering
to back up the deputy, ways he'd left behind. Even if

Dillingham had accepted his help, they would have parted before the deputy's murder, but Shane couldn't help feeling somewhat responsible for his death. He'd known of the man's troubles and done nothing. Dillingham had sworn Shane to secrecy, but Con would have understood a request to watch over the deputy, if Shane had sent him one.

Now it was too late for anything but regrets.

Con had mentioned similar problems with the deputies in Bannack. Con, who was still alive. Shane whistled for Archibald. It seemed high time he looked up his cousin.

Finding him was another matter. None of the miners Shane asked had seen Con or knew where his camp might be. With dark coming on, Shane quit for the day and set up camp on the banks of Alder Creek. He would try again tomorrow. Meanwhile, he and Archibald both deserved a rest.

He woke with the sun's morning rays filtering through the willows above his head and a meadowlark greeting it with a rippling song. He bundled his bedroll, lit a fire, and made coffee. With a steaming cup in one hand, he reached for his Bible, an early-morning habit.

His fingers caressed the worn pages, searching for a comforting passage after so many traumatic events. He stopped at Psalm 121 and moved his lips as he read. "I will lift up mine eyes unto the hills, from whence cometh my help. My help cometh from the Lord, which made heaven and earth. He will not suffer thy foot to be moved. He that keepeth thee will not slumber."

A miner with a rusty beard and dressed in denim carried a pail down to the water. When he came up, Shane called to him. "I'm looking for my cousin, Connor Walsh. Do you know where he is?"

"I'll say!" The man grinned. "You almost camped on top of him." He pointed to a brush wickiup a little farther along the creek.

As Shane watched, Con came out of the wickiup. With his

hair rumpled, his clothing dirt-stained, and his face in want of a shave, he looked worn but no worse off than any of the other miners.

Shane started toward his cousin carrying his coffee pot. "Hello there, stranger."

Con's head turned, and his face brightened. "Shane! It's wonderful to see you again."

"I'm glad to see you too." Shane perched with Con on the tailgate of rough cart sitting outside his wikiup. He raised the pot in his hand. "I thought you might want a cup."

"I'd welcome one, thanks." Con untied a tin cup from his belt.

Shane poured a dark stream of coffee into the vessel. "How have you fared here?"

"Pickings are good, but the living conditions leave something to be desired. If I stay long, I'll have to build myself a cabin." Con raised his cup in salute. "I'll be off to Idaho City as soon as I can."

Shane chuckled. "I have the hardest time keeping track of you, cousin." He sobered. "But I'm glad to hear it."

"Why?" Con swilled coffee and wiped his mouth with the back of his hand. "Are you still out to save me from myself?"

"Actually, I was thinking of saving you from other threats."

"Well, yes, there is that to think about." Con winced. "I suppose you've heard about Dillingham."

Shane gave a quick nod. "I met Jared Stone and George Dalton on the way from Deer Lodge. They gave me some of the details. I found them difficult to hear."

"I took it hard myself." Con shook his head. "That's why I'm planning to leave. I'd rather avoid being shot in cold blood for what I know. Once I've mined enough gold, I'll set myself up somewhere else."

"You always land on your feet." Shane saluted him with his cup.

"What about you?" Con cocked a brow. "Want to come

along?"

"Thank you, but I've decided to stay."

Con frowned. "Watch yourself then." He glanced around. "There's a gang of road agents who call themselves The Innocents. They're after gold."

"I'm fairly certain my poverty won't recommend me to them." A leaf floated down the creek, spinning as it struck a rock. "Dillingham told me some things too."

"Don't speak of that to anyone else, assuming you prefer to remain alive, of course."

"Rest easy, will you?" Shane punched Con's arm. "We already discussed my mortality in Bannack."

Con's forehead creased. "Yes, well. Don't expect me to remain silent while danger threatens. I'd sooner see you alive than dead, if it's all the same to you."

Shane's lips curved in a smile. "That's my preference too, just so you know."

"Truly? The way you behave makes me wonder."

"You can remind me of a mother hen sometimes."

"Do you blame me?" Con flashed a grin. "I want to bounce your children on my knee someday."

Shane laughed. "Now you're meddling."

"Have you forgotten? You once wanted a family of your own."

"That was before—" Shane broke off and turned away.

Con squeezed his shoulder. "Don't give up *all* your dreams."

The dirt Nate shoveled into his sluice box darkened when water ran through it. The current pulled the silt downward and out to wash away. Water splashed and gurgled as it flowed past. It occurred to Nate that life was a lot like a creek and a sluice box. Time swept by with no way to catch it, carrying off everything extra until only the grit remained.

He smiled at his flight of fancy. Spending so much time in nature made him think more deeply than he might have otherwise.

He'd staked his claim farther from Addie than he would have liked. But he'd spent so much time helping her set up her cook tent while the ranks of the miners swelled that he'd been forced farther downstream. Not that he had anything to complain about. In the couple of days since he'd started mining, he'd found good pickings. At this rate, he'd be able to help Addie build her restaurant in no time. He didn't suffer from an addiction to alcohol as many of the other miners did. This left him in a better position to save what he earned for a better tomorrow.

The distance from Addie helped Nate stay away from her as she needed. Her aloofness when he'd first offered to help her establish herself in town had discouraged him. Hopefully, her attitude would change in the future.

He dipped his pan into the sluice box and began swirling. Dirty water slopped out of the pan, carrying lighter particles with it. The heavier flakes would stay in the pan, provided he handled this task with finesse.

Nate smiled to himself. Panning for gold reminded him of wooing a woman. You had to go easy and take your time.

Addie stirred a batch of soda biscuit dough in her enamel bowl and listened for Liberty. Travis had charge of the baby while America paid her respects on Boot Hill, but another pair of listening ears never hurt. Her son wouldn't take kindly to her watching over him, but he didn't have to know.

Travis wanted so badly to become a man that at times it

terrified Addie. When he'd taken over his father's duties in the wagon train, she'd quietly protected him in ways he hadn't known about. She'd asked Nate to look out for him on night watch, kept an eye on him while he drove the oxen, and let him scrape the supper pot clean when she could have eaten more.

Addie might be more protective than other mothers, but with her husband gone and her family far away and out of reach, Travis was all the kin she had. She would do whatever it took to keep her son safe.

A scruffy miner walked toward the cook tent. Thinking he would go on down the street, she didn't pay him much mind until he ducked inside.

"I'm not open yet," she called over her shoulder.

"Don't you know me?" He laughed, a pleasant sound that had her turning toward him.

"Nate Whalen! You're unshaven." She wanted to clap her hand over her mouth after making the personal remark.

He rubbed a hand across the shadow on his face and grinned. "Time to shave was in short supply, Addie Martin, beings as how I needed my hands for panning more gold than a man could ever hope to find."

She looked at him in surprise.

Nate went on before she could ask the questions clamoring in her mind. "I'm wealthy now, with enough money to buy you five restaurants." He took her hand and twirled her in a dance to music only he could hear.

Addie stepped away and touched her palms to the warmth in her cheeks. It hardly seemed fair. While she had been working hard and laying her money by, Nate had gathered the gold to purchase building supplies for her. Not that she was doing poorly with her cook tent. Business couldn't be better and the miners, when they had the means, were generous.

It wouldn't be seemly for her to take money as a gift from a man not her husband, nor would it be fair to him. His charity could rob her of the chance to make her own dream come true.

She hadn't realized before what that meant to her. She'd spent her life until now being guided by others. What would it be like to make her own way? Suddenly, clearly, she wanted to know.

Nate's blue eyes shone. "Addie—Widow Martin, would you allow me the great pleasure of courting you?"

A part of Addie wanted to say yes more than anything. She had loved Clyde and would always miss him, but to once again be sheltered by a man who would cherish, guard, and fend for her would spare her so much. If only it wouldn't take away from what she wanted to do, or deny everything she had become.

She had to think about Travis too. He might stand against anything that could result in his mother remarrying. She stared at Nate, so torn she couldn't form words.

His smile faded. "Won't you say yes? I promise to take good care of you."

She knew what to say then. "I'm sorry, but I can't."

"Of course you can." He gazed at her beguilingly. "If only you will."

She shook her head and turned to the side to quiet her longing to give in. "I must remind you that I have not yet been widowed a year."

Nate cleared his throat, and for the first time Addie sensed his nervousness. "I took that under consideration, don't think I didn't," he said. "But we don't stand on ceremony as much in the West. I'd like to think that your husband, God rest his soul, would thank me for helping you."

She hadn't thought of it that way, but he could be right. Clyde wouldn't want her to struggle alone. Weakening, she reminded herself that what *she* wanted also mattered. "I can't get used to how fast things happen in the West. I'm not one to cast away the traditions I was raised with."

"I love you, Addie." Nate said in a tortured voice. "Surely that counts for something."

She closed her eyes and took a deep breath. "I can't let it."

"Well then, I guess there's nothing more to say." His words held regret. "I'll just have to wait for you to be ready, Addie Martin."

She looked back to him. "It wouldn't be right to ask you to do that."

Nate's smile didn't quite reach his eyes. "Now, did I say you asked me?"

She gazed at him in sorrow, feeling closer to him in this moment of shared grief. "I want you to know that you're dear to me, and I'm honored to have received your offer." She spoke the words haltingly, wanting to comfort but fearful of bringing him hope that could hurt.

"Thank you." He captured her hand and brought it to his lips. "I can get by on that much."

"Ma, I—" Travis's voice cut in abruptly.

Pulling her hand out of Nate's grasp, Addie turned toward her son. About to ask him what he wanted, she froze at the look of rage on his face.

He glared at Nate. "Keep your hands off my ma!" His shout jangled Addie's already stretched nerves.

"Travis, that's enough." Her voice shook with anger. Travis couldn't know what he had just seen. She could sympathize with his feelings, but he had no right to interfere.

"It's all right, Addie," Nate said.

Travis swung toward her. "When did he start calling you by your given name?"

"Don't speak to your mother in that tone of voice," Nate scolded him.

Travis's face went scarlet.

Addie clasped her hands together. "Nate—"

"You're not my father!" Travis bellowed. He swept her with a scornful glance. "You're as bad as *Nate*."

Fury shot through Addie. "Stop this right now!"

Liberty cried out in America's wagon. The shouting must

have woken her. Addie didn't want to think about who else might have overheard. "Travis, get the baby."

Travis stayed where he was, balling his hands into fists.

She stepped forward to stand between her son and Nate. "Go on."

Travis gave her a look of disgust. "What would Pa think?" He turned on his heel.

Nate came up behind her. "Addie, I—"

"Please go." She couldn't look at him. Not now.

He squeezed her shoulder. His footsteps crunched in the street outside the cook tent.

America stopped down the street from the cook tent. Shane had talked of God's love, but this sounded like an argument. How sad to come from that to this, and sadder still to recognize the raised voices. She could guess what the problem might be, something their words made plain, and out of delicacy she skirted the cook tent on the way to her wagon.

Liberty started wailing before she reached it. No wonder, what with Travis shouting that way. She climbed into the wagon and picked up her baby. Liberty cried harder. America was doing her best to soothe her when a boot thumped on the wagon step. She looked up.

Travis appeared with a scowl on his face. His eyes widening, he backed down the wagon steps.

America carried Liberty and looked after Travis, already disappearing down the street. He was a good boy, but she didn't know where he was going or what he might do in such a state.

"Wait!" she called. He looked back. "I put the oxen out to graze along Alder Creek this morning," she went on. "Will you check on them for me?"

He stared at her distantly but then seemed to focus. "All right."

"Thank you. If you'll stay by the creek, I'll bring Liberty down in a bit and we can take a stroll."

She waited for him to decline her offer. Suggesting a walk in the middle of supper preparations was something she never did. He would probably guess she wanted to talk about the fight.

His scowl vanished. "That would be nice."

America's heart went out to the boy. The loss of her own father, not to death but to his withdrawal after her parent's divorce, had been hard to suffer.

She had almost finished tending to Liberty when Addie peered into her wagon. Her friend's swollen eyes and red nose revealed that she'd been crying.

"You're back." The pucker eased from Addie's brow but then returned. "Have you seen Travis?"

"I sent him down to the creek to check on the oxen."

Addie came into the wagon and perched on the edge of the feather tick beside America. "Did he tell you we had a fight?"

"He didn't have to. I heard."

Addie blushed. "I feel terrible about what happened."

"If you don't mind, I'll take Liberty and go down to see how Travis is doing."

Addie gave her a grateful look. "Thanks. I planned supper around having your help, but I can change things out. Making sure my son is all right matters more than impressing a bunch of miners with my cooking."

"They'll be grateful, whatever you serve. Even your plain fare is better than most."

"Thank you. I'm glad you think so." Addie's smile pushed aside some of the strain in her face. "And thanks for talking to Travis. I found myself at wits' end with him today."

America hesitated, then decided to ask the obvious question. "What happened? I don't mean to intrude, but it might help me to know a little more."

Addie examined her hands. "Nate asked to court me. I told him no, but Travis didn't hear that part. All he saw was Nate holding my hand, and that set him off."

America didn't ask why Nate would be holding Addie's hand if she'd told him he couldn't court her. If she'd learned anything in life, it was that matters of the heart made people do things that didn't always make sense. "May I explain that to Travis?"

"I hope you will."

"I think you're right to refuse Nate, if you want my opinion. You and Travis need more time to adjust to your husband's death."

"Agreed, although I fear I'd forgotten that with Nate." She gazed toward the rear of the wagon as if looking into the past. "I've been so lonely that I lost all sense and encouraged the man. I should have been more sensitive to my son and respectful to my husband's memory."

"Whatever is true about that, you can't change anything you've done. All you can do is learn from what went wrong and go on in a better way."

The irony of giving advice to Addie that she needed to take herself did not escape America.

CHAPTER THIRTEEN

LIBERTY GURGLED WHILE AMERICA CARRIED HER along Daylight Creek. The oxen, hobbled by leather straps to keep them from wandering, were easy to spot in the open countryside. Still green this early in summer, the grass felt soft to walk upon. Finding Travis gave her little trouble. He was casting stones into the water at the edge of a wide pool, not far from where the oxen grazed. She waved to him, and he started toward her.

He seemed calmer than he had earlier. Going off into nature had done him good.

"I brought you some food." She handed him the packet of crackers and a hunk of cheese Addie had sent with her.

"Thanks." He crammed his mouth full and ate with single-minded focus.

Rocking Liberty in her arms, America waited for him to satisfy his hunger. "Are you ready for a walk?" she asked after he crunched the last cracker.

Travis seemed quieter than usual, but that was only natural. She took her cue from him and remained silent. Along Daylight Creek, willows bent toward the water that flowed across the rocky bed in bright currents. They stopped at a wide place where the water took on a brownish cast shot with green. The sky arced above them, its blue bleached by the sunlight to a pale shade. A fish jumped in the creek, spreading ripples in a wide circle.

He turned to her. "Shall I carry Liberty now? Your arms must be getting tired."

Travis will make a loving father someday, America decided. She handed the baby over. Travis was a gentle soul, which made his rage today all the more appalling. "Your mother sent the food." She hoped the comment would give the boy an opening to talk about his troubles. She also wanted to remind him of his mother's love for him.

He scowled. "She's going to marry Nate."

That didn't mesh with what Addie had told her. "Did she say that?"

"No, but I can tell," Travis snarled.

Liberty startled and puckered her face. America reached to snatch her away before she could start crying. In that moment, Travis spoke to the baby in the singsong voice he reserved for her. Liberty quieted, but America wasn't sure how long that would last. "Maybe we should start back," she suggested. "Walking usually lulls her."

They fell into step together.

"You were saying?" America prompted.

"I don't want Nate to replace my father."

"No one can do that, and I doubt that Nate would want to."

"If Ma marries him, he'll be my *father*."

"Aren't you assuming some things?"

He glanced sideways at her. "What do you mean?"

"From what I understand, Nate won't be courting your mother."

"That's not what it looked like to *me*." His voice became agitated, and Liberty's mouth puckered.

America thought she might have to claim her baby after all, but Travis cooed and lifted her against his shoulder to pat her back. Liberty calmed down, and so did Travis. The scowl on his face disappeared. "Appearances can be deceiving," America went on. "Your mother told him no."

His eyebrows drew together. "Then why—"

"I only know what Addie told me," she forestalled him. "I didn't ask about private matters." She stressed the last two words, hoping to plant a seed in Travis's mind. Hopefully it would grow into the realization that his mother's personal affairs didn't have to be open to his opinion.

Shane walked into the brush wickiup on the main street of Verona, where a group of miners were drinking, swearing, and gambling. "Gentlemen, have you forgotten it's Sunday?"

The proprietor squinted his direction. "What's that you say?"

"Have you forgotten, Riddler? It's Sunday, a day dedicated to our Lord."

A burly miner glanced up from his cards. "Throw him out. Or else grease his holler with a shot of forty rod." His remark sparked laughter from the other miners.

"You tell him, Ezra!"

"The preacher tangle-legged. That'd be a sight to see."

"Maybe he wants a cigar too." More laughter followed.

Blake Riddler's shoulders shook. "Whadda ya say, Shane? Shall we celebrate the Sabbath with a round?"

"I don't want your whiskey, and be careful how you speak of the Sabbath. God will not be mocked."

"Oh, now you've gone and hurt his feelings," Ezra crowed.

"What exactly did you want, preacher?" the proprietor asked from behind him.

Shane faced him. "Do you know the Bible, Riddler?"

The man shrugged. "I went to Sunday school."

The other men hooted at this information.

"Then you know the story of how our Lord Jesus Christ cleansed the temple with a whip. He threw out those buying and selling in the House of Prayer."

Riddler's gaze slipped away from his.

Shane pressed his advantage. "Must you do business on the Lord's Day?"

"Don't let him talk you into anything," Ezra said.

Shane strode toward Ezra.

Ezra leveled a pistol. "Hold it right there, preacher."

Shane stopped.

"Put the gun away," Riddler commanded in a heavy voice. "All right, Shane. I'm not willing to shut down for the whole day, but I'll give you an hour. Bar's closed, boys!"

"Give that hour to God, not me. I am but His messenger." Shane remained watchful, keeping his eye on Ezra in particular. He suspected that those present might not appreciate being cut off from their source of liquor.

"If he's going to hold church, make him sing for us."

"Yes, a song!"

"Maybe he'll dance too. What do you say, preacher?"

"He can dance at the end of a gun as far as I'm concerned," Ezra growled, but he put away his pistol without further comment.

Shane addressed his congregation. "You're welcome to sing along if you know the words. I apologize for the lack of an accompanist, but I'm told I carry a tune well enough to follow. How many of you know the hymn, 'All Creatures of Our God and King?'"

"Oh, sing that one. I haven't heard it since I was a boy," Riddler said. He looked a little weepy-eyed.

"Well, then . . ." Shane cleared his throat and began. "All creatures of our God and King, lift up your voice and with us sing . . ."

Riddler joined in on the Alleluias, which might be all he remembered. A clear tenor voice piped up to sing above Shane's baritone. A bass and another baritone chimed in.

Shane kept to simple choruses. He repeated them so that the miners who didn't know them could learn the words and sing along. By the end of the hour, he had everyone singing, including Ezra.

He sent up a silent prayer of thanksgiving when he left the wickiup, feeling as if he may have made a few friends. He'd rushed into the shelter out of frustration and had landed himself in hot water, as usual. But this time, something good had come out of a bad situation.

America threw out the dishwater and dried her hands with a sigh. She wouldn't complain, but she had certainly grown tired of washing dishes. Her hands were chapped from so much soapy water, and the chore gave her too much time for introspection.

Her thoughts flew annoyingly often to Shane. If she wasn't thinking about him, other memories rose to torment her. Sometimes the image of Richard's body in the snow came back to her, along with the helpless feeling of finding herself widowed and alone.

At other times, the last words Kyle spoke to her repeated themselves in her mind. *"How do I know the baby is mine?"*

America loved Addie dearly, but she couldn't wash dishes forever. If only sorting out what else she might do wasn't so confusing. The puzzle revolved in her mind endlessly, with no solution. She might be able to hire out as a maid. However, she'd grown up without needing to cook and clean and had only developed those skills after her marriage.

Something told America that housekeeping on the homestead did not necessarily qualify her to clean a finer dwelling. Hiring out as a cook's helper presented similar drawbacks. It was much the same as what she did for Addie right now. In any case, her life would have to change eventually, or her soul would bleed into the dust and perish.

She went back into the cook tent for more dirty dishes. During the supper rush, they weren't hard to find. Addie's fame as a cook had spread throughout the mining camp.

"I tell you, Addie. I never heard the like of it." A rusty-bearded miner seated at one of the tables chuckled. "I'm not sure if that man is tetched in the head, a complete idiot, or the bravest person on the face of this earth. They say he walked right into that wickiup like he owned it and held church."

America nearly dropped the tray of dishes she'd gathered. The man could only be talking about one person. What had Shane done this time?

"My goodness." Addie sounded impressed. "He's certainly a force to be reckoned with."

"Had them miners singing like angels, he did." The miner laughed outright.

Intrigued, America listened for more details about Shane's unusual church service.

"Do you recall that fellow Charley Forbes?" The miner switched topics, much to her disappointment.

"The name rings a bell." Addie laid a plate of corn dodgers on his table. "Wasn't he one of the men accused of shooting Deputy Dillingham?"

"That's right. The miners' court declared him innocent but the other two guilty. Turns out, that might have killed him."

"What do you mean?" Addie asked.

America stopped pretending to clear away dishes.

"Some believe the other two deputies murdered Charley out of anger because of the way he went and got himself a separate trial. Heard they killed Charley's horse along with him and buried them both to hide what they done."

America shivered. How horrible if it had really happened that way, but letting convicted murderers loose could not fail to bring more grief. Whether or not Charley Forbes had shot Dillingham, he had once been an innocent child in his mother's arms. What had gone wrong in his life that caused him to fall in with his chosen companions?

The conversation moved on to the recent renaming of Verona to Virginia City. The mining district judge who reviewed the town's charter, a staunch supporter of the Union, refused to name it after Jefferson Davis's wife. He crossed out the name of the first lady of the Confederacy and wrote "Virginia" instead. His choice of a southern state represented a compromise that appeased the town's Confederate sympathizers.

Unable to justify eavesdropping instead of working, America squared her shoulders and carried another load of dirty dishes outside. After scraping the plates into a bucket, she replenished the dishwater from the pot steaming on the fire, fished out the washcloth, and picked up another plate to scrub.

Her mind returned to the puzzle of Shane. His brand of faith didn't make sense to her. He put himself in danger without a second thought, seemingly, and all for the sake of people who couldn't care less about him. He used his faith to bludgeon anything standing in his way with a single-mindedness America couldn't fathom. In putting himself in jeopardy, he appeared to fight for his very life.

She rinsed the plate and chose another.

Shane strove to save the lives of others as if they belonged to him. To do that, a man would need absolute faith in what he believed and a depth of love for humanity she didn't understand. If that were true of Shane, it should recommend him, not make her want to hide from him whenever he spoke of his God. She shook her head, giving up the riddle.

The next time she entered the cook tent, more miners than before bent over plates of Dutch oven trout alongside corn dodgers and wilted greens. She and Addie had gathered the greens that morning, while the dew still glistened on the grass. Travis had gone fishing early and come back with stringers full of trout.

America had long ago thrown in her food with Addie's, but their stores were now running low. After the long haul from Bannack, the last thing they wanted to do was hitch the oxen and make the journey all the way back to replenish their provisions. They needed to do so, however. A few enterprising men with wagons did make supply runs, but they charged more than Addie wanted to pay. Once the freight wagons came to Virginia City, keeping enough provisions would become easier.

Sensing that someone watched her, America looked up from clearing one of the tables—and straight into Virgil Henry's face. She started, shifted away, and returned her attention to the task at hand. He moved on to claim a seat. She quickly piled dirty plates on her tray, anxious to escape his scrutiny.

Outside, America stoked the fire and drew more water to boil from the barrel strapped to Addie's wagon.

Liberty cried, and she dried her hands. Travis waved as she hurried to her wagon. Knowing he would take over the dishes, America picked up her baby. She was grateful for the chance to spend time alone with her sweet daughter. Now in her fifth month of life, Liberty smiled more and liked to touch faces. She also stayed awake longer.

With her baby's belly full, America brought her out to Travis. He usually took Liberty on a walk at this hour. The supper rush had ended, and Travis had finished most of the washing up. She had only to dry the remaining dishes and put them away. She worked quickly, eager to be done for the day.

Daylight softened into evening as the sun hovered close to the horizon. High above, a hawk spread its wings, seeming hardly to move. Addie had closed the cook tent, but she lingered in conversation with a late comer.

Travis should have returned by now. America put aside the dishtowel and started off in the direction he had followed. Where had he gotten to? She didn't like him venturing so far from her wagon with Liberty this late in the day. Maybe he'd gone down to Alder Creek to talk to the miners camped there.

She headed in that direction but didn't see him right away at the creek and didn't want to go any farther. With so many miners in the area, she didn't need to worry about Indians, but being a woman alone among rough men carried its own dangers. Besides, the hair on the back of her neck had risen with the uneasy feeling of someone watching her. She turned to go.

A hand clamped over her mouth. "Caught you, fair and square, now didn't I?" The man restraining her murmured close to her ear. She twisted her head to look at him and met a pair of familiar gray eyes. Virgil Henry chuckled. "Come along now, darlin'."

The alder bushes scraped her arms as he hauled her backward and out of sight from the road.

CHAPTER FOURTEEN

"THANKS FOR SERVING ME PAST CLOSING." Shane pushed away his empty plate. "I enjoyed that fine meal."

Word of Addie's trout dinner had spread around town. Shane hadn't been able to resist sampling it, but truth be told, he'd also hoped to see America in the cook tent. She hadn't come in during his meal, but he'd put off supper too long and stopped by after closing. No doubt she'd departed for the day. He shouldn't have kept Addie any longer at her duties, but she didn't seem to mind.

"You're welcome." Addie closed the stove's air intake duct. "There's plenty more if you want another helping."

He patted his stomach. "Thank you, but that will hold me a while."

Addie's gaze shifted past him. She stood up slowly, transfixed by something behind him.

Shane turned around. Clutching Liberty, Travis rushed toward them along the main road.

Addie ran out to meet him, but Shane passed her and reached Travis first. He grasped the boy's elbow. "What's wrong?"

"I saw a man make off with America," Travis shouted above the baby's wails and between breaths. "He hauled her into the alder bushes."

A sick feeling jolted through Shane. "When?"

"Just now, while I was walking back. With the baby in my arms, I couldn't do anything to save her. I hollered for help, but no one came."

"Most of the miners with gold dust to spare will have gone

to town at this hour." Addie said.

"Who took her?" Shane jerked out the words.

"He comes by the cook tent sometimes. I think he's called Virgil."

Addie relieved Travis of Liberty. "I bet it was Virgil Henry. I've noticed him watching her."

"Show me where it happened," Shane demanded.

The two jogged off together, leaving Addie on the side of the road rubbing the baby's back.

"He took her right here." Travis pointed out the spot.

Shane picked up the trail. It wasn't difficult, since Virgil had not been careful. He knew the man pretty well from their association in Bannack and could guess at Virgil's lack of sobriety when he grabbed America.

He'd worried something like this might happen. Prostitutes flourished in these mining camps, some so wealthy they flaunted themselves in fine silks, jewelry, and furs. But the two widows presented a challenge a certain breed would find irresistible.

The trail followed the creek at a little distance. Scuffed ground and broken brush made it obvious America had tried to escape, but the trail continued. Shane winced, imagining what might be happening to America. Shutting his mind to the horrifying possibilities, he pressed onward. If he'd had any doubt about his feelings for her, his reaction to her peril removed them entirely.

He seemed doomed to repeat this sort of situation—hunting a man to confront him over a woman who mattered to him. The night his sister died, Rory had come home whistling, hands in his pockets, obviously not expecting trouble.

Shane had tensed to spring out at the sight of Rory rounding the corner, but Con had held him back. "Let him come to you," he'd whispered.

Shane found himself grateful for the advice when Rory waved to a group of friends who stepped into the road behind him. The group continued out of sight along the cross street. Rory went on alone, drawing near the alley.

Quivering with anger, Shane strode out to challenge him.

Rory jumped back. "Sean! You startled me. How are you?"

By the light of that long-ago moon, Shane had seen Rory darting nervous glances into the darkness, clearly checking for others who might have come along. Con, stationed behind a couple of garbage cans in the alley, would be too well hidden to spot.

Shane's jaw tensed. "I'm all right, but it's Ailish you want to ask about."

Rory flicked a glance over him. "What do you mean?"

"You've killed her." Shane's voice shook in a rush of rage.

"Talk sense, will you?"

"I'm not here to *talk*. Come into the alley, and we'll settle this." He'd issued the challenge, having been taught from boyhood that a real man settled matters with his fists. That had been his way until he'd learned a better one.

Shane shook free of the memory. He hoped he could remember that lesson when he caught up with Virgil. With the light leaching from the sky, it had better be soon.

Footsteps and the sound of branches breaking came from just ahead. He put up a finger to warn Travis to silence. "Wait here," he whispered. Travis might act older than his years, but he couldn't hold his own against a grown man. And if anyone was going to be shot today, he didn't want it to be Travis.

Ignoring the boy's frown, Shane burst from the concealment of the alder bushes.

Virgil spun about. He'd been dragging America by a rope tied to her bound hands, but he must have loosened his hold from surprise for she jerked away. Shane saw why she hadn't screamed. She couldn't yell with a cravat gagging her.

Virgil stepped between Shane and America.

She looked past her captor and met Shane's eyes. Virgil jerked the rope, and she fell.

After a quick glance to make sure America wasn't badly hurt, Shane kept his eye on Virgil's gun hand. "What are you doing? You can't steal a woman."

"No?" Virgil laughed. "You going to stop me?"

From the corner of his eye, Shane caught sight of Travis creeping toward America. If Virgil noticed him, anything might happen. He had to keep the man talking to distract him.

"You know the miners favor the two widows. Once they know what you're about, they'll set the law on you."

"Who's going to listen to them?" Virgil scoffed. "Ain't no one around here to stop me."

Shane didn't want to discuss that particular topic, especially not with a man who had so few scruples.

"Where are you taking her?"

Virgil smirked. "I'd have to be tetched to tell you that."

Travis had nearly reached America. If Virgil turned his head, he'd see the boy. Shane eased a little closer to Virgil. "Tell me, is your mother alive?"

"Died the winter afore last."

"My condolences. Were you able to attend the funeral?"

"No, but I hear her wake was really something." He smiled. "All the cousins and Uncle Leroy brought whiskey and took turns toasting her."

Travis bent to untie America's hands.

Shane forgot to breathe.

Virgil looked sideways. "Hey!" His pistol snaked out, pointed at Travis's head. "Stop right there."

Travis froze with an expression of terror filling his face.

America's eyes widened.

"Let him go. He's only a boy." Shane kept his voice calm. He knew people like Virgil fed on fear.

"Too bad." Virgil shook his head. "Looks like he won't make it into manhood." He cocked the trigger.

Travis's muscles tensed as if he might try to jump Virgil. If the boy moved at all, he'd probably wind up dead.

"Say, that's a nice gun." Shane said the first thing that occurred to him, anything to take Virgil's mind off Travis. "May I see it?"

Virgil roared with merriment, but his finger eased off the trigger. "I'll say this for you, preacher, you're good for a laugh. No, you may *not* see my gun."

Travis leaped. He latched onto Virgil's shooting arm. Virgil bellowed and tried to shake him off. Travis hung on doggedly. Shane launched himself at Virgil in an instinctive move from long ago.

The rope connecting America to Virgil slackened. She kicked herself backward, away from the fighting men. The cravat gagging her shifted lower. She clawed it away from her mouth with her bound hands.

A gunshot blasted the air.

Someone screamed.

America averted her eyes for fear of seeing Shane or Travis shot and bleeding.

"My leg! My leg!" someone shouted.

She whirled. Virgil Henry lay writhing on the ground, clasping his thigh. Blood oozed from between his fingers.

Shane bent over him. "He'll bleed to death." He unsheathed his hunting knife and cut a length from Jack's rope. Working quickly, he wrapped the rope around the injured leg above the wound and pulled tight.

Virgil stopped screaming and fell to moaning.

Shane tied off the rope and lifted his head. His gaze searched America's face. "Are you all right?"

She nodded.

"Travis, untie America then go for Doc Steele. Tell him a man's life is at stake. If he hurries, he might cheat Boot Hill of another grave."

Travis loosened the knots at America's wrists. He tugged her hands free, exposing angry rope burns. After helping her to her feet, he lit for town.

America put her tongue to a cut at the corner of her lip and tasted blood. Virgil had hurt her in ways that were not physical too. She wanted him to suffer for what he'd done, but she didn't wish him dead.

Virgil grasped Shane's arm with a bloody hand and pulled himself partway up. "I can't figure you out, preacher. Why do you care about me?"

"Because God cares, Virgil." Shane pushed him back down. "Now, shut up and lie still."

America chopped carrots with more force than necessary. Shane had stopped by while she and Addie prepared vegetables for the night's stew and had taken Addie aside. Now they sat at a table murmuring together. If they didn't stop, she would go mad. It wasn't hard to guess that they were discussing what had happened while keeping their conversation low to shield her feelings. Everyone tiptoed around her, treating her like some delicate porcelain plate that might break.

Yes, she had taken harm from Virgil, but she wasn't so fragile as they thought her. She had weathered far worse in her life than Virgil had meted out. Travis and Addie had shouldered her chores on the day following Virgil's misdeed, but determined to pull her own weight, she'd insisted on helping today.

Shane and Addie probably wanted to spare her the strain of hearing Virgil Henry's name. She knew from Travis that Doc Steele had patched him up and taken him home to recover, after which he would be slapped into custody. Whatever came of that, she was glad he wouldn't be coming around the cook tent anymore. She never wanted to see Virgil Henry again.

Shane pushed back his chair, stood up, and raked her with a glance. Addie found something else to do outside the cook tent.

America laid her knife down and gave Shane her attention.

"How are you faring?" he asked in a soft voice.

She shrugged. "It comes back to me at times, almost like I'm there again, but I suppose that's normal."

"I've heard of such a reaction to a terrifying event. It will pass in time. I want you to know that I mean to make sure Virgil never bothers you again."

The way he jutted his chin told America he meant what he said. His words sounded reassuring, but she doubted his ability to carry them out. She had seen him thrown into the mud outside the hotel when they'd first met, and she knew how the trial for Dillingham's killers had gone.

She smiled at him, touched by his sentiment. "Thank you for what you did for me."

"I'm thankful to have been available to help you." His forehead creased. "I'll tell you truthfully that I'm concerned it could happen again. Virgil Henry isn't likely to try anything, but someone else might. A beautiful woman like you who also has moral fiber is both a treasure and a challenge in a mining camp."

"You have a backhanded way of paying a compliment."

A smile touched Shane's lips. "Can I persuade you to take a walk in my company? We won't go far."

He must have wanted to talk to her about something in particular. Well, that was an improvement over being handled with kid gloves. "All right." Aware that her response had come out less than graciously, she tacked on an awkward-sounding thank-you.

They struck out eastward along the main road, in the opposite direction of Alder Creek with its memories. Walking at his side seemed natural, as if they had always matched their steps.

Trees and brush covered a swell on one side of the road while grasses waved on the other. Birds sang a rippling melody, and the breeze lifted tendrils of America's hair about her face. She glanced sideways at him. "How far does the road go?"

He squinted into the horizon. "East to Bozeman and beyond to Yellowstone Country, although that's dangerous to travel due to Indian activity."

She frowned. "Aren't all roads dangerous these days?"

He looked back to her. "That's true to a certain extent. With the war distracting folks in the East and taking soldiers away from the forts, traveling in the West these days is not for the faint of heart."

"And yet you do." She swung away from him to hide her expression. The idea of him riding off into peril troubled her more than she cared for him to know.

"It's a risk I willingly take." He turned her toward him and laid his hands on her shoulders. "And what of you? Are you comfortable living in a mining camp?"

She didn't meet his eyes. "I'm not certain, to tell you the truth. When I first came west, it was my husband's decision." She flicked a glance at him. "Now that the choice is mine, remaining is probably the right one."

"Why do you feel that way?"

"For a lot of reasons. The West may be lawless, but there's also freedom and the feeling that you can make anything of yourself if you try hard enough. Maybe all of that is worth a bit of risk."

"If you could do anything, what would you want your life to be like?"

"Something better than before."

He picked a wild iris from a patch growing alongside the road and cupped her hand around its stem. "Hold it and tell me what you see."

She gazed at the petals of the blue flag. Yellow stripes radiated from the blossom's pure white heart to its indigo tips. The flower unfurled in arcs more graceful than a poem. "Beauty."

"Yes, it has that. If you closed your hands, what would happen?"

"I'd crush it." She glanced at him questioningly.

"If you destroyed the flower, would the plant die as well?"

The silly notion brought a grin to her lips. "No."

"Do you see? The roots sustain the plant. Even though a flower wilts, the plant goes on to bring forth more beauty." He closed his hands over hers on the stem. "A life can resemble a plant."

She caught her breath. "Thank you."

He gazed at her across the flower, his hands caressing hers. The sweet scent of the blossom, the warmth of the sun, and the simple joy of living melded into a breathless moment. His smile faded, replaced by an unmistakable look of desire that awoke a wild longing within her to be comforted and cherished in his arms.

Shane moved closer until his lips hovered only a breath away. He cupped her face with one hand. "Whenever I think of you while on my circuit, I'll remember this moment." He lowered his lips to hers and caressed her mouth in a lingering kiss.

America submitted herself to every heady sensation, forgetting that she shouldn't allow him to kiss her. Only here, now, this instant of delight mattered.

He led her in the kiss, and she yielded in an age-old dance that ended too soon. He rested his forehead against hers. "I've wanted to do that for some time."

"I have too." Saying those words was playing with fire. America knew it but didn't care. Perhaps she even reveled a bit in her power to unsettle him. She stepped into his arms, and they folded around her. He claimed her mouth in a kiss that carried her into storm-tossed waters. She could only cling to him as wild emotions surged within her and every defense washed away.

He broke from her with a moan, lurched backward, and pushed a hand through his hair. "That shouldn't have happened. Forgive me."

America's conscience smote her. "No, it's my fault." She'd taken delight in tempting him, but it had backfired on her.

"I am responsible for my own behavior," he corrected her in a dry tone.

Shane might be liable for his actions, but she was to blame for hers. Regrets crowded in, bringing tears to sting her eyes. Everything would change between them now. If only they could go back to before, but that couldn't happen.

Shane's jaw firmed. "We should go back."

The flower swam into sight through her tears, crushed in her fingers.

CHAPTER FIFTEEN

ADDIE WATCHED FOR AMERICA TO COME down the road with Shane. One thing that would make a perfectly reasonable woman forget her duty was a handsome man. She smiled to herself, glad that two people she liked admired one another. From the glances she'd intercepted, their attachment had become more than simple admiration. Love was one thing, and filling a man's belly another, although some likened the two. With a passel of hungry miners about to descend, Addie needed her cook's helper to return.

She called Travis to watch over the stew and free her for other duties. He came in carrying Liberty and stirred the pot while the baby in his arms stared in fascination.

Addie rushed to set out plates, fetch a ladle, cut the vinegar pies she'd made as a frugal measure with fruit running low, and do a hundred other things simultaneously. She spun about . . . and ran square into a solid masculine chest.

"Whoa there, woman. Where's the fire?" Nate caught her in his strong arms, and they swayed together.

"What are you doing creeping up on a body?" she scolded with a trace of humor.

He laughed. "Is that what I was doing? My mistake. I thought you barreled into me."

She shifted out of his embrace and spared a glance for Travis, who was scowling at her. "Since you're here, perhaps you could be of use."

"What do you want me to do?"

"Would you mind slicing the rest of the pies?"

"Let me wash my hands first." His voice dropped to a

murmur. "I want to ease your burden however best I can."

Warmth spread through Addie. "You are very kind."

"I mean it, Addie. Say the word, and I'll do whatever you need me to."

"Would you consider . . ." She bit her lip. "Oh, never mind."

He tilted her face with a finger under her chin. "For you, anything."

"It's a lot to ask, but we're running low on supplies and—"

"You need someone to drive the wagon to Bannack and purchase more."

She shook her head. "No, it's too much to expect you to do."

"That's for me to decide, don't you think?" He grinned. "You are worth the trouble, Addie Martin." He glanced in Travis's direction. "I'll need help, though."

Addie swallowed. How would her son respond to being asked to go to Bannack with Nate? Should she even ask him?

"If you mean me, of course I'll go," Travis piped up.

Addie hid her surprise. That wasn't what she'd expected him to say.

"Well then, it's settled," Nate said. "Can you leave in the morning?"

"Sure can." Travis looked uncertain. "Can't I, Ma?"

America hurried into the cook tent, breathless. Shane followed behind her. "Forgive me," she apologized. "I forgot the time."

"It's all right." Addie gave her a forgiving smile. "But please take Liberty or stir the stew."

America took Liberty from Travis.

"Did I hear that you're going to Bannack?" Shane asked.

Nate dipped his head. "You did. I'll haul supplies for Addie. Care to ride along?"

Shane sent America an unreadable glance before focusing back on Nate. "I'd be more than happy to do so."

"Thank you, Reverend Hayes." Addie tried not to show her relief. "Now I won't need to send Travis along." Tension sloughed from her shoulders. Her son would have been exposed to danger on the open road. And she had no idea how he'd have gotten along with Nate.

"But, Ma, they need me." Travis turned to Nate. "Don't you?"

Addie understood with sudden clarity why her son had volunteered to go on this trip. A lump formed in her throat. With his father gone, Travis needed masculine company more than ever.

Nate grinned. "That's up to your ma, Travis, but I'd surely like you to come along."

She bit her lip. With everyone watching her and the first of the miners coming down the road to the cook tent, it wasn't the best time for such a decision, but she needed to make it now. "All right, go."

Shane rode beside Travis in the wagon while Nate drove the oxen. They reached the place where four trails converged on the afternoon of the second day. Finding wagons and horses with gold pans tied to their saddles at the camp was no surprise. They'd passed miners on the road since leaving Virginia City on their supply run to Bannack. With so many hands in the pot, and more hopefuls arriving every day, the pickings would dwindle in time.

The sooner that happens, the better. Shane didn't like what lust for gold did to men. He hated how many miners wasted their new-found wealth on riotous living.

A bearded miner wearing a red shirt and denim trousers hailed them at the crossroads.

"Whoa!" Nate called from beside the oxen. The wagon shuddered to a stop.

"You folks from Alder Gulch?" the bearded miner asked.

Several others wearing friendly smiles came up behind him.

"That's right," Nate answered. "We've come from Virginia City, the biggest town in the gulch. You headed that way?"

"Yes sirree!" The bearded miner chuckled. "We aim to git some of that gold that's lying around for the taking."

Nate squinted at him. "It could be a mite harder than that."

"Can you tell us the best place to stake a claim?" one of the others called out. His apple cheeks highlighted a fresh face. Suspenders held up his britches, and he didn't look much older than Travis.

Nate laughed. "If I knew that, I wouldn't have to drive this ox team."

"Gentlemen." Shane climbed from the wagon, and Travis jumped down beside him. "I can tell you where to find gold."

"Is that so?" The miners pressed toward Shane.

"That's right. You'll find gold fit for the King of kings and precious gems aplenty in the Word of God."

The bearded miner screwed up his face. "The *what*?"

"He means the Bible, Otis," the apple-cheeked miner jeered. "You didn't go to Sunday school like us decent folk, now did you?"

"Shut up, Danny."

Shane eyed the boy. "You could do with a few more lessons."

Danny blushed.

"Cherish the Bible," Shane said, "for it is a precious stream flowing from the mouth of God. Beware any substitute."

"What are you, *Irish*?" Otis asked. "Some kind of preacher?"

"Don't take that tone with him." Travis came up beside Shane with his hands fisted.

"You are speaking to Reverend Hayes." Nate idly tapped his bullwhip against his boot. at the same time pinning the miner with his gaze.

Shane's throat tightened. The derision he suffered seemed all the darker in the light of his friends' support.

Otis threw up his hands. "Far be it from me to offend a man of the cloth."

"Good thinking," Nate approved. "You don't want to wind up on the wrong side of the Almighty."

"Shall we pray?" Shane seized the advantage.

Danny bowed his head, as did several others. Otis followed suit.

"Heavenly Father, who loves us despite our weaknesses, I ask that You guide as You see fit and protect us from any waywardness we chance upon. Teach us to lay up treasure in heaven that no thief can steal and neither moth nor rust will destroy."

Shane's small flock concluded the prayer in a round of amens and glanced at one another sheepishly.

"Shane, the oxen are restless so near water," Nate said. "If you're finished—"

"Yes, of course."

"Thanks, preacher," Danny called. The miners moved off.

They pitched camp a small distance from the river bank, hoping to avoid the excited chatter likely to go into the night around some of the other firesides. Shane built a fire while Nate took care of the oxen and Travis started supper.

Shane had expected the supply run to be more of an ordeal, but he'd enjoyed taking his turn driving the oxen or riding along in the wagon in fellowship with the others. His memories of his father had faded long ago, and his uncle had proven a poor substitute, but Nate's association with Travis struck a chord deep within him. When he watched the boy respond to the older man's gentle guidance, Shane felt more of an orphan than ever before.

David had suggested that Shane should find a wife and start a family. In this moment of introspection, that seemed wiser than the lonely life he'd planned for himself. He pushed the stray thought aside, determined not to give in to weakness, and gave his attention to the task at hand. A spark caught, and he blew on the tinder until it flamed upward to lap the logs with appetite.

It was clear Travis had inherited his mother's cooking ability. Tonight's supper included roasted rabbit, hoe cakes, and wild greens harvested from the riverbanks. Shane said grace, and after they ate, Nate filled the air with the wailing of his harmonica until the fire burned low and the dying sun splashed the sky with red.

The company made an early start the next morning, hitting the trail while the sun peeked over the shoulders of the Tobacco Root range. Travis started out driving, and Archibald kept pace with the oxen-led wagon. Nate rode alongside him. They planned to switch back and forth throughout the day.

They followed the shining waters of Beaverhead River through waving grasses. Distant peaks thrust into the sky. They reached their halfway point at Beaverhead Rock. This monolith, rather than the furry creatures themselves, gave the river its name.

That night they camped at the edge of a slough and reached Bannack the next day. The town drowsed in the sun and looked much the same on the surface as when Shane left. Yet, everything had changed. He knew only a few of the miners who chewed the fat in Chrisman's store. The Merrick Hotel loomed against the sky, undisturbed by voices. Those with active claims remained, but everyone else had gone to Alder Gulch. Bannack, though still busy, served as a freight stop and supply station for outlying areas as much as a mining center.

The small cabin set back from the road listened for the footfall that would never sound within its walls again. Con had no reason to return to this place. Shane turned the handle, and the door creaked open. He went inside, his boot heels echoing hollowly on the floorboards. He touched the rough wood of the table as memories awoke. He had laid his head in his hands here and wept for Chief Snag. Con had pounded his fist on this very table while challenging Shane to believe his own teachings.

Nate and Travis set up camp in Yankee Flats for the night. Not planning to stay long due to the lack of forage for the oxen, they would conduct their business in town and head back right away. Shane planned to remain in Bannack for a brief rest, then continue along his circuit.

Time away from America might help Shane recover his perspective. He should never have kissed her. It had weakened his resolve, and he'd given in to his desires. He might be a preacher, but he was still a man and vulnerable to temptation.

The incident with Virgil had shaken Shane. He'd surrendered to instinct and gone back to his street ways when he leaped on Virgil. But what else could he have done to save Travis? A question whispered in his mind: *Could defending an innocent life be wrong?* The idea didn't sit well with him, but neither did the idea of fighting. Weariness prevented Shane from giving the matter his full consideration.

He brushed off the mattress of the rope bed, untied his bedroll, and fell instantly asleep. Waking in the night, he listened for his old friend, the owl in the wood, but it had moved on.

He woke early the next morning and walked down to Chrisman's store. The men who were gathered around the stove broke off their conversation and stared at him when he entered. Shane sighed. It was always the same here in Bannack with the miners closing forces against him.

Chrisman gave his ready smile. "Shane! I thought you were gone for good."

Chrisman's expectation came as no surprise to Shane. After all, he'd left town with both his eye and his spirit bruised. "Ah, but that would be quitting." He spoke the words loudly for the sake of the listening ears in the room.

Humor lit Chrisman's eyes. "Well then, welcome back. You staying in Con's cabin?"

"As long as I'm able." Shane spared a glance for the closed

door to the sheriff's office at the back of the store.

Chrisman grinned, obviously taking his meaning. "There's not much call for a sheriff's sale with folks more interested in leaving Bannack than buying it up."

The door creaked open. Nate and Travis came in. After a nod to Shane, Nate turned to Chrisman. "Good morning. I'm purchasing supplies for a restaurant in Virginia City. I have a list for you."

Chrisman frowned. "Let me see it."

Nate unfolded a piece of paper and handed it over.

Chrisman read the list. He looked up. "I'm in short supply of some of these items. The wagon freighters are working double time, but we still can't keep up with demand. I'll do the best I can for you, though."

Nate concluded his business in good time. Shane helped load the wagon, shook hands with Nate and Travis, and stood in the road watching his last connection to America roll out of sight.

CHAPTER SIXTEEN

LIBERTY WOKE CRYING ONLY A FEW minutes after America settled her in her cradle. She sighed and picked up her baby. Living in town had become harder. By day, construction noises rang out from buildings going up, and dance halls blared music late into the night.

They also had to endure the revelry of drunken miners. The quarreling and curses made America flinch. Poor Addie despaired over protecting Travis. He had already begun to learn more than a boy his age should know about soiled doves. Prostitutes strolled freely down the boardwalk in their expensive clothing, unashamed to show their painted faces.

Not long after Nate and Travis returned from Bannack with supplies, the freight wagons started running to Virginia City. That made attaining provisions easier for everyone, and the town flourished. With hopeful miners arriving daily, all the towns along Alder Gulch would soon be overrun.

Where money and human need coincided, businesses followed. Addie's cooking had won her a devoted clientele, even as other businesses offering places to eat crowded in, but she would do well to trade her cook tent for a building. Nate visited the cook tent more often now, helping Addie plan her restaurant.

America would appreciate the chance to wash dishes in less primitive conditions, and sleeping behind solid walls might block out some of the nighttime noises. It would also be wonderful to have a more substantial roof protecting them from the weather. That became more important now that the first breaths of autumn stirred the air.

With the money America had earned for her labors

accumulated in a cracker box in her wagon, she had a decision to make. Should she continue working for Addie to save more money or leave Virginia City and start a new life on what she had already put aside? Whether she quit her job now or later, she would leave town. Shane had helped her make that choice.

America frowned. Shane hadn't come back after the trip to Bannack. He was either staying away from Virginia City or avoiding her, possibly both. He was probably right to put distance between them, although everything in her wanted the opposite. She tried not to mope around pining for the man, but sometimes she couldn't help feeling sad. If they had parted on better terms, perhaps his absence wouldn't hurt so much.

She settled Liberty back to sleep and laid down on her feather mattress. After punching her pillow with more force than necessary, she rolled over and tried to go back to sleep.

Virgil Henry's face rose before America in yet another flashback. He had spent only a short time behind bars before being set free. She'd never been called upon to testify to how he'd traumatized her, and she hadn't seen him again. Last she'd heard, he'd returned to Bannack. Good riddance, but she wished he'd gone farther away.

She tossed and turned then fell into a restless sleep troubled by a monster who chained her to him and went about roaring.

"You look tired," Addie noted when America emerged from her wagon. Bright-eyed this morning, her friend had already started a fire. The inviting fragrance of coffee wafted from a pot on a rack above the flames.

America accepted a cup of the dark elixir Addie pressed into her hand. "Thank you. Liberty didn't sleep well."

"I'm sorry." Addie replenished her own cup. "Travis can take her for a walk so you can nap before it gets too busy."

"You are so kind to me." It would be hard to say goodbye to Addie when she left Virginia City.

Addie waved a hand. "You would do the same for me."

After a breakfast of spotted pup, a sweetened rice mixture

dotted with raisins, America felt restored. She put a pot of water on the grate above the fire to wash up their dishes, but Addie elbowed her out of the way. "I'll do it this time. Why don't you sit for a spell?"

America moved a crate closer to the wash station so they could visit while Addie worked. Soft light shone in the sky and birds sang their melodies around the sleepy town. The mining camp lay quietest in the morning, providing a respite from the feverish activity that intensified throughout the day and peaked at night.

Addie washed out a cup, her hands working with deft skill. She still wore her wedding rings, but America couldn't help wondering how long she would continue to do so. The fact that Nate had remained a friend after she'd turned him down spoke well of the man and suggested they might one day be together.

The dishcloth swished across a plate. "Nate stopped by last night after you'd gone to bed. He told me he saw Shane in Nevada City."

"Oh?" America pretended not to care.

Addie rested her hands in the dishwater and gave her a sympathetic look. "Did something happen between you two?"

"Nothing important." She willed that to be true, but it felt like a fib. She'd had enough of sitting, so she picked up a dishtowel and a plate to dry.

Addie's hands resumed their task. "We're going to start building the restaurant next week. It should go up quickly, but we'll have to close down while we work on it."

"What will we do with ourselves with time on our hands?" America enjoyed having Sundays off, but it would be nice to take a longer break and exciting to see the restaurant go up.

Addie laughed. "I expect there will be plenty of work for us. We'll need to move everything out of the cook tent and feed Nate and the other workers."

Travis hurried down the road toward them, carrying wooden buckets filled with water, one in each hand. Every morning, he made sure the water barrels strapped to the wagons remained full. America restrained the impulse to take one of the buckets from him. She'd bruised his masculinity once before by offering to help.

"Ma!" He set down the buckets. "Guess what? I ran into Nate down at the water. He's going to let me pan for gold once my chores are finished. Can I?"

Addie's brow puckered. "Just be careful in the water. Stay in the shallow part, okay?"

"Ma, I'm going on fourteen."

Addie rounded on him. "Age doesn't matter when you're drowning."

He rolled his eyes. "I'm not going to drown. I can swim."

"Your father could swim, but that didn't help him."

America sucked in a breath, understanding a little better Addie's fears for Travis.

Scowling, Travis stomped over to fill the water barrel on the side of America's wagon.

She followed him. "Travis, your ma loves you. She only wants to make sure you'll be safe."

He gave her a sheepish look. "All right. I'll stick to the shallow part."

From habit, they kept their voices down, but they must have woken Liberty. She started talking to herself from within the wagon. Smiling at the sound of her baby's sweet voice, America climbed inside to play with her while Addie and Travis talked. Words Gramma had read aloud from the Bible returned to her memory.

America smiled. Shane might have admired her intervention, for blessed are the peacemakers.

The wind rattled the leaves on either side of the road. Shane pushed Archibald into a gallop, unwilling to be caught out after dark. He'd left Nevada City much too late. Traveling even a short distance after nightfall made a man vulnerable to outlaws. Without material wealth, he could offer nothing to line a road agent's pockets but still might not escape unscathed. He'd heard tales of travelers being threatened or shot when they carried too little cash.

Shane had meant to leave earlier, but he'd gotten into a conversation with a miner bent on testing him as a preacher. Walking away would appear like conceding, so he'd felt obligated to stay.

His excuses for remaining longer in Bannack didn't mollify his conscience. He'd finally moved on, only to linger at the other stops along his circuit. Now, duty pointed him toward Virginia City. As Chrisman had said, the sheer numbers of humanity in Alder Gulch demanded his attention. In the face of that, he had to return.

Truth be told, he longed to see America again, the very reason he'd stayed away so long. He pictured her as she'd looked during their last walk together. The image of her beautiful face above the flower she held—her lips slightly parted as she gazed up at him—had the power to drive all other thoughts from his head. That he loved her was not hard to understand, but he didn't know what to do about it. When he'd given his life to God, he'd extinguished the desire to have a family. The best he could do for America was persuade her to settle in a more suitable location.

He would look up his cousin as soon as he arrived in Virginia City. Spending time in the cabin had caused him to miss Con, and he looked forward to catching up with him.

Something moved at the corner of his vision. Shadows shifted beneath the trees on the side of the road.

Heart pounding, Shane reined Archibald to a slower pace. "Who goes there?"

A masked man brandishing a pistol spurred a black horse onto the road in front of him. Screaming, Shane's horse reared and flailed the air with his hooves. A hooded figure sped on horseback from the brush on the other side of the road. He seized Archibald's bridle. Archibald snorted and shuddered.

"Have a care, will you?" Shane demanded. "You're frightening my horse."

The masked man leveled his gun at Shane. "Well, well. Caught us a preacher now, have we? Let's see if we can make you say your prayers."

The road agent obviously knew him. Shane felt certain he would recognize the outlaw without a mask. The odd accent coloring his voice probably disguised it, but the ring of his tones sounded familiar.

"Might as well shoot him." The hooded man at Archibald's head pulled his gun. Eye holes cut in his hood revealed his light eyes narrowed on Shane.

"Simmer down." The masked road agent reprimanded in a bored voice. "I'd rather not cross the Almighty by killing a preacher unless I have to."

"Well, I like that!" The hooded man roared with laughter. "When did you turn into a Sunday school teacher?"

"He has a point." Shane found his tongue. "God has a way of punishing those who make his servants suffer."

"No one has to get hurt today," the masked road agent insisted. "All I want is your gold."

"I'll give it to you gladly." Shane reached for the pouch on his belt.

"Careful there!" The masked road agent pulled back the hammer of his pistol.

Shane froze, uncertain of the man's commitment to not angering God.

"Take it nice and slow," the man advised.

"Certainly." Shane recovered his composure and untied his buckskin pouch from his belt. He tossed it to the man. "I would have given it as willingly if you'd asked without pointing your gun at me."

"Sweet of you." The masked road agent sneered. He flipped the pouch into the air and snatched it back. "Considering there's nothing here, that's not hard to understand."

"The treasure a man can lay up in heaven surpasses earthly gain," Shane informed his wayward charge.

"That won't do me any good." The masked road agent snickered. "I don't expect I'll wind up in that place."

Shane tensed his jaw. "May God forgive you for speaking of your eternal destiny so lightly."

"You gonna let him preach at you?" the hooded man protested. "Let's get out of here."

"God has a few other sins to forgive on my account before He gets to that one," the masked road agent went on as if the other man hadn't spoken. "Guess I won't have to burn for killing a preacher, though." He took off his hat and swept it in a mocking gesture. Then he lashed his horse with the reins and started off in the direction of Nevada City. Galloping hooves echoed through the night air.

Shane faced the hooded road agent. "I'll pray for your redemption."

"I didn't ask you to." The pistol in his hand shook.

"What a man prays rests between himself and God. The road you're traveling won't take you anywhere pleasant. I'll pray that you discover the truth of that in time."

"Don't waste your breath on me." He snarled the words but lowered his gun.

"No soul can sink so low as to lie beyond God's reach."

"Thank you." The whisper carried to Shane on a breath before the man melted into the night.

"May God preserve your soul," Shane murmured. He turned his horse toward Virginia City and remained upright in the saddle, alert for further trouble the rest of the journey. Con wasn't on his claim, but his rusty-bearded neighbor advised Shane of his whereabouts. Shane gave Archibald a rest and a handful of oats before heading after his cousin.

He found Con at a gambling table in Daily's Saloon, stinking of whiskey and with a fancy lady hanging on his arm. Con tilted a shot glass to his mouth, threw back his head, and drained the contents. He set the glass down. It tipped over, hinting that other shots had already gone down Con's throat.

Shane frowned. He wasn't a gambling man, but he knew playing cards while drunk was an efficient way to empty a man's pockets. How much gold had Con brought with him?

"Good evening, gentlemen." Shane nodded to the men gathered around the table. He clenched his hands into fists. "Con, what are you doing here? I've never known you to gamble."

Silas Brown, whom Shane had seen at the Merrick Hotel's bar, returned his nod with a guarded look. Virgil Henry gave him a tight-lipped smile from beneath his flop-brimmed hat. Not trusting him an inch, Shane kept an eye on Virgil's gun hand. The fourth man was dressed in white shirtsleeves and a satin vest. A bowler hat covered his flame-red hair. He glared at Shane above his fanned-out cards.

"Hello, Atticus." Shane smiled. "What are you doing in Virginia City?"

Atticus Merrick selected a card and threw it down before replying. "I get around."

Shane didn't doubt it. He had the man's measure by now, and Atticus would follow any easy money available. With Con impaired by alcohol, Shane could guess what was going on here.

"Go 'way, Shane." Con half rose from his chair, but the fancy lady pulled him back, laughing with her arms slung around his neck.

"Do you really want to do this, Con?" Shane asked.

His cousin stared at him with glassy eyes. "Why wouldn't I?"

The saloon girl draped herself across Con's lap and murmured in his ear.

Con pushed her back with a smile. "Stop that and let me be." He ruffled his cards. "I need to think."

"Come on, Con," Shane urged. "Let's get out of here."

Virgil Henry's gun appeared. "I suggest you leave him alone."

"I must say, Saint Preacher"—Atticus scowled at him— "You have a remarkable capacity for intruding."

Shane tightened his jaw. "I won't apologize for looking after my family."

Con stood up, blocking Virgil's line of fire. "Don't take this to heart, gentlemen, but I've changed my mind about playing tonight." He threw in his hand. "I'll be going."

"This way." Shane guided Con through the tall doors. Once outside, he paused to peer back into the saloon. Virgil had put away his gun, which he seemed remarkably fond of drawing on people. Shane, however, had never seen him pull the trigger. Atticus sat as before with his cards spread. The fancy lady had transferred her favors to Silas.

Con swaggered off in the opposite direction from his claim.

"Hold on!" Shane caught up to him. "You want to go the other way."

Con displayed a beatific smile. "I'm glad you're back."

"That makes two of us. Hard telling what you'd have gotten yourself into back there without me." Shane turned him about, and Con started off with an unsteady gait.

Shane kept pace, watching in case called upon to prevent a fall.

"*The pale moon was rising above the green mountain,*" Con belted out the first line of "The Rose of Tralee" and careened perilously close to the edge of the boardwalk. A muddy puddle waited in the street below. "*The sun was declining beneath the blue sea!*"

"Careful, there." Shane hauled him back to safety.

"*When I strayed with my love to the pure crystal fountain that stands in the beautiful Vale of Tralee.*" Con rolled the last words out with dramatic emphasis.

"You *would* choose a romantic song."

Con grinned. "Wha's the matter? Strike close to home?"

"I've had my fill of the subject lately, that's all. But you—I never thought of you as a romantic."

Con laughed. "I'll tell you something if you'll keep it to yourself."

"Oh?"

"I am the author of poetry." Con spoke near his ear in a stage whisper.

"Go on with you!" Shane could barely conceal his amusement at the thought of Con's future reaction to this admission.

"'Tis the honest truth." Con nodded.

"I suppose you have your poems hidden away somewhere."

"Indeed I do." Con tapped his chest in the region of his heart.

"Ah." Shane nodded in understanding. "Are they all love ballads?"

"I wrote them for Aileen." The stage whisper stirred the air near his ear. "But that's 'tween you and me."

"Aileen O'Grady?" The picture of an awkward girl with frizzy hair and blemished skin arose in Shane's mind, soon replaced by that of a beautiful young woman. Aileen had improved with time. "You delighted in teasing her as I recall."

Con laughed. "That I did. She only wanted you, so I never told her my feelings. I've always regretted leaving her for you, since you didn't take up with her when she gave you the chance."

"She did? I must not have noticed."

"'Twasn't the first time I wanted to be you."

"What?" They left the boardwalk and started down the trail that followed the banks of Alder Creek. Moonlight and the glow from smoldering campfires guided them. "Why would you want such a thing?"

"You do everything right, at least most of the time." He hiccupped. "I always make a mess of things."

How had Con come by such a notion? "Don't turn me into a hero, or I'm bound to disappoint you. And don't sell yourself short."

"I wish I had your faith."

"Then look to God." Con stumbled, but Shane caught him. "I've got you."

His cousin threw an arm around Shane's shoulders and lapsed back into "The Rose of Tralee."

Shane guided him along the path, watching the shadows for hidden danger—a habit he'd acquired by necessity. The wickiup loomed ahead, a dark hulk against the moon-washed ground. Beyond it, Alder Creek flowed in a bright ribbon. Shane pulled back the flap of the wickiup, leaving it open as he half-dragged his singing cousin inside.

Shane lowered him to his bedroll, pulled off his boots, and tugged a blanket over him.

"*Oh no, 'twas the truth in her eyes ever dawning that made me love Mary, the Rose of Tralee.*" Con blasted him with the stench of whiskey on his breath. He finished the song with a flourish, rolled over, and rasped out a snore.

Shane retrieved his own bedroll from against the wall, where he'd stashed it before going to the saloon. He unrolled it near the entrance flap and stretched out with a long sigh. Sleep didn't come readily. His mind, less weary than his body, turned over the events of the day and reached through time to childhood memories he'd rather forget.

Shane knew the source of Con's low self-esteem. Uncle Bradan's criticism had ground it out of him from boyhood. The impact a father could make on a son had become apparent on his circuit as well. Those who received nurture had an advantage over sons who did not. It didn't escape him that Con had transferred his need for masculine guidance to Shane. He hoped he wouldn't fail his expectations.

Con's groans woke Shane from a restless sleep. He rolled out of his blankets and bent over his cousin. The light shining into the wickiup from a gap at the edge of the door flap lit the dried brush matting of the walls. His cousin looked decidedly unwell. "How do you feel?"

"Like death." Con quit his feeble attempts to rise and fell back to lie prone.

"Wine is a mocker and beer a brawler. Whoever is led astray by them is not wise. That's from the book of Proverbs."

Con glared at him through half-closed eyes. "I suppose you think that's comforting."

"I was more concerned that it's true." Shane began pulling on his boots. "I've never known you to indulge."

He winced as if his head ached, which Shane knew it must. "Yes, well. I don't want to be like Uncle Seamus."

Shane heartily approved that sentiment. "Whatever possessed you to go into that saloon in the first place?"

"I cashed in on a strike." He put a trembling hand to his brow. "And I decided to celebrate."

"By going to the saloon?"

"I ran into Cyrus, who happened to be celebrating too. I told myself I'd only have one shot of whiskey. I guess you saw how that went."

Shane lifted an eyebrow. "I thought you were saving money for a new start somewhere else. Do you have anything left?"

"Yes, thanks to you." Con attempted to sit up again but fell back with a moan, holding his head with both hands.

"You're welcome." Shane lifted him into a sitting position.

"Help me outside," Con cried with sudden urgency.

Shane obliged.

After Con emptied the contents of his stomach behind the wickiup, Shane dipped a tin cup into a bucket and offered it to his cousin. Con rinsed out his mouth and spat before swallowing any water. He leaned over, heaving again. Shane half-carried him back to bed, breathing through his mouth to avoid inhaling the stench on his cousin's breath.

Con grasped Shane's shirt. "Should I ever decide to drink again, remind me about this, will you?"

"You can count on it." Shane gazed down at his cousin with compassion. "Try to sleep it off."

Con slept most of the day and woke in a better condition around supper time. Shane sat next to him at the fire. Sparks flew into the air like so many fireflies. Dusk crouched in the shadows, and wavering light climbed the alders at the edges of camp. Lively sounds started up in town, but the trees and brush deadened the noise at this distance. Shane spared a prayer for the mortal souls drinking to the god of confusion in the saloons and dancehalls.

Con crunched the last of his crackers and finished his bowl of potato soup. "That's better." He swilled water from his tin cup and slanted a sideways look at Shane. "Thanks for taking care of me."

"I'll always watch your back." Shane poked the fire. "Do you have enough money left to go somewhere else?"

Con shook his head. "Some of it vanished for no reason I can figure."

The laughter of the saloon girl who had draped herself around Con came back to Shane. "That's unfortunate."

Con gazed into the crackling flames. "There has to be more gold where that came from. I'll dig again."

Shane knew the process by which miners washed gold out of the dirt using a sluice box. It seemed back-breaking labor. An idea presented itself, one he rejected at first but then entertained. The wind dragged through the tops of the alder trees. Water gurgled, and a rock thumped over in the creek bed.

"I'm willing to help you," he said in sudden decision. "Anything so you can get away sooner."

Con laughed. "I never thought I'd see the day you'd become a miner. Be careful, Saint Preacher. Your halo is slipping."

Shane smiled. "Go ahead and have fun at my expense, but remember I know your secrets."

"Secrets?" Con gave him a guarded look. "What did I say last night?"

"Nothing much." Shane shrugged. "You mentioned that you write love poems and carry a torch for Aileen O'Grady."

"I remember that, anyway." Embarrassment colored his laugh. "I shall never drink again, dear cousin."

"Wise man."

Voices murmuring outside brought America to peer from the opening at the rear of her wagon. Several men, talking quietly together, climbed down from their horses on the side of the street. Construction of Addie's restaurant would start today, but she hadn't expected the workers to arrive before breakfast.

Nate greeted them, cutting off her view. Angling her face to take a better look, she shifted to avoid exposing herself in her shift.

Her breath caught in her throat. She knew the way Shane wore his hat, the fit of his jacket across his shoulders, and how he carried himself. Nate had run into him in Nevada City, Addie had told her, and he must have asked Shane to help out.

After their unhappy parting, America had no idea how she would make it through a day that threw her into Shane's company. She would have to brazen it out, though, and treat him exactly like the other workers. That required her to smile and say hello. She wasn't a naïve schoolgirl, after all, but a woman grown. She could face a man she had kissed with regrets.

Her hands shook while buttoning her blue wool dress. The air held a nip this morning. The weather was easing into fall, so she pulled on her wool coat as well.

Liberty woke before she could leave the wagon. The need to

care for her daughter delayed the inevitable meeting with Shane but also gave America time to collect herself. She clothed Liberty in a blue dress and added a white pinafore and pantalets for extra warmth. For good measure, she wrapped her baby in the small quilt she'd sewn to pass the time while waiting for her birth on the homestead. She gathered Liberty into her arms and left the wagon, determined to face Shane with composure.

Huddled beside Connor Walsh around the fire outside Addie's wagon, Shane laughed at something Nate said. Smoke embraced Addie's coffee pot. It drifted on the breeze toward America, mingling the fragrance of burning pine with the dark aroma of coffee.

Addie called a greeting at America's approach, and Nate gave her a nod before crouching to add wood to the flames. She summoned a smile, but it faltered when Shane's blue gaze meshed with hers.

Time and distance melted away. The longing that had swept over her on the day their lips touched returned in full measure. Her heartache fled, and she forgot each sleepless night. Nothing mattered between them now but here, this moment, and the desire that flared between them.

Liberty fussed in her arms, breaking America's bemusement. She cooed to her baby, grateful for the interruption and the opportunity to recover her poise.

"You're looking well, Mrs. Reed." Shane spoke in a neutral voice that had nothing to do with the ardent look he had given her.

Her heartache came back to roost. "Thank you." She acknowledged his compliment in what she hoped was a detached voice. She couldn't return it, however. He looked rough and unsettled, as if the road had not been kind.

"Have you met my cousin, Connor Walsh?" Shane glanced at the man beside him.

Addie had pointed him out to America the first time he'd

visited the cook tent. With dark hair and blue eyes, the man resembled Shane, but he carried himself with a roguish air, while Shane seemed overly serious.

Con took off his hat with a flourish. "That she has, for she's fed me often enough. I'm always delighted to find myself in the presence of a fine lady in these rough parts." He spoke in the same lilting Irish accent as Shane, but with more charm.

She rewarded his gallantry with a smile. "You are very kind."

Con smiled, an act that made his already-handsome face even more appealing. "No matter how I respond, I am trapped. Should I say I am not kind or that you are mistaken?" He shook his head. "Either way, my admiration is sincere."

"Thank you." America's cheeks warmed with pleasure at his words. "If you'll excuse me, I'll go and make myself useful."

To clear the ground for construction of the restaurant, they'd taken down the cook tent and dismantled most of the tables Nate had improvised from sawhorses and planks. Addie, with Travis helping beside her, stationed herself at the table they'd set up for food preparation.

America navigated the piles of quarried stones, stacked boards, picks and shovels, and all manner of carpentry tools that crowded Addie's property and spilled over at the edges of the broad street. She reached the table and asked Travis to watch Liberty in order to work with her hands free. As she suspected, he jumped at the chance for a break from kitchen duties. She mixed and shaped dough for quick donuts, watching in amusement as he carried the baby around to be admired in turn by each of the workers Nate had rounded up.

While Addie fried the donuts, America reloaded the coffee pot and cracked eggs for the skillet. With the food ready, Addie called the workers for breakfast. They assembled around the largest of the tables set up in front of the wagons.

America waited for Shane to sit down before taking a seat as far away from him as possible. She fed Liberty applesauce in between eating her own scrambled eggs and bacon. Nibbling a vanilla-glazed cake doughnut, she listened to the conversation flowing around her and remained silent. The excited mood around the table proved contagious, however. Liberty pealed with laughter and did her best to claim attention, which made keeping to herself more difficult for America.

Liberty engaged in a lively game of peekaboo with Con, who seemed to have a natural affinity with children. "What a darling child," he called to her from down the table.

The other men chimed their approval. Liberty's antics often won her admirers.

"She's a beauty like her mother." Con's eyes warmed.

She smiled at him. Shane turned his head, and their gazes clashed, but an invisible cord tugged them together. She blinked and looked away to dispel the sensation. When she turned back, Shane was listening to Addie say something from across the table. He wore an intent expression. The yearning to smooth the creases from his brow took hold of America.

Con intercepted her gaze, a question in his eyes. He divided a glance between her and Shane and frowned at his plate.

After breakfast, Nate and the other workers assembled to plan the day's duties. America took Liberty from Travis to allow him the freedom to help build the restaurant. She spread Liberty's quilt in a patch of grass behind the table where she and Addie washed dishes and stole glances at the baby playing with her toes. By the time they finished the dishes and started in on lunch, Liberty had fallen asleep. America admired the beauty of her small face and the curve of her lashes, although with so much to do she couldn't stand over her daughter for long.

The men ate sandwiches during the breaks they took from excavating the root cellar where Addie would store potatoes, onions, apples, and other produce. After laying the stone foundation, they measured and sawed boards for the next day's work.

At supper, Nate lowered himself to sit beside Addie, while Travis glared at him from her other side. America, distracted by Liberty's squirming, took a spot across from Addie, leaving empty places on either side of her. Thinking better of that arrangement, she decided to move toward Travis at the end of the table. Before she could shift, however, Shane and Con settled on either side of her. Feeling surrounded, she resigned herself to being sandwiched between the two men.

"This meal looks wonderful," Nate murmured to Addie.

"You're most welcome. I wanted to thank you all for your hard work." Addie smiled at each worker. "I can't tell you how wonderful it is to see my restaurant finally going up. I can't wait to try out my new root cellar."

Nate grinned. "I'm glad you're pleased."

Shane turned to America. "Thanks for your service, as well."

"Yes, indeed." Con gave her a brilliant smile. "Food tastes better when lovely hands prepare it."

"Thank you, Mr. Walsh. You have a way of turning a phrase that is downright—" America broke off, searching for a suitable word.

"Poetic?" Shane supplied.

Con looked past America to his cousin. "I'm certain she meant something else."

"No, that's the perfect word." America lifted Liberty to her shoulder and patted her back.

"Perhaps you should consider a career as a writer," Addie suggested.

Shane smiled. "I'm certain you could pursue such an occupation after leaving Alder Gulch."

"Thank you for the suggestion." Con matched him smile for smile.

"Reverend Hayes, will you say grace?" Addie asked.

America bowed her head and lost herself in Shane's Irish lilt when he thanked the Almighty for their sustenance. Then they passed the food around the table. During her trail days, Addie had mastered the art of cooking over an open fire. Now she expressed her gratitude to the workers by cooking a feast. Platters of fried trout, bacon, potato cakes, and reconstituted dried vegetables went around, with currant bread alongside. Addie and America had indulged in a baking session the day before the cook tent came down, and dessert consisted of pies made from dried apples and the buffalo berries Travis had gathered in the wild.

Chatter flowed around the table, accompanied by the clink of tableware and occasional laughter. Addie and Nate entered into a hushed conversation while Travis and Shane discussed the best way to catch a trout.

Liberty fussed but soon settled down when America fed her small tastes of soft vegetables.

"What brings you to this part of the world, Mrs. Reed?" Con asked.

America sipped the water in her glass to give herself time to come up with an answer. Necessity had driven her here, but saying that could lead to a discussion of painful subjects she'd rather avoid. She settled on telling the surface truth while keeping deeper matters to herself. "I came to help Addie and to provide for myself and my daughter. What about you? Why did you come to Alder Gulch?" She asked the question to take the focus away from herself.

Con tilted his head. "I needed somewhere to go."

Recognizing a tactic similar to her own, America wondered what he didn't want to say. She didn't press him to clarify his statement. "I hope you find living here worthwhile."

"How can I complain?" Con gave her a reverent smile. "I've landed in the company of an angel."

"My cousin will be leaving town as soon as possible." Shane spoke in a sharp voice America had never heard him use before.

Con narrowed his eyes. "It's bound to take a while."

"Not if I can help it," Shane replied.

America took a bite of potato cake and tried to ignore the tension brewing between the two men. She didn't understand it, but she sensed it might have something to do with the attention Con paid her. She could almost convince herself Shane was jealous, but his rivalry with his cousin might have nothing to do with her.

Con returned his attention to America. "Where are you from originally, if I may ask?"

She broke off a bite of currant bread to hide her dismay. Unable to think of a way to dodge his direct inquiry, she answered, "St. Louis."

"I stayed there on my way West. It's a nice city." He sipped his cup of cider. "Does your family still live there?"

"Yes." She volunteered no further information and hoped he wouldn't want to know more.

"Would you ever consider returning to them?" Shane asked.

Her smile slipped. She could never go home again. She shook her head and took a drink of water to hide the emotions rushing in to choke her.

"Well, I for one am glad you're here." Con's sympathetic expression told her she had found an ally. "And I appreciate the chance to get to know you. Would you consider—?"

"We should be going, Con, don't you think?" Shane cut off whatever his cousin had been about to say. "We have an early start tomorrow."

"You can't leave before dessert," Addie protested.

Con gave Shane a puzzled look. "You can go back to camp if you want, but I'm not finished with supper. I don't plan to miss the dried-apple pie. It's famous, from what I hear."

"How can I argue with dried-apple pie?" Shane scowled and subsided.

Liberty reached for her toes, giggling.

Everyone burst out laughing.

"May I take your baby while you eat?" Con asked her.

"She can be an armful, but you're welcome to hold her." America transferred her daughter to his arms.

Liberty looked slightly alarmed, but then Con made a game of raising his eyebrows, to her great hilarity. The two carried on an extended conversation.

"Con seems to have found a playmate," Shane said with dry humor.

"I'm grateful to eat my supper with my hands free," America replied mildly.

Shane nodded toward Liberty. "I'd be happy to take a turn with your baby."

"Thank you, but you might have trouble getting her away from your cousin. She's quite smitten with him."

"He has a way with women." Shane kept his voice low. "But they shouldn't take him too seriously."

"Is that a family trait?" America couldn't resist the question. From the way he frowned, her barb had gone home, but she couldn't rejoice in the victory.

"You never know, Cousin. That could change." Con rested his gaze on America. "Given the right woman."

Shadows stretched across the road before Shane. He kicked a rock and avoided looking at Con, walking beside him.

"What was that about back there?" Con asked.

Shane darted a glance at him. "What do you mean?"

"I wasn't born yesterday. You glared at me all through dinner, and made comments unlike yourself. What's the matter? Was I poaching on your territory by paying attention to America?"

"She is not my territory."

"Well, *something* has you riled," Con pointed out. "You all but dragged me out of there. Since when are you concerned about getting to bed early? It's not yet dark. I had half a mind to let you traipse back to camp on your own."

"I'm tired. I worked hard today." That was the simple truth, but Shane knew his desire to remove Con from America's company was a bit more complicated.

"I'll give you that much. We both did. But there's something more going on here. I never saw a woman trying so hard to pretend to ignore a man, and you were doing the same to her. I played up to her to find out how you'd react." He grinned. "You didn't disappoint me. Now, do you want to tell me what's going on between the pair of you?"

Shane considered his request. "No, I don't."

Con laughed. "So I'm to mind my business, thank you very much? I was never any good at that, as you well know."

"Try harder." Shane didn't want to have this out with Con right now, but he knew his cousin wouldn't let him off that easily. He waited for the next remark.

Con shot him an impish look. "She would make a good preacher's wife."

"Now you *are* meddling." Shane scolded, but lightly. How could he blame his cousin for seeing more than he wanted him to? "For your information, I have no intention of marrying."

"Ah now, Shane. Not everyone has as poor a marriage as my parents."

For Con's sake, he wished that could have gone differently. When Shane had arrived at Five Point with Uncle Seamus all those years ago, he'd expected to live with his cousin's family, but Con's parents refused to take in another mouth to feed. Shane understood their concern now that he was older, but it had stung his young heart. If they had allowed Shane to live with them, however, their fighting might have traumatized him as much as it had their children.

"It's not that," Shane said. "My profession stands in the way."

Con gave him a startled look. "Marriage isn't forbidden to you, is it?"

"No, but I don't want to bring a woman into my unsettled way of life." They turned aside onto the path toward Con's claim. A breeze scented by water lifted off the creek.

"You wouldn't consider giving that up and settling down for the love of a woman?"

Shane sighed. "It's hard to explain a sense of duty."

"Virginia City is in need of a church, I understand."

Shane raised a brow. "What are you saying cousin? Would you have me go back on my word and abandon the other charges on my circuit?"

"I don't know what to say about all that, but one thing I know for certain. If the God you serve would take all a man has or can be, I want nothing to do with Him."

"He multiplies all we surrender twenty-fold, but not always by the same coin."

"I don't understand that kind of arithmetic," Con pointed out. "All I know is if you don't marry the widow Reed, someone else will. Maybe I will. I waited on you for Aileen, and look where it got me. I won't stand by and wait for you again."

Shane shook his head. "I can't grasp the idea of you as a married man, and certainly not married to the widow Reed."

"Why not?" Con asked in an offended voice. "She's easy on the eyes and can cook besides."

"What about *you*?"

"Me?"

"What will you bring to a marriage?" Shane asked.

Con went silent.

Shane smiled. "Settle that, then look for a wife."

As for himself, Shane had chosen duty over sentiment. He would help build the restaurant, give Con a hand on his claim, and then continue on his circuit. If the image of America holding a fragile blue flower and gazing at him with tender eyes haunted his dreams, he would try all the harder to remove the memory of holding her in his arms.

CHAPTER SEVENTEEN

AMERICA GAZED OUT THE WINDOW OF the small room at the back of the restaurant where she and Liberty slept. The glass panes gave a view onto the brush, where meadowlarks trilled and sang. Addie slept in the room next to hers, and Travis bedded down in the loft. The restaurant occupied most of the building, with the kitchen off to the side. In the pantry beside the kitchen, a trap door opened to steep steps leading down into the root cellar.

Nate and his helpers finished building the restaurant before the rains set in, thankfully. With the temperature plummeting and the leaves turning, Addie's potbelly stove kept them cozy. Winter would arrive soon, the season she had lost Richard. Had it truly been only a year since he'd frozen to death in an early blizzard? It seemed so much longer. Reflections dogged America, taking her from Richard's proposal to their wedding, onward to the homestead, and finally back to the day he died . . .

The wind had wailed across the prairie like an abandoned child that long-ago day. America had huddled beneath the quilts on her bed, bracing herself to endure a storm-tossed night. Gusts moaned under the little sod house's door. She should have plugged the gap with rags before lying down. Now she had to steel herself to leave the bed to stop the draft. She pressed a hand to her swollen belly but drew no response from within her womb. Perhaps she'd worn the baby out along with herself when she'd clawed through the snow looking for Richard. She'd come near to freezing before giving up.

The oxen had warned them of the storm's approach, lifting

their wet noses to sniff the air. They bawled, and Richard paused from drinking out of the jug of water she'd brought him. He wiped a hand across his mouth and turned his head northward. America followed his gaze, a sinking feeling in her stomach.

Above the horizon, a huge white cloud piled into the sky.

"I'll get this corn cribbed and take Curly and Sam in." He returned the jug and nudged her toward the house.

America nodded and went to make coffee to warm Richard when he came in. She turned back at the door to look for him. He was walking with his limping gait to unhitch the oxen. His hair needed cutting, and dirt etched the seams of his skin, but he had breadth of shoulder and a careless, loping grace despite his handicap.

How could either of them have guessed the swift advance of this storm or its unrelenting fury? When it abated days later, America found Curly and Sam in the sod stable, barely alive. The wagon had never moved from beside the crib and still held its load of corn.

Her calls to Richard remained unanswered.

A tear had trickled down her cheek, and she could still feel its warmth where she'd brushed it away. Another followed, and she'd pulled the quilts over her head, weeping for Richard, and for herself. She'd meant to spend the rest of her life with him, to grow into loving him. Now it was too late. God had taken her husband and, for her sins, she deserved to lose him.

The child had stirred and stretched within her, and she'd caressed her baby through the thin veil of flesh. No matter how deep she burrowed into her quilts, the cold reached her. When she could ignore her discomfort no longer, she rolled to her feet, clutched one of the quilts about her, and groped her way to the Franklin stove. Shivering, she opened the stove door and lifted the lid of the firebox beside it, thankful she'd had the presence of mind to fill it to overflowing with logs Richard had split, even in the teeth of a bitter wind. She hoped her supply would see her through the storm.

She remembered straightening and putting a hand to her back to ease its aching when a wild keening throbbed in the air. Even now the hair on the back of her neck bristled at the recollection.

America had pushed aside the linen at the window and glanced outside. The storm had passed, and the wails of the buffalo wolves gave way to snarling and yelping. A full moon shone above the rangy creatures and lit their coats with blue light. They were fussing at something in the snow. Pressing against the glass, she tried to make out what the creatures were dragging. She pushed the back of her hand against her mouth and fought to keep from vomiting. The urge to retch still threatened to seize her at the image of what she'd seen that night.

The buffalo wolves had found Richard's body.

With a shudder, America forced her thoughts back to the present.

"Someone come and help me, please," Addie called from the kitchen in the urgent voice people used when they needed rescue.

America hurried to see what she needed.

Addie had caught a large porcelain platter against her forearm and the edge of the shelf. In her other hand, she held a large punch bowl in an equally precarious position. She'd evidently been trying to take it down from the shelf and had dislodged the platter. She couldn't save one without sacrificing the other. Addie herself was in none too secure a position, since the chair rocked beneath her feet.

America rushed to steady the chair. "How did you wind up in this situation?"

"Never mind how it happened!" Addie snapped. "Take this platter before it falls."

"Hold on." America hauled over another chair from the nook at the far side of the kitchen.

"Hurry!"

America climbed onto the chair and reached for the platter.

"Oh, no!" The platter slipped from Addie's fingers and crashed onto the floorboards. Shards of porcelain flew everywhere.

The punch bowl wobbled alarmingly just out of America's reach. "Careful!" she called out.

Addie steadied the punch bowl with both hands, preventing it from following the platter.

America stepped down from her chair and lifted her hands to take the punch bowl.

After transferring it to her, Addie came down from her perch. She picked up one of the shards. Her shoulders slumped. "My platter." She looked up with tears glistening in her eyes. "That was my mother's favorite."

"I'm so sorry." America's words seemed inadequate in the face of her friend's pain.

Addie brushed away her tears. "Oh, why didn't I take better care of it?"

"You couldn't have known it would fall."

Addie shook her head. "I shouldn't have put it up so high on a shelf that I couldn't see what I was doing." She plopped onto her chair and heaved a deep sigh. "Clyde didn't want to bring it along in the wagon, but I insisted. Now, I wish I had left it behind. At least it would still be in one piece." She put her face in her hands and wept.

America touched her shoulder. "Why don't you lie down? I can clean this up."

Addie scrubbed her face with her hands and shook her hair back. "Ma gave me her platter, along with the matching punch bowl, on my wedding day. I didn't want to take her things, but she insisted. She never let on she was dying. I wish I hadn't dropped it!"

"It's a shame, but at least you have the memory."

Addie heaved a breath. "We never really know when we

part from someone if we'll ever see them again, do we?"

America's thoughts flew back to Richard. "No. My husband turned away to tend a simple chore the last time I saw him alive."

"Clyde went quickly too."

"What happened?"

Addie looked away, then back to America again. "You've never asked me that."

"I've wondered."

"It happened while Clyde was fording the Laramie in our wagon. The oxen panicked, and the wagon nearly capsized. He fell in when it tipped. The current carried him downstream. We found his body later." Addie remained silent for a span of time then shifted her shoulders as if to throw off a burden. "Can I ask you a question?"

A spurt of alarm surged through America. "What do you want to know?"

"How do you feel about Reverend Hayes?"

America hadn't anticipated that question, and it rendered her speechless. She pulled in a breath. "He's a good man."

Addie shook her head. "I didn't ask what you *think* of him but how you *feel* about him."

The impulse to confess her feelings for Shane gripped America. "I honestly don't know. He's the most maddening man I've ever met. Sometimes I want to slap his face. Other times, well . . ."

"You want to kiss him," Addie supplied.

America nodded. "I don't know why he affects me that way, but he does."

"Nate tells me that Shane is leaving town tomorrow."

She'd expected as much, sooner or later. Shane came and went as if blown on the wind. "I hope he keeps safe and stays warm."

Addie's face took on a smug expression. "He'd probably want to hear you say that, unless I miss my guess."

"What are you suggesting?" A touch of shock laced her voice.

Addie took her hand. "Don't let him go without a goodbye."

America backed into the shade of a cottonwood tree alongside the path. "Maybe this isn't such a good idea."

Travis frowned. "Do you want me to ask Shane to come over and talk to you or not?"

"I'm not sure." She pressed a hand against the sinking feeling in her stomach. Whatever had possessed her to do this?

Travis stared at her then turned his head to look elsewhere. "Of course you do." He strode toward the wickiup he'd told her belonged to Con Walsh.

America opened her mouth to call Travis back. Then she closed it and leaned against the tree. After what had happened with Virgil Henry, she wasn't all that comfortable waiting alone like this. Hopefully, Shane would come soon.

Travis stood at the entrance to the wickiup, speaking to someone inside. After a pause, Con emerged and started toward her. "Hello! Travis tells me you're looking for my cousin."

America wanted to crawl behind the nearby tree and hide. Maybe she shouldn't have taken Addie's advice, after all. Chasing a man was foreign to anything she had ever learned, and this seemed a lot like that.

"My cousin is right there." Con pointed to a figure bending over a gold pan with the water rushing at his feet.

"That's Reverend Hayes?" Amazement lilted America's voice.

Con's eyes danced. "Indeed, it is."

America stared at Shane. His string tie, jacket, and slouch hat had vanished. He worked bareheaded and with rolled-up shirt sleeves. Her breath clogged her throat. "I won't disturb him. Perhaps you'll tell him goodbye for me. I heard he's leaving soon." She turned to flee.

"Wait!" Con called.

She couldn't very well ignore him and run off like a coward, even if she wanted to. She turned back.

He gave her a heartening smile. "I'm sure he'll want to talk to you. Why not tell him yourself?"

How could she say that she'd changed her mind about speaking to Shane? "All right."

"Wait here."

Travis touched her arm. "I'll be going now. Will you be okay?"

"Yes." She smiled at him. "Thanks for doing that for me."

His ears pinked. "I didn't mind."

Con spoke with Shane on the banks of the creek then strolled to his wickiup and went inside. Shane turned toward her, his brow furrowed. With his hair and clothes rumpled, he looked windblown and utterly masculine. He strode to her. "Con said you wanted to talk to me. Is something wrong?"

America's face heated. "It's just that Addie—I mean Nate said—" Oh heavens, she was getting muddled! "Are you leaving tomorrow?" She managed to ask.

"Yes. I've spent longer than I intended in Virginia City, and I must see to the needs of my entire flock." He stared at her a moment, as if trying to read her mind. "Did you have a question for me?"

"I came to say goodbye."

His face registered surprise. "Well, thank you." He spoke the polite words in a guarded tone.

"You're welcome. I'm sorry to have intruded on your . . . *mining?*"

The hard light in Shane's eyes softened. "You could never intrude. And yes, I'm panning for gold to help Con move elsewhere."

"Of course. I recall your mentioning that he meant to leave after you helped build Addie's restaurant." She remembered a lot of other things from that supper, as well. Had Shane been jealous over her then?

"About Con," Shane said. "I hope you won't take everything he says to heart."

She leaned against the rough bark of the cottonwood tree, taken by a sudden desire to find out if he *was* jealous. The tree lifted its twisting arms and draped yellowing leaves above her. "Don't you know that women find such men irresistible?"

Shane's jaw tightened. "America . . . I mean Mrs. Reed—"

"You can call me by my given name. After all, we have kissed." A trifle shocked by her own temerity, America considered abandoning her test.

Shane leaned his arms against the tree on either side of her, trapping her between them. His face hovered inches from hers. "Tempting me, are you?"

America had hoped to draw some sort of reaction from him—anything to let her know where she stood with him—but she hadn't expected this. He was watching her face in a way that challenged her to continue. And, for the life of her, she wasn't going to back down. "Do you remember?" Her voice came out huskily.

"Didn't it go"—the tree's shade shifted around them as he lowered his head and paused his lips above her mouth—"something like this?"

America caught her breath, and Shane closed the gap between them. His lips glided over hers in a sweet embrace. She grasped the front of his shirt and held on for all she was worth. Nothing could take him away from her in this moment of delight—no duty, no concern, no road.

He showered kisses on her mouth, eyes, and neck, shattering her reserve. Her hands climbed to clasp him behind his head as she returned his kiss.

Shane made a sound in his throat and broke away from her

but remained with his face inches from hers. "You'll be the ruin of me yet, woman."

America curled her fingers into his shirt and whispered, "Stay safe and come back to me."

He caught her hands, turned them, and kissed each palm. "Leaving you in the first place becomes troublesome." His eyes gleamed with humor. He caressed her cheek a final time before slowly turning away.

CHAPTER EIGHTEEN

ADDIE SMILED TO HERSELF AND SWISHED the dishcloth through the soapy wash water. Travis had gone walking with America, allowing her to get ready in secret. She wanted everything to be perfect tonight. Last year for Travis's birthday, his father had taken him hunting as a rite of passage into manhood. She'd restrained the urge to counter her husband's wishes and keep Travis close and had watched with a lump in her throat as father and son tramped into the woods carrying their rifles across their shoulders. Now she was glad she'd let him have that precious time with his father.

Jaundice had almost taken Travis from her a few days after his birth. She'd shielded him from the darkness by shining lantern light above his crib by night and bathed him in sunlight during the day. Oh, how she'd watched over him.

As he grew, she'd taken every one of his scrapes and bruises as a personal affront. She could never stop them all, no matter how hard she tried.

The terror of his first fever had sent Addie into Clyde's arms. He'd comforted her, hiding his own fear, she later discovered. Her son had looked so feeble, lying in his cradle with a pale face, death but a hand's breadth away.

Addie shook her head to dispel her gloomy reflections. Travis had survived his childhood, and so had she. Now her son was growing up too fast, a luxury not afforded to her brother John. She remembered the sound of her father's weeping when he returned from the lake carrying her older brother's limp body. John had fallen through the ice while skating. Her younger brother Arthur had tried to save him and had nearly drowned as well.

She washed out the dust coating her punch bowl, her fingers lingering on its contours. If only she hadn't broken her mother's platter. America had cleaned up the fragments, but Addie hadn't been able to sweep the bitter disappointment away. Tears pressed at the back of her throat. She swallowed hard to avoid giving way to them.

She rinsed the punch bowl and reached for the dishtowel.

"Hopefully I picked enough buffalo berries," Nate said from behind her.

Addie started. The bowl slipped from her grasp. "No!" The cry tore from her throat.

Nate's bucket thudded to the floor. He dove for the punch bowl. Berries scattered at their feet.

She put a hand to her chest. "You saved my punch bowl."

"Thankfully." He placed it on the wooden counter with care. "But there go my berries."

Relief made Addie lightheaded. She grasped his shirt. Giggles bordering on hysteria broke from her. "I'm sorry."

A smile grew on Nate's face. He joined in, clasping her by the arms as they laughed together.

Addie found herself standing too close to Nate. Her laughter faded, and she stepped away.

He tugged her back. "Addie." He dwelled on her name with lingering tenderness.

Gazing into his gentle eyes, Addie lost her inner battle.

Nate lowered his head and feathered his lips over hers in a question of a kiss, then drew back with a smile.

Addie tilted her face, inviting him to return.

He touched her cheek. "You are so beautiful."

She went into his arms, utterly captivated. To be cherished by a man was a treasure she hadn't expected to find again.

"Ma! How could you?" Her son's voice couldn't have sounded more shocked.

Addie broke away from Nate. "Travis. What are you doing

here?"

Tears stood in her son's eyes. "Didn't you even love Pa?"

Addie stared at him, at a loss for words.

Nate imposed himself between them. "Careful what you say to your ma."

"Don't tell me what to do!" Travis bellowed.

"That's no way to speak to Mr. Whalen," Addie chided her son.

"It's all right, Addie." Nate touched her arm. "Travis and I can have a talk once he calms down."

"I have nothing more to say to you." Travis hurtled out of the kitchen. The front door slammed, shaking all the windows.

Addie started after him.

"Let him go." Nate called to her. "He needs time to adjust."

She faced him. "Adjust to what?"

"He'll have to get used to us as a couple."

She shook her head. "I can't ask that from him."

"Your son can't expect you to live the rest of your life without a man. It's time to cut some of those apron strings he's knotted up in."

She rounded on him. "Don't you tell me how to raise my son."

"That's not fair."

"I don't care about what's fair. I care about my son. He's out there, crying on his birthday, because I gave in to a moment of weakness."

He flinched. "Is that all it was to you, Addie?"

"Nate, I—" She broke off, unwilling to lie to him.

"I guess I thought we had something special going on between us."

She squared her shoulders. "I should apologize for my behavior, Mr. Whalen."

"Never mind, Mrs. Martin," Nate replied. "We'll call it my mistake."

She trembled. "I must ask you to leave."

Nate stared at Addie like he'd never seen her before. "If that's the way you feel about it . . ." His boots thumped across the floorboards. The front door opened with a creak and thudded shut.

The silence that followed clanged so loudly Addie could swear it spoke, blaming her for everything—Clyde's death, America's coming to Virginia City, Travis's pain, and now Nate's disappointment.

She had to find Travis.

Cold air hit her face as she stepped outside on the porch. Nate rounded the corner of the house. She'd thought he'd already left. Their eyes met, and she cringed when he firmed his jaw. "If you're looking for Travis, he's not in the wagons. I took a last look around for him before leaving. I don't know where he went, but I reckon in time he'll cool off and come home."

She folded her arms. "Thank you for checking on him."

He tipped his hat in reply, turned his back, and left her standing alone.

Addie watched him move out of sight, staving off the impulse to run after him. That would only confuse matters when she needed to sort them out.

Where could Travis have gone? Possibilities ran through her mind, none of them happy ones. She needed to calm down and stop imagining the worst. Travis would come back, and then they'd settle matters. When he did, she'd have his birthday decorations hung and the food ready and waiting. She nodded, pleased to have settled on something constructive to occupy her hands and help her son feel loved.

She'd just finished frosting the cake when the door opened. She turned toward the sound. "Travis?"

"No, it's me, America." She stood in the kitchen doorway. "He should be here, though. He came back from our walk before I did."

Addie spoke around the lump in her throat. "I'm afraid I

upset him."

"What happened?"

Addie sank into a chair at the table. "He walked in on me kissing Nate."

America's eyes widened, and she sat down across from Addie. "I imagine that didn't go well."

Addie propped her forehead on one hand. "He accused me of not loving his father."

"It must have been hard for him to see you with Nate."

"Don't you think I know that?" Addie snapped, but regretted doing so at once. "Forgive me. I'm worried about my son. It's his birthday, and I don't know where he is."

"I'm sure everything will turn out all right." America stood behind her and massaged her shoulders. "He probably went down to the creek and will come home soon."

Addie held onto that hope until nightfall arrived and dark settled in.

Travis was still gone.

America peered outside through the panes in the kitchen window, watching the lantern brighten and dim in time with Nate's strides. He'd tapped on the door around sunset and asked for Addie. America had hovered in the background while Addie and Nate spoke to one another in stilted voices she'd never heard either of them use before. Nate had searched down at the creek for Travis and come up empty-handed.

Addie was now beyond consoling, and America couldn't help but fret about Travis as well. He normally wouldn't stay out this late, and for good reason. All manner of dangers lurked in the night. America stopped herself from grabbing a lantern and searching for Travis herself. For Liberty's sake, she couldn't risk going out alone at night.

Besides, Addie needed her. America had prevented her from running out into the dark, calling for her son. Addie shouldn't put herself into danger. She needed to be ready and waiting when Travis came home. Because, of course, he would. *He must!*

A knock sounded at the front door, and they exchanged glances. Addie rushed to the door and yanked it open.

Con stood in the doorway with his lantern sending shadows into his face. "Have you found Travis yet? Nate told me he'd gone missing."

America put an arm around Addie's shoulders and spoke on her behalf. "He's not back yet."

"Well then, I've come to join the search."

"Thank you for your trouble," Addie said.

"You're welcome." He gave her a reassuring smile. "Don't worry, Mrs. Martin. We'll find that boy of yours." He thumped down the porch steps.

America shut the door behind him. Addie slumped into a chair at one of the tables. Silent tears ran down her cheeks. America sat beside her, helpless to change the situation. If anything ever happened to Liberty, she would suffer in the same way.

Addie wiped her eyes. "I've always thought of myself as a good mother."

America put an arm around her shoulder. "And you are."

Addie shook her head. "I've been selfish, so caught up with losing Clyde and starting my own restaurant that I didn't give my son the attention he needed. I let Nate turn my head without considering how Travis would feel."

America put a hand over Addie's clasped hands on the table. "You've been going through a hard time."

Addie sighed. "That doesn't matter. I'm a mother."

America's lips curved. She understood what Addie meant. She would do anything to protect Liberty and never count the cost. "You're not perfect. None of us are. We make mistakes.

All you can do is try harder from here on out."

"None of this would have happened if Clyde was still alive." Addie wrapped her arms around herself as if she felt chilled.

America frowned. It wouldn't help for her to become ill. "Maybe you should lie down. I'll stay up and let you know if anything happens."

Addie shook her head. "I couldn't sleep." At some point, her hair had slipped from its pins and now tumbled about her shoulders in a tangled cloud. With her eyes wide, she resembled a child afraid of the dark.

"I meant that you should rest. It might make passing time easier to bear until they find Travis."

"All right." Addie stood up. "But promise you'll tell me if you hear anything at all."

"Of course."

After Addie closed her bedroom door, America checked on Liberty, who was slumbering in the room they shared. Then she went into the kitchen to put on the kettle for a cup of tea. She occupied herself with tidying up from the quick supper she'd made.

America couldn't imagine what could have happened to keep Travis from home. Even when upset with Addie and Nate, Travis didn't have the nature to do something so spiteful as worrying his mother into the night. Trouble must have come his way. He might have fallen prey to a marauding Indian still irate over Chief Snag's death despite Tendoy's attempt to diffuse his people's anger. Other tribes who might travel through these parts weren't as friendly as the Shoshone.

America returned to the main room of the restaurant then slipped into her chair at the table. She sipped her tea and let its warmth uncurl within her stomach. In all honesty, the danger from Indians paled in contrast to the threat of road agents and drunken miners carrying guns. One man in particular had most of them spooked. Jack Slade seemed nice enough when sober, although rumor had it that his wife did not always find him so. When drunk, he was given to riding his horse down Wallace Street while firing his six-shooter in all directions. This could happen at any hour, night or day.

The clock on the hearth ticked away the time while America strained for the sound of returning searchers. She waited up until her head nodded and she jerked upright in her chair.

Liberty cried for her during the dead of night. With no word yet of Travis, America put out the lantern and went to hold her baby close.

Nate lifted his lantern higher, casting eerie shadows as he tramped through the brush near the base of Boot Hill. A night bird whistled from the branches of a cottonwood, making him jump. The dead of night had to be the worst time for combing such a site. He wouldn't have attempted it if finding Travis hadn't called for a thorough search.

His boots crunched along the trail worn by those who had trod there before him. Dillingham lay, dead and buried, at the top of the hill. Did he rest easy in his grave or seek the justice life had denied him? Others had joined him since, their graves marked by wooden crosses, piled stones, or no markings at all. The feet of the faithful coming to honor the memories of those they had loved and lost would need no guide.

Some of those buried here languished in graves that saw no visitors. The loved ones of the dearly departed resided in eastern towns where life in the West took on the form of a dime novel. Few of the bereaved would make the long journey to pay their respects.

Would someone mourn him at his own death? How easily he had turned away from his mother and father, eager to begin the journey west. He'd never suspected that he wouldn't see them again. They'd died, along with his younger brothers and sisters, in the Dakota uprising. His grown brothers had left for California's gold country in forty-nine, and he'd lost touch with them.

Nate shivered as the chill wind fingered his collar, but he huddled into his coat and went on. Finding Travis for Addie's sake—and to spare the boy from suffering a night out of doors in this cold—meant more to him than his own comfort.

The book Ma had bent her dark head over in the lantern light every night contained a passage Nate remembered well. In the mornings when he came down from the loft where he slept with his brothers, he often found her worn Bible lying on the kitchen table and open to the same page. Reading the passage she'd penciled a box around so many times, it had etched into Nate's memory. *"But the fruit of the Spirit is love, joy, peace, longsuffering, gentleness, goodness, faith, meekness, temperance: against such there is no law."*

Addie had rejected his advances. Nate would respect that, but he'd do whatever lay within his power to ease her burdens. As his ma had taught him by her example, loving someone had more to do with giving than expecting anything in return. If Addie allowed Nate to court her, he would rejoice, but if not, he could show her love in the ways open to him.

A mockingbird perched in the cottonwood, singing its heart out at the moon. The fullness of that heavenly light guided Nate's feet up the hill. At the top, the wind buffeted his face and tore at his hair. Below him, Virginia City's streets lined up in neat squares. Moonlight gleamed along the rooftops. Light reached out from the saloons and dancehalls, but most of the town reposed in darkness.

Nate turned his back to the wind and let it carry his voice. "Travis!"

Only the mockingbird answered. Light from his lantern raised shadows among the graves and made the trees jump. The hair on the back of his neck bristled, although he didn't fear the dead but the living. Shouting into the darkness with a lantern in his hand could make him an easy target for road agents or renegade Indians.

Nate yearned to leave this place, but first he would walk along the edge of the hilltop and call out in all directions. In the middle of the night in this place of death, the idea that Travis had come this way struck him as unlikely, but he couldn't shake the idea.

On the far side of the hill, away from town, the moonlight picked out a lighter patch among the rocks that reflected the moon's blue light. Nate peered downward, sucked in his breath, and started downhill.

Waking out of a fitful dream, Addie bolted upright. How could she have fallen asleep when Travis might be lying injured and alone in the dark? She refused to consider what else might have happened, but the fear of it haunted her. Had her son's anger cooled? He'd always looked to her more than his pa. That came naturally, she told herself, since he spent more time with her.

Still, Addie couldn't help but wonder if she'd stolen her son's affections from his father. In some ways, Clyde had given up on Travis, leaving to her certain decisions they might have otherwise made together. Now, with the distance of time, she could admit the truth and try to forgive herself.

Someone knocked at the front door, the sound carrying through the restaurant. Heart pounding, she threw back her covers and hurried to the door. America reached it first and flung it open. The light from America's candle revealed Nate standing in the doorway with Addie's son in his arms. Travis's eyelashes lay on his cheeks, and his arms hung limp.

"What happened?" The words seemed wrenched from Addie's soul.

"Looks like the ground gave way under his feet, and he went sliding down the far side of Boot Hill. I think he hit his head, and it knocked him out cold. He's cut up some but still breathing." He carried Travis inside.

"Put him in my bed." Addie led the way to her room. Travis wouldn't make the trip up the ladder to his bed in the loft tonight.

Nate lowered him to the bed. "I'll fetch Doc Steele and let Mr. Walsh know we found Travis."

Addie touched her son's bruised face. "What was he doing on Boot Hill of all places?"

"I saw him coming down from there once and asked him the same thing." America spoke from behind her. "He said he liked the spot because it's quiet but close to town."

Addie gazed down at her son. "He looks so pale."

"I'm sorry, Addie." Nate touched her shoulder.

She rested her hand over his. "Just fetch the doctor."

America went into the kitchen to boil water for the doctor while Addie took off Travis's boots and pulled the covers over him. She stood looking down at him in the same way she had in his childhood after he'd fallen and hurt himself. She brushed the hair back from his forehead in a gesture she had repeated many times in his life. Closing her eyes, she uttered a prayer for her own son to God's Son, who cared about him.

When Doc Steele arrived, Addie greeted the doctor and led him to Travis. She held her breath while the doctor bent over her son. America came into the room and stood beside her.

The Doc straightened and turned to Addie. "When he wakes, he'll probably have a whale of a headache. Don't let him sleep too much, though. Time will tell us for sure, but I think he's going to be all right."

Addie exhaled a deep breath. "That's good news."

Doc Steele offered her a weary smile. "It's the kind I prefer to give. Now if you'll excuse me, I'll return home for whatever sleep remains to me."

Addie nodded. "Thank you, Doc."

America saw the doctor out. After a while, Addie recognized Nate's voice in the other room. Nate came in and stood behind her, his hat in his hand. "I should be going too, unless you want me to take a shift watching Travis."

Addie shook her head. If Travis woke, he might not welcome the sight of Nate. "I can't thank you enough for finding my son."

"Whatever I can do to help. That's all I want."

"Nate . . ." She drew a painful breath. "I have to ask you not to come around anymore."

He sent her a wounded look. "You don't mean that."

"I do. I've been thinking, and I need to provide a stable life for my son. I'm all he has."

"I don't understand," Nate said. "How is denying yourself and your son a man in your life *stable*?"

Addie sought for words but couldn't find an answer.

His jaw firmed. "You're going to let your son decide your romantic life for you?"

"I don't mean to do that." She hauled in a shaky breath. "It's just that I almost lost Travis today, and it would have been my fault. I need to do better by him."

"I won't say I believe that completely, but you seem to. I told you this once before, and I'll tell you again, Addie Martin. I love you, and I'll wait for you."

It would be selfish of her to let him make that promise. "No!" The word came out more sharply than she'd intended. "I can't let you do that."

"I'm not certain I have a choice in the matter." He spoke with wry humor. "What I do with my heart is my own business, but I guess that *no* was loud enough even for a hard-headed fellow like me to hear." He kissed her forehead. "If you ever need me, you can call on me."

Addie stood in the doorway, watching Nate walk away from her until the light from his lantern faded into the night.

CHAPTER NINETEEN

ADDIE GAZED DOWN AT HER SON'S face, pale and still in the candlelight. She couldn't sleep, not while she needed to watch over Travis.

Believing she could enjoy a friendship with Nate while keeping him at arm's length romantically hadn't been wise. Even if he'd managed to be a friend without making advances, her own response to him refused to allow such a thing. Her mother wouldn't have approved of their association, having brought her up to observe proper social customs. A widow grieved for her husband for a year of deep mourning, wearing dull black and veiling her face on those rare occasions when she went out in public. A widow turned down social invitations except those from relatives.

After a year and a day, a second mourning period began. During this time, she could relieve the plainness of her dresses with lighter cuffs and lace. She could wear the veil back on her head rather than in front of her face.

Nine months later, a third mourning completed the year of full mourning. Half-mourning would then commence, allowing a widow the freedom to wear soft purples instead of black. The total time required to mourn the death of a spouse had once lasted two and a half years or more, but that had begun to change.

Mourning garments had gone up in price due to the demand caused by the War Between the States. This demand forced women to dye their existing clothing black or give up traditional customs. In the West, women had even less of a desire—or the means—to keep up appearances. The rapid pace of life meant that a young widow usually didn't remain unmarried for very long.

Circumstances hadn't allowed Addie the luxury of mourning her husband in the conventional way, but after Travis's reaction to discovering her in Nate's arms, she couldn't help but wonder if the old ways might be best.

The linen curtains in Addie's bedroom glowed with dawn light. Birdsong greeted the sun outside the window. Travis's color looked better this morning. Addie closed the bedroom door and went to the kitchen to make coffee, slice a rasher of bacon, and stir up a batch of biscuits. While breakfast cooked, she chopped vegetables and prepared an elk roast for supper. She worked feverishly to keep from dwelling on her son's condition and on what had happened with Nate.

"Why are you up so early?" America stood in the doorway, looking remarkably rested for having missed so much sleep. But caring for a baby taught a woman to manage without as much rest as she needed.

"I need to get this roast in the oven." Addie's voice wobbled.

"You're not opening the restaurant today!" America started toward her.

Addie set her jaw and sliced potatoes with quick strokes. "The regulars will want their supper."

"No one will fault you for staying closed today."

Addie let out her breath, and her shoulders relaxed. "You're right, of course. I don't know what I was thinking. My son needs me, and he matters a whole lot more than this restaurant."

"You've had a rough night. Why don't you let me do this?"

Addie batted away tears. "Thank you. I'll go and sit with Travis. I don't like leaving him alone. He might wake up confused."

America picked up the knife. "I'll watch over him a little later so you can sleep."

Addie hastened back to her bedroom and sank into the ladder-backed chair beside the bed. Travis frowned in his sleep, and she leaned forward to watch him. He didn't move again, so she sank back and closed her eyes to rest them for a moment.

"Ma?" Travis called out.

She jerked awake. Her son's eyes were open. "You're awake. How do you feel?"

Travis grimaced. "My head hurts."

She took his hand. "Do you remember what happened?"

"I fell." His forehead creased. "Sorry for yelling at you."

"Oh, Travis, it doesn't matter now."

He frowned. "How did I wind up back here?"

"One of the"-- she hesitated --"searchers found you and carried you home."

He swallowed. "I'm thirsty."

She picked up the glass of water on the bedside table. "Can you sit up a little?"

"I think so." He levered himself into a sitting position and gulped from the glass.

"Are you hungry?" She tried not to hover over him but couldn't resist asking the question.

He shook his head and winced. "Ouch. That hurt."

"Na—Doc Steele thinks you hit your head when you fell."

"I don't remember." His voice faded, and the lids swept down over his eyes.

"I love you, Travis." She pulled in a sharp breath. She hadn't known if she would ever be able to say that to him again in this life.

"I love you too, Ma." A faint smile lit his face before his mouth slackened in sleep.

Addie leaned her head against the back of the chair and breathed a prayer of thanksgiving. She'd been given a second chance to make things right.

Shane's boots crunched the newly fallen snow as he started down the boardwalk toward Chrisman's store. He hadn't meant to spend Christmas in Bannack, but the snow had blown in early this season, making him reluctant to leave the warmth of Con's cabin.

That wasn't his only reason for staying, however. Traveling the open road brought many adventures and rich experiences, but since meeting America, a part of him yearned for a more settled existence. The only taste of a decent home life he'd ever known had been as a young child in Ireland when his parents were alive. He could still feel the brush of his mother's hand against his brow and hear the sound of his father's deep voice beckoning him home from playing with his friends.

His baby sister had followed him everywhere then, keeping up on her stumpy legs with strong-willed devotion. He'd found it necessary to avoid her at times. Another sister had not survived her birth, and he could remember his mother weeping endlessly in her bedroom.

With food hard to come by, they hadn't always eaten well, which made the times they could feast all the more special. Shane smiled to himself, remembering Mam serving Christmas pudding she had made with pride from a recipe handed down through generations of their family. He'd helped her prepare it and could still recall how to make it even now.

He would never have his family around him again, but baking plum pudding on Christmas Eve might bring them back to him.

Con had left a few provisions—dried fruits, nuts, and a sack of flour—but Shane lacked some of the items he would need for plum pudding. The general store might be in short supply the day before Christmas, but Shane would do his best with what he could find.

Warmth greeted him in Chrisman's store. After the brightness of the snow, it seemed dim inside the mercantile. Miners gathered around the potbellied stove as usual. He picked up baking soda, dried lemon peel, and a few other items for his plum cake while listening to their discussion on the conviction of George Ives for the murder of a young man named Nicholas Tbalt over the gold he carried.

"I guess Nevada City got a hanging for Christmas," one of the miners crowed.

Shane cringed at the glee in his voice. Whatever his sins, a man had lost his life.

Others chimed in.

"Must have surprised George when he couldn't cheat the rope again."

"He got his fixings if you ask me."

"I guess they taught them road agents what's what."

The meager scraps of Christmas spirit Shane had managed to scrape together shredded away. He collected what he needed and went to the counter, eager to leave the unsettling conversation behind.

"Merry Christmas to you, preacher." Chrisman greeted him with a smile.

"And the same to you. I hope you will have a wonderful celebration of our Lord's birth."

Chrisman's face wreathed in smiles. "It's in the making. Get all you need today. The store will be closed tomorrow."

"As is only right on such a glorious day." He gathered his purchases and made for the door.

"Road agents better tremble in their boots," one of the miners growled. "Good men don't aim to stand by and let them murder people."

Shane went out the door, pondering that remark. George Ives had been brought to account by a group organized to ride out after him. He'd heard that Virginia City had formed a vigilance committee, and that Bannack would soon dispense mountain justice as well. Lust for gold had fueled most of the stagecoach robberies and cold-blooded murders. A long list of atrocities that went back much further than the murder of Tbalt had sparked the outcry leading to George Ives's hanging

The winter sun sparkling in the snow made such dark ruminations appear outlandish, and death seemed a strange prospect on the cusp of the Christ-child's birth. The Bible called it an enemy, and Shane had met no one yet who could take it in stride. For immortal souls inhabiting mortal bodies, that made sense. The body would fail while the spirit continued. Each person's instinctive knowledge of this gave death its rudeness. If only he could make them understand that Jesus had taken away its sting.

Shane tamped the snow from his boots on the cabin's tiny porch, flung the door open with his free hand, and carried his purchases inside. The conversation he'd overheard had robbed his desire to make his mother's Christmas pudding, but he put himself to the task anyway. He'd survived much worse in his lifetime than a holiday spent alone.

His thoughts turned, as they usually did in idle moments, to America. The memory of their last kiss wouldn't leave him, and an ache to gaze on her again seized him. Would she think of him this Christmas, as he thought of her?

"I'll take that." America snatched the tray of shortbread cookies from Addie's hands. "Let me help you more, or you'll wear yourself thin."

"Thank you." Addie gave her the frenzied look so often on her face these days before rushing back into the kitchen.

America set the platter down on the lace tablecloth Addie had neatly ironed. Whatever was wrong with her friend must have to do with the reason Nate wasn't coming around anymore. Addie seemed determined to work herself to death. She stayed up late and rose before the sun to prepare elaborate menus consumed by her customers in a matter of minutes. Her restaurant clientele grew as a result, but she seemed oddly dispassionate about the realization of her dream. Instead, she focused on mothering Travis to the point that he'd begun acting hunted.

Christmas served as a showcase for Addie's talents. Evergreen wreaths with candle lanterns at their centers hung from velvet ribbons in every window of the restaurant. She had shifted the tables to accommodate a festive tree, cut down by Travis in the forest and decorated painstakingly by his mother. America had tried to help, but she gave up after realizing Addie needed the tree to be a masterpiece of her envisioning.

Addie had planned Christmas dinner as an elaborate affair, complete with a turkey she'd had freighted in, oyster stuffing, and cranberry sauce. America helped with the food preparations, but the bulk of the cooking required the special skills only Addie possessed. They only had to cook for themselves today, but Addie's menu called for a major effort.

America followed her into the kitchen. "What else can I do?"

Addie gave her an assessing look. "Can you stuff the turkey?"

Her attempt to repress a smile failed. "Of course I can. Any child could do that."

Addie retained her serious expression. "All right then. I have the dressing already prepared."

America completed the task and sewed up the bird while Addie fussed over the elaborate yule log centerpiece she'd made for the table.

Travis came in carrying Liberty. "I think she wants you." With her daughter leaning over and extending her hands, that seemed an obvious conclusion.

"Let me wash my hands before I take her."

Travis sampled a handful of chopped walnuts sitting on the cutting board.

"Hands off!" Addie scolded him with a smile.

"But Ma, I'm starving."

Addie sighed. "Sit down and I'll make you a sandwich." She pulled a loaf from the breadbox and reached for a block of cheese. "Do you want one too?" she asked America.

"Thank you, but I'll wait. I'd hate to ruin such a delicious meal." She dried her hands and retrieved her daughter from Travis. Liberty set herself to charm her with smiles and captivating stares. America caught her breath. Smiling like that, Liberty looked a lot like Gramma.

At Christmas, America still hung the stocking Gramma had knitted for her, one of the few things she'd taken away when she had left home. It reminded her of Gramma's Christmas cookies, the eggnog she'd always made to go with them, and her joy while singing Christmas carols.

Travis finished his lunch, and America returned Liberty to his arms. By the time they had finished preparing the intricate menu, America felt dead on her feet. Addie had started much earlier in the day and could only be in worse shape.

America sat down with Addie and Travis to the sumptuous meal with little appetite due to her exhaustion. Liberty, however, overflowed with energy. Having picked up on the heightened emotions of the day, she giggled and chattered. America plowed her way through the meal and did her best to make conversation, but weariness dragged at her.

Addie brought out a Christmas cake with silky white frosting and presented it with a flourish. America groaned and laid a hand over her full stomach. "I can't."

Addie smiled. "Maybe in a little while?"

Travis proved his mother's claims that he had a bottomless stomach by eating two slices.

America stirred from her listlessness to help Addie clear the food away while Travis started the dishes. Liberty finally fell asleep. After laying her down, America returned to the kitchen.

Addie sat at the table, leaning her head on one arm. "Travis has gone to bed, but I'm not ready to sleep yet."

"I'm glad to have your company. Do you want a slice of Christmas cake?"

"I was about to cut one for myself." She sighed. "Only, I couldn't seem to move."

"You don't have to." America took two plates down from one of the shelves and cut slices from the cake. She retrieved forks from the drawer where they stored silverware.

"Thanks." Addie accepted one of the plates. "My feet really ache."

"I can imagine. You worked yourself too hard today." America bit into the dark fruit cake and closed her eyes in delight. "My, but this is good."

"I'm glad you like it. The recipe came down through my family. My mother made it for us every Christmas." Addie's forehead puckered. "I sure miss her."

America put her hand over Addie's. "She gave you a lot to remember her by. That should comfort you."

"It does." Addie laid aside her fork and dabbed the corners of her eyes with a red-checked napkin. "You never talk about your own family. Do you ever wish you could go home?"

"My parents divorced before I left home." America brought out the shameful truth. "Even before that, we never acted like a family. I don't think my parents knew how."

"I'm sorry to hear that. It must have been hard growing up in such a household."

"Gramma made it easier at first, before she died. After that, I didn't know how to go on without her." Her mother had seemed even more lost without Gramma. Looking back, America could see how her parents had slid toward divorce from that point onward, with her father withdrawing from Mother's histrionics.

"I'm glad your gramma gave you something worthwhile."

Addie picked up her fork.

"She did." America smiled at the memory of Gramma holding her up to blow out the candles on the tree. She could still feel Gramma's strong hands clasping the waist of the child of seven she had been. Afterwards, Gramma had tucked her in with a song and a prayer. Now, whenever she heard "O, Come All Ye Faithful," she thought of Gramma.

"My ma made cookies on Christmas Eve morning." Addie licked frosting from her fork, looking little older than a child in that moment. "We all pitched in, but I'm not sure how she managed it with us to pack off to church and supper to get ready as well."

"It must have been wonderful having a mother so dedicated to her children." Her own mother had always seemed faintly surprised that America existed.

"She did well by us." Addie studied her. "You devote yourself to Liberty in the same way. That little girl of yours had an enjoyable Christmas."

"She fell asleep clutching one of her wooden blocks in each hand."

Addie laughed. "They sure kept her busy today." She stopped laughing and touched her temple. "I'm not feeling well all of a sudden." Two spots of color invaded her cheeks, but the rest of her face gleamed pale in the lamp light. Her eyes seemed glazed too.

America pressed the back of her hand to Addie's forehead. "You're burning up."

"Oh, no," Addie wailed. "I don't have time to be sick. I have a restaurant to run."

"Travis and I can take care of things while you rest." She hoped that was true.

"I can't expect you to do that."

"Don't be silly."

Addie burst into tears. "I've tried and tried, but I just can't do it."

America put an arm around her shoulders. "What can't you do?"

"I can't make up for what I should have done." Tears slid down Addie's cheeks.

America sat down in the chair beside hers. "I'm sorry, but I don't understand what you mean."

Addie wiped the tears from her cheeks. "I'm not making sense, am I?"

"You do have a fever."

"I should have done so much more for Travis, and I've been trying to atone for that. I wanted to create a perfect Christmas for him to make up for—" She broke off, pressed her lips together, and averted her eyes.

"For his father not being there?" America prompted.

Addie shook her head. "It's all my fault."

"I don't see how."

Addie stared at America with glazed eyes. "I wanted my stove and dishes, so I made Clyde bring them even though he told me they were too heavy. They overloaded our wagon, which is why it tipped him out." Her shoulders shook. "He drowned because he married a selfish woman."

"Oh, Addie." America held her until her weeping eased. She passed her a linen napkin. "You can't blame yourself for that. Whether you should have insisted on bringing your stove or not doesn't have any bearing on an accident." She rubbed Addie's back. "May I make a suggestion?"

Addie nodded. "Go ahead."

"Stop trying so hard. You can't make up for past failures. It's not possible. It's better to forgive yourself for them, apologize where it's needed, and go on in a better way."

"Thank you." Addie took her hand in a gesture of gratitude. "I'll do my best to follow that advice."

Addie went to bed, but America took a few moments to sit in the light of the candle-lit wreaths before taking her leave of Christmas for another year. Her reflections turned to Shane.

Had he spared a thought for her today? She hoped he had found a family to take him in for Christmas. If not, she hated to wonder how he had spent the day.

Other Christmases came to mind. Those with memories of Gramma sent smiles flitting across her lips, but the last one, alone on her homestead, brought her pain. How could she fully celebrate when Richard was dead because of her? If she had told him the truth about her pregnancy, he never would have married her. Without a wife, he might not have filed for a homestead, and he wouldn't have been out in the blizzard that took his life.

She'd encouraged Addie to start anew, but the words rang hollowly in her own ears. The irony of giving advice she herself needed to take pressed on her. But here in the dim restaurant, with the clock on the fireplace mantle ticking away the time, she admitted that she didn't have the faintest idea how to let go of the past.

CHAPTER TWENTY

SHIFTING LIGHT AND RAISED VOICES DREW Shane to the window. Lanterns glowed in the gathering dusk and cast long shadows down the hill behind the cabin. The veil separating the spiritual and physical worlds all at once thinned. He could give no other explanation for the uncanny energy sizzling in the air.

"Company! Forward, march!" the call went out.

Nine men walking three abreast trudged along the road toward him. Others stood watching at a short distance, holding lanterns.

Shane pulled on his jacket, seized his hat, and threw open the door. The wind chilled his face with the kind of cold that made a man grateful for the warmth of hearth and home.

High on the hillside above him, three men waited on the platform beneath the gallows. Their presence explained the grim fate of the men in the middle of the procession and the mission of those delivering them to it.

"Not *you*!" One of the men in the middle of the procession cried out in a passionate voice to a dark figure watching from beside the road, one of the vigilantes he obviously knew. Shane started, recognizing Sheriff Plummer's voice. "I never thought you would betray me. Would you hang an innocent man without a chance to clear his name before a jury? I beg of you, don't do this!"

"It is useless for you to beg for your life," the answer came. "That affair is settled and cannot be altered. You are to be hanged. You can't feel harder about it than I do. But I cannot help it if I could."

Henry Plummer's shoulders slumped.

The prisoner behind Henry threw a punch at one of the guards. Before anyone could react, he spun and kicked the other.

The guard he'd sent sprawling scrambled to his feet. Lantern light gleamed on the barrel of his pistol, leveled at the combative prisoner's chest. "Settle down or I'll shoot you before you can hang."

The prisoner's curses blistered the air as the procession continued to the foot of the hill.

Men brandishing pistols rode on horseback in front of the crowd. "Anyone with a mind to venture farther will be shot," one of them shouted.

Breaking free of the inertia gripping him, Shane hurtled himself down the porch steps and toward the crowd. He had to prevent three souls from going to perdition without a chance to repent for their sins.

"Bring up Ned Ray," a voice rolled down the hill from the gallows.

"What are you doing?" Shane shouted into the dull air. "For the love of God, stop this!"

Several heads turned his direction then away.

A man wearing a bowler hat stepped in front of Shane before he reached the crowd. "Leave them alone. These men are simply doing their duty in the interest of law and order."

Shane made out Atticus's face in the dimness. "If they want law and order, they should give these men a fair trial."

Atticus laughed. "You know as well as I do that a miners' court would be a sham. A trial by their peers would release these road agents to murder again."

Ned Ray struggled against his guards, still raining curses on them.

Atticus turned his head. Torchlight etched his features. His mouth twisted in the semblance of a smile. "That is one of the charming citizens you wish to save."

"It is God Who wants to save him," Shane explained. "He yearns to redeem every soul, to bring freedom and new life."

Atticus pivoted and grabbed Shane by the shirt. "I've had

about enough of you, preacher." He hauled his fist back and smashed it into Shane's jaw.

Shane's head snapped sideways as pain slammed through his face. He tumbled backward into the snow. This couldn't happen right now. He needed to tell the condemned prisoners about God's mercy for those with a contrite heart. He rolled to his hands and knees and tried to stand.

The toe of Atticus's boot hooked into his stomach.

Shane clutched his middle, fighting to draw breath.

"If I were you, *Saint Preacher*, I'd think about leaving town." Atticus crunched the snow as he left him behind.

When Shane could breathe again, he lifted his head to stare up the hill. Lantern light flickered over the gallows, where a lifeless body hung. He heaved the contents of his stomach.

"Bring up Buck Stinson."

Shane shoved away from his vomit, gasping. Agony clawed at him. His head swam, but he staggered to his feet through a mist of pain. The awful sound of a rope rubbing against a body alerted Shane to what had happened. He gazed on the second man swinging at the end of a rope.

"Bring up Plummer."

No one moved.

"Let me pray with him!" Shane summoned the energy to shout.

The voice repeated the summons. "Bring up Henry Plummer."

"Give a man time to pray," one of the guards called out. Beside him, the sheriff knelt with his head bowed.

"Certainly," the answer came back. "But let him say his prayers up here."

Shane drew breath to bring the voice of sanity to those who seemed to have lost all reason. Something slammed his skull. Darkness swarmed over him.

His shivering body jerked him awake. He moaned and touched a lump where his head throbbed. Gritting his teeth,

Shane dragged himself from the snowdrift where he'd fallen. The crowd had dwindled, but guards stood sentinel on the platform, watching over the three stiff bodies dangling from the gallows.

Shane lurched to his feet, sucking in air. Pain knifed his stomach. His body's discomfort paled in comparison to the agony in his heart. With the ashes of defeat bitter in his mouth, he stumbled to the cabin and locked himself inside. At the basin, he washed blood from his face, but long-ago images plagued him, and he couldn't cleanse them from his mind . . .

"I don't want to fight you, Sean." Rory met his challenge even as he shifted into a fighting stance. "Is there something wrong with your sister?"

"Don't pretend you don't know!" He rushed in to take the first shot.

Rory blocked Shane's punch and came around with a left hook that knocked him back.

He shook his head to clear it and rushed in again, but Rory was ready for him.

This time he didn't return so quickly but cupped a hand around the eye Rory had bruised. Shane attacked with a plan this time, feinting with one fist while striking with the other.

Rory faced him again, fingering blood from his lip. He smirked. "Your sister wasn't worth this trouble."

Shane barreled into him, bludgeoning with both fists until he drove Rory to the ground.

The click warned him. He jumped back in time to avoid Rory's switchblade.

Rory sprang to his feet. He crouched with his back to the moon, which shadowed his features while revealing Shane's.

Metal clattered in the alley where Con hid. Rory swung toward the sound.

Shane saw his chance and tackled him.

Rory screamed and went silent.

Shane turned Rory over. He wanted to weep at what he'd

done. He felt frantically for a pulse, while Rory stared sightlessly at the sky.

Con bent down. "He fell on his knife. It must have gone through the heart. Come on, let's get out of here." Con dragged Shane off of Rory. "He's dead, Sean. Come on."

Shane shook himself free of the memory and lowered himself gingerly into the rope bed in Con's cabin. He groaned at the agony in his stomach. He knew—more than anyone—how blood on your hands could steal your soul. He'd wanted to spare others the torment, but they didn't care and wouldn't listen.

He couldn't keep trying and failing.

Shane fell off his horse and sprawled spread-eagled into a snowdrift. He shook his head, trying to clear the mists surrounding him.

Footsteps crunched the snow. Arms lifted him from behind. He struggled against them, uncertain whether they belonged to friend or foe.

"Easy there, Cousin."

Shane sank into darkness.

"Will you sleep forever?" Con's inquiry wrested Shane into wakefulness. He groaned, all at once reacquainted with the aches and pains that had worsened during his ride from Bannack.

Con propped him with an arm at his back and touched his lips with the edge of a ladle. "Drink."

Shane's throat worked with the effort to swallow, but water flowed into his throat too quickly. He jerked back his head, choking.

"Sorry." The ladle tilted at a better angle, and he drained it. "That's better."

Shane didn't need his sight to know he lay in Con's wickiup

with his cousin bending over him. He opened his eyes anyway. Casting back in memory, he tried to piece together a series of disjointed images, thoughts, and words, finally giving up. "What am I doing here?"

"If you don't know, I doubt I will. You rode in from somewhere. Do you recall?"

Shane passed his tongue over his cracked lips. "I came from Bannack, where I watched three men die." He struggled to sit up.

"No, lie back." Con pushed him down. "You're weaker than a newborn calf."

"I'm fine," Shane blustered, but he didn't try to rise again.

"I can tell. Just so you know, there are better ways to get off a horse." Con's brow puckered. "Were the men anyone I would know?"

"Haven't you heard? Vigilantes hung Sheriff Plummer and two of his deputies."

"I'm not so surprised, I guess. The news will probably hit town today. I'm not sure I should hang around and wait for it. Being a deputy from Bannack doesn't seem terribly popular these days." He touched the tender place on Shane's jaw. "Who did this to you?"

He winced. "Atticus Merrick."

"I suppose you were preaching uninvited." Con's tone perfectly expressed his opinion of that idea.

"No, but I did try to save a few souls."

"God is more capable of such a thing, I would think," Con snapped.

"Yes, but under the circumstances He seemed in need of a little assistance."

"What am I going to do with you? This attitude always lands you in trouble." Con gusted a sigh. "Never mind. I'll stay and take care of you."

"You don't need to do that."

"No, but I will."

"Maybe you shouldn't." Shane tried to lever himself into a sitting position, the better to argue with his cousin.

"Quiet now." Con lowered him again. "Don't deprive me of the chance to feel needed."

America pushed a lock of hair out of her eyes and dropped dumplings by the spoonful into the bubbling mixture of rehydrated apples, brown sugar, and spices. Making a nice dessert like apple and dumpling soup was a task Addie normally reserved for herself, but she still needed rest. Observing Addie had taught America how to improvise most of the recipes, and taking over the cooking gave Addie the break she needed to recover her health.

America was thankful she'd found a way to repay her friend for the care she'd given her on the wagon train. She enjoyed the change of pace that relieved the tedium of her own duties. Travis, now restored from his fall, pitched in by doing the dishes and other chores that normally belonged to America.

The miners didn't seem to notice the change in cooks, although a few commented on the delay in service. America could hold her own in the kitchen, but she didn't match Addie's skill in greeting the miners and keeping their food coming.

Addie appeared in the doorway with Liberty in her arms. "What can I do?"

"You can play with the baby," America answered, holding onto her patience. She'd shooed Addie out of the kitchen several times already. It wasn't difficult to understand her friend's frustration. America had suffered similar feelings during the journey from Fort Bridger. Being on the receiving end of someone else's ministrations didn't always come easily. It required a person to surrender pride and self-sufficiency. That had been good for her, as it turned out, and it would be good for Addie as well.

A furrow appeared between Addie's dark brows. "I hate to see you slaving away."

This struck America as ironic, coming from a woman who had worked herself into her present weakened condition. She had the subtlety not to mention it, however. "I'm only too glad to spare you."

She applied herself to preparing the food in time, and Travis helped carry out plates and beverages to wave upon wave of hungry miners. She slipped between them, delivering food and catching bits of conversation.

"Did you hear about Sheriff Plummer?"

"All three danced at the end of a rope."

"They'll be after the other road agents now."

America pieced together that Sheriff Plummer had been lynched in Bannack, along with two of his deputies. Buck Stinson, one of the deputies who had met his end alongside the sheriff at the hands of the vigilantes, had cheated the grave dug for him after being convicted of Dillingham's murder. Had Shane witnessed the hanging? She couldn't imagine it sitting well with him.

By the time the last miner left, America's feet ached. She sank onto one of the chairs at the kitchen table.

Travis finished washing out a cup and glanced at her. "Tired?"

"It's been a long day."

"Thank you for all you've done for me," Addie said from the doorway. "I know it wasn't easy. Why don't I help Travis clean up while you spend time with your baby?"

America stood and stretched. "I guess there's no holding you down."

Addie smiled. "She needs you, and I've had all the rest I can stand." She transferred the baby to America's arms. "I can't tell for certain, but she seems a mite poorly tonight. I hope she hasn't come down with my sickness."

Liberty, fussing in her arms, appeared pale. America carried her into the room they shared and sat down in the ring-backed side chair Addie had given her for Christmas. She ran a hand over her baby's limbs, enjoying the softness of her skin but also noting its warmth. Liberty took a long time to fall asleep but didn't wake all night.

Morning sunlight filtered into the small room, highlighting dust moats in the air. America touched Liberty's tiny form then drew back with a start. Her baby burned with fever!

America bathed Liberty's face with a cloth wrung from cool water, and she woke screaming. Her skin looked waxen, and her breathing came fast and shallow.

Addie knocked and opened the door. "Is she all right?"

"I can't get her to eat, she has diarrhea, and she's burning up." Hearing the note of terror in her voice, America took a deep breath and willed herself not to panic.

Addie touched Liberty's forehead. "Mercy! I'll send Travis for Doc Steele."

When she returned, they took turns holding the crying baby and waited for Doc Steele to arrive.

Boots stomped on the porch, and Addie hurried out to open the door, calling, "That'll be the doctor."

She caught a glimpse of Travis stomping snow from his boots on the porch.

Addie pulled him inside and shut the door. "Where's Doc Steele?"

"He's attending a birth at a ranch near Laurin." Travis glanced at Liberty, wrapped in her baby quilt in America's arms.

America had kept her baby back from the cold drafts but now came forward. "What about Doc Bissell? Did you look for him?"

"He's gone to a wedding in Ennis." Travis gave her an apologetic look.

"There's no doctor?" America asked in a bewildered voice.

Coming to Virginia City had put her into contact with more people than she would have known by remaining at her homestead. With doctors living in town, she had never considered being without one during a crisis.

Travis stood a little taller. "I'll ride after a doctor."

"Both of them are too far away for you to reach alone," Addie protested.

Travis scowled. "I can do it."

"No." America shook her head. "Your ma's right. I couldn't live with myself if anything happened to you. We'll think of another way."

Addie drummed her fingernails on the table. "I know. We could ask Mr. Walsh to fetch Doc Steele. If he can't, Reverend Hayes may be willing."

America hid her surprise. "Shane—Reverend Hayes is in Virginia City?"

"Yes." Addie hesitated. "I thought it might upset you, so I didn't mention it. He took a beating in Bannack, but his condition may have improved by now. Travis, go and tell them what's wrong."

Travis's face brightened. "Sure enough."

Addie took a turn walking Liberty while America went into the kitchen to stir a little sugar and salt into some water. Hopefully, the sweet taste would stimulate Liberty's appetite, and the salt would keep her from dehydrating. Working together, they managed to get the baby to suckle a little of the fluid from a nursing bottle America kept on hand for just such an emergency. Liberty soon broke off, crying.

"It must hurt to swallow." Addie gave Liberty back to America.

"That must be why she's not nursing either." America held the wailing baby against her. "I don't know what else to do."

"I'll make some onion syrup. That's what my ma always did for me." Addie went into the kitchen.

America stood in the doorway, swaying and patting

Liberty's back.

Addie cut an onion into slices and layered them with sugar in a jar. "It needs to steep a while, but maybe it will ease the poor lamb's throat so she can drink."

Travis returned, a crestfallen look on his face. "Neither of them was at the cabin. Mr. Walsh's neighbor didn't know where Con went, and he said Reverend Hayes left for Idaho City two days ago."

"This is a nightmare!" America wailed.

"Just a moment." Addie went to her room and came out bundled in a coat, ear muffs, and gloves.

"Where are you going?" America asked in alarm. Surely Addie hadn't taken it into her head to go after the doctor.

"Mr. Whalen invited me to call upon him should I ever need help." Addie sounded confident, but her face told another story. Casting herself on Nate's kindness after she had rejected him must hurt, and she might have to ward off his advances afterwards.

Gratitude at her selflessness rushed through America. "Thank you."

One glance at Travis's face explained why Addie preferred to go for Nate herself. Emotions warred across his face, but he made no protest.

"Travis, see if you can track down Mr. Walsh," Addie instructed her son. "If you find him, ask him to ride out after Doc Steele. I'll ask Nate to bring back Doc Bissell."

While they were gone, America managed to coax her baby into nursing. Liberty fell asleep, and she laid her in the new crib Addie had hired one of the miners to build in exchange for free suppers.

A knock came at the door. America hurried to answer it.

"Good afternoon, Widow Reed." Virgil Henry tipped his hat. With his other hand, he aimed a gun at her head.

Her throat tightened. She'd thought he would never come around again. "What are you doing here?"

"I've been watching this place, waiting for a chance to finish what I started." He lowered his hat. "Reckon this is it."

America stared at him. "I don't understand."

"It's simple, darlin'." He smiled in a way that made America's skin crawl. "I've come for you."

She heaved air into her lungs, ready to scream.

"Uh-uh! Don't do that." He waggled a finger at her. "I'd hate to shoot such a pretty lady. Now come along. I have a horse saddled for you."

"But my baby—" America struggled to take in what was happening. A sense of unreality threatened to suffocate her.

"Sorry, but you'll have to give her up. He's not going to pay many horses for a bride with a baby, if he'll take you at all."

"*What?* Who wants a bride?"

"Never mind that for now. I don't aim to wait around all day long. We don't have much time to head out of sight down the road. Are you coming, or do I have to knock the daylights out of you and sling you across the saddle?"

Who knew what this crazy man would do if Travis or Addie came home and challenged him? What would he do if Liberty woke up? She ventured onto the porch and closed the door after her, leaving her baby sick and alone. Tears bathed her cheeks as she stumbled down the front steps with Virgil's gun at her back.

A sorrel horse and a spotted Indian pony waited behind the restaurant. Virgil prodded her forward until they stood beside the Indian pony. He pulled a rabbit skin coat decorated in the Indian fashion with feathers on the upper arms from across the pony's saddle. "Put this on." He held the coat out to her.

She stared at him mutely. She didn't like to think how he had come by the Indian pony and the coat. He waved his gun, and she complied with his request. "Where are you taking me?"

His face lit in a slow smile. "Somewhere no one will follow us."

CHAPTER TWENTY-ONE

NATE HAD KEPT BUSY ON HIS claim since Addie had first seen it. Where his tent had once stood in a small clearing above the banks of Alder Creek sat a log cabin. Smoke curled from its stone chimney and caught in the branches of the cottonwood and alder trees.

Addie climbed the rough-hewn porch steps with a lump in her throat. She hadn't spoken to or seen Nate since that awful day when she'd asked him to leave her alone. Coming back to him for a favor seemed an awful imposition, but she would do it to help Liberty. Swallowing her reluctance, she raised her hand to knock. Before she could, however, it swung inward.

"Addie? I saw you from the window." With tousled hair, his face unshaven, and wearing rumpled clothing, Nate stood with one hand on the door frame. The stench of burnt bacon wafted around him.

"Goodness, is something burning?" She peered past him into the cabin, forgetting her nervousness.

"Thanks for your concern, but I've dealt with the matter." His lips curved in a rueful smile that put hollows in his cheeks that she'd never noticed before. Had he suffered an illness?

"I'm sorry to disturb you, but—" She broke off, the words suddenly tangling her mind.

His forehead creased. "Is something amiss?"

Nate gazed at her with such compassion that Addie had to overcome the yearning to cast herself into his arms. "Liberty is ill, and we need someone to ride after Doc Bissell. Would you be willing to go?"

"By all means." He straightened away from the jamb. "I'll

leave right away."

"Thank you." She sighed her relief.

"Where will I find him?"

It occurred to Addie that she didn't know. "He went to a wedding somewhere in Ennis, but I'm sure Travis can give you more details."

He nodded. "I'll stop by before I leave and ask him."

"See you then." She hurried away, anxious to reach home and ease America's mind.

Shane breathed the bracing air of a clear winter's day and let his gaze wander over the broad, bunchgrass-covered valley that swept to the feet of far-flung mountains. The Indians had named this valley Lodge of the White-Tailed Deer because the warm springs at the top of a mound rising forty feet or more attracted the creatures.

He stiffened his spine and climbed the wide steps before passing beneath the wooden archway into the interior of the church. At the end of one of the side aisles, he stopped before a smaller arch that overshadowed a round-topped door.

At his knock, spinster Bradley admitted him with a delighted smile. "Welcome back." Her smile slipped. "What happened to you?"

Shane rubbed his bruised cheek. "Nothing time won't heal. I'm here to see Bishop Masters." He hadn't meant to speak so curtly, but with his errand occupying him, he couldn't summon the presence of mind to satisfy the finer points of etiquette.

"Certainly. He's expecting you." She spoke in a polished voice and showed him into David's office.

David rose from his desk when Shane entered. With his brown hair trimmed and his jacket well cut, he looked as impeccably groomed as ever. "Hello, Shane. It's been a while." He flicked a glance to Shane's bruised jaw but made no comment. "Won't you have a seat?"

Shane lowered himself into the leather-upholstered oak chair across from the desk. "It's good to see you again."

David smiled. "What brings you to me today?"

In the presence of the man who had brought Shane out of the slums, the speech he'd so carefully rehearsed vanished from his memory. He sought for words to replace the lost ones.

David settled back and waited in silence.

"I've come to resign," Shane blurted out the ugly truth.

"I see." David lifted an eyebrow. "What prompted your decision?"

He'd anticipated this question, but for the life of him couldn't decide how to answer it. All the reasons that had propelled him to this point jumbled together in an incoherent mess. "I'm not cut out for the job," he blurted.

"Please clarify." David sat up and folded his hands on the desktop. "Why do you say that?"

"I'm not any good at it, that's why." Shane took a steadying breath before going on. "They don't listen to me, David. I preach until I'm blue, and they continue to ignore me. If I've learned anything in all this time, it's that I can save no one."

"I begin to see the problem." David rose and strode to the window, looking out with his hands clasped behind his back. After a long stretch, he turned back to Shane. "You're right, in point of fact. You can't save your charges. I suggest you stop trying."

"What do you mean?" Shane asked, miffed. How could David say such a thing? Shane had expected him to try and persuade him to go on with his circuit—not encourage him to give up.

"Shane, Shane." David smiled at him. "Every once in a while, one of my circuit preachers tries to carry more of a burden than God intended. No one can do the Almighty's work for Him. All God expects you to do is speak for Him when you should, bend your knees as often as possible, and move out of the way when necessary."

Shane shook his head. "I don't understand."

"I'm afraid you've been laboring under the wrong conviction, and it has you unraveled. To tell you the truth, I'm surprised you held out this long. Must be that strong mind of yours."

"It's not anything to do with that. If left to myself, I'd have quit before this, but I couldn't bring myself to abandon my charges."

"That's because you have a shepherd's heart. Do you really think you'd be happy if you left your flock out of frustration?"

"I don't know what's best anymore!" The words tore from Shane's throat. "Sometimes it's as if I can hear lost souls crying out for a Savior. It breaks my heart, and I can't do anything else but try to help them."

"That's the call of God."

"Then why, when I try, do I fail? How can that be God's will?"

David's eyes shone with compassion. "You'll make a wonderful preacher, Shane, once you stop striving for results. Will you do one thing for me? If afterward you still want to resign, I'll give you my blessing."

"What do you want me to do?"

David smiled. "Travel your circuit, but this time let God work through you without trying to force anything to happen on your own."

"You don't want much, do you?"

David smiled. "Take it to prayer for a couple of days. Think it over, then come back and tell me your decision. Can you do that much?"

How could he refuse to pray? "All right."

"Thank you." David came around the desk and shook his hand.

Shane summoned a smile for the spinster Bradley on his way out. Mind reeling, he resolved to go for a walk. Before he could give David an answer, he should fully grasp the concepts the man had raised. How was it possible to save people without *striving* to save them, let alone do the work of God without *doing* God's work?

Whatever else Shane did in life, he needed to answer those questions.

Nate stomped onto Addie's porch and lifted his hand to knock at the door.

Addie threw it open before his knuckles came down against the wood. "Thank goodness you're here. I don't know what to do. Honestly, it makes no sense." Her strained face, furrowed brow, and panting breaths told Nate that something was terribly wrong.

Closing the door with his booted foot, he grasped her by the arm and guided her into the restaurant. "What's wrong?"

"I came back to find the baby here alone and America gone. Where can she be?" Panic throbbed in her voice.

Nate pulled Addie against him and patted her back. How should he handle this situation? He decided to tackle practical matters first. "How's the baby?"

She drew away to arm's length. "Liberty's fever has gone down some. She's sleeping now, but she'll want her mother when she wakes."

Of course she would. What sick child wouldn't? "I hope she'll be all right." He glanced around the restaurant for anything out of the ordinary. "Any sign of violence?"

Addie shook her head, her eyes huge. "No, but she wouldn't have left her baby willingly."

From what he'd observed of the widow Reed, Nate agreed.

"Why don't you sit down and collect yourself while I take a look around?"

"Thanks, Nate." She lowered herself to a nearby chair. "This has really thrown me."

"Don't worry, Addie. We'll figure it out." He hesitated, not wanting to worry her further, but he had to ask. "Is Travis back yet?"

"He'll be home soon."

She spoke in a voice that brooked no argument, and he didn't want to make one.

He gave her a bracing smile. "I'll be right back."

Nate went over the restaurant twice before moving outside. He found no signs of a struggle on the porch. In the fading light, he almost missed the hoofprints in the snow behind the restaurant. He crouched over the tracks, reading a story of two horses, one of them unshod.

Travis leaped up from the chair beside Addie's when Nate entered the restaurant. The boy's nostrils flared at the sight of him, but he made no protest.

Nate nodded to him and directed his question to Addie. "Why would an Indian pony walk through your property?"

"I have no idea." She looked to Travis. "Do you?"

"No, Ma." Travis's face turned red. "You'll find Mrs. Reed, won't you?"

"I'd like to try, but I need to go for the doctor."

"No, you don't," Addie informed him. "Mr. Walsh went after Doc Steele. I appreciate your willingness to help look for America."

Her face wore a fragile expression, as if he could crush her with a word. The urge to take her into his arms and smooth all the worries from her brow plagued him. He tamped down his wayward emotions. "I'll ride out tonight."

A chill wind blew down from the Tobacco Root Mountains, ruffling the mane of America's Indian pony. She huddled into her fur coat, thankful for its warmth. Virgil had bound her hands and feet and kept her pony's lead as he rode ahead of her. He never wavered and seldom allowed the horses to rest. She suspected he feared they might be followed.

America strained at her bonds, trying to free her hands, but Virgil had tied them well. Worries about Liberty filled her mind. Had the doctor come? How would she eat? Could she be crying for her at this moment? Had she breathed her last breath without knowing the comfort of her mother's arms? No, she couldn't allow herself to believe that.

Whatever Virgil's plans for her, they could hold no merit. What sort of person would pay for a bride with horses? Her mind churned with possibilities, but none of them made sense.

A hush fell over the snowy landscape. She felt somehow separate from her aching body. But for the cords rubbing her wrists, she could believe herself more spirit than flesh.

Virgil left the road, dismounted, and untied her. "Don't try anything funny." Walking on foot, he led his horse and the Indian pony she rode toward a tall building with numerous windows. It loomed against the cobalt sky.

"What is this place?" she asked.

"A roadhouse." Virgil stopped in front of the building below a long balcony, tied the reins around a hitching post, and reached up to help her from the saddle. "They call it Robbers Roost."

America's heart sank. She'd heard of this haven for road agents who watched from the balcony for stagecoaches and lone riders carrying gold between Bannack and Virginia City. This must be the place Virgil had meant when he'd said no one would follow them. Decent folks avoided Robbers Roost or rode past as quickly as possible.

Rejecting his help, America slid from the Indian pony on her own, but her legs shook so badly she had to grasp the saddle to keep from falling. Virgil threw an arm around her and tugged her close to his side. "Play along now, darlin', and you'll come to no harm," he said in a cordial tone. He released her and pushed her through the wooden turnstile gate. She stumbled before him along the path to the front door.

America shrank from going inside the dreadful place, but with the barrel of his gun pressed to her side, Virgil propelled her through the open doorway. A man with a flowing brown beard looked up from behind a tall desk. His gaze traveled over America's body in an insulting way. "You two looking for a bed for the night, Virgil?"

"The lady wants the cabin. We'd like a little privacy."

"Sure thing." Gold exchanged hands, and the man gave over the key.

Virgil dragged her out the door and across a wooden footbridge. The grass gave under her feet, damp from the stream. Cottonwoods lifted skeletal branches high over the one-room log cabin that awaited them. He opened the door and pushed her inside.

"What do you want with me?" Whatever he told her could be no worse than her fears.

He kicked the door shut behind them. "I saw the way that Indian looked at you when he rode into Bannack."

She massaged her temples, trying to relieve the headache behind them. "What are you talking about?"

"You're worth quite a few horses in trade, I'd say. 'Course, Tendoy has more'n a few horses to spare."

"Tendoy?" She stared at him. "What does he have to do with me?" But she'd taken his meaning. Indians gave horses for brides. She should have realized Virgil's intent from the fur coat he'd given her and the pony he'd made her ride.

"I saw the way he looked at you." Virgil smirked at her. "He fancies you."

If she hadn't needed to cry so badly, she might have

laughed. If Tendoy had wanted her for a bride, he could have made off with her when he'd had her on the back of his horse. Instead, he'd returned her to her wagon train. Virgil must have drawn his own conclusions after noticing Tendoy's look of recognition after catching sight of her on the hotel balcony.

America did not point this out, however. She wasn't certain what would happen if she did. At least, Virgil didn't appear to want her for himself.

He made a sweeping gesture. "Make yourself to home. I'll fetch supper after I see to the horses. We ride out tomorrow."

He closed the door behind him, and the key rattled in the lock.

She sank onto a chair, head whirling. Tendoy had shown her kindness once. Perhaps he would again. She hoped he would purchase her from Virgil and then release her, although she had no guarantee he would do anything of the sort.

Her arms ached to hold her baby. She clasped them about herself and gave way to tears. She wept for Liberty, who couldn't understand what had happened to her mother. She wept for herself as well. Lost and alone like a small child without her mother, America vented the emotions she'd held back all day. Every circumstance in her life had led her to this moment, and it seemed nothing would ever come right again.

Shane strode down the boardwalk toward the livery stable, carrying a new container of liniment. Archibald's hooves still troubled him from spending so much time on muddy roads. He wanted to make sure his horse had a chance to heal before moving on.

His horse nickered as he entered the livery barn. "Miss me, did you?" He applied the liniment and left Archibald munching hay. The day outside seemed brighter after the dim building. He didn't notice the horse and rider coming down the street until they entered the livery yard spraying mud.

He squinted up at the man in the saddle. "Decide to follow me, did you?"

"You're not the only one who wants a new start." Con ran a hand over his face in a weary gesture. "Having been a deputy in Bannack serves as a recommendation for a noose these days. It seemed provident to put distance between myself and Virginia City."

Shane eyed his cousin's frothing horse. "You rode here in a hurry."

"The prospect of a posse after you has a way of focusing the mind."

"*Are* they after you?" Shane asked in sudden alarm.

Con's lips quirked into a faint smile. "I don't think so, but I didn't like to inquire." He dismounted and led his horse around the livery yard.

"I see your point." Shane walked alongside him as he cooled his horse.

"I also thought you might want to know that the widow Reed's baby took ill. Travis told me about her when I was riding out. I stopped at the Ruby Fork ranch on the way here to ask the doctor to hurry home. Poor man. He'd been up half the night with a birthing. Let's hope he can help the baby."

"I'm sorry to hear of Liberty's illness." America would be frantic and in need of support. Shane rubbed the back of his neck and considered what to do.

Con tilted his head. "She asked for you first. Before me, as it happens."

"I suppose that means something, but the baby could be over the crisis by now."

"Or else lying in her coffin. Does that matter to you?"

Shane dropped his hand to his side. "Of course it does, but you know why I came here. I'm not sure about going back to Virginia City."

Con stepped in front of him, blocking his path. "Whether or not you go on as a preacher, I would think you'd want to continue living as a man worth his salt." He turned away, still leading his horse.

Shane caught up. "You've no call to say such a thing."

Con rounded on him. "You didn't mind being in Virginia City when you kissed her in the shade of that cottonwood tree." He started off again.

Shane followed him. "I shouldn't have done that."

"The fact that you lost your head over the woman says a lot more than you know. Why not marry her and be done with it, for pity's sake? Giving up preaching should make that an easier decision for you now."

Con continued walking his horse, but Shane didn't follow this time.

Virgil vanished for most of the night, and the voices and laughter from the roadhouse told the story of where he'd gone. He'd been clear-eyed all day but would probably make up for that now. He'd locked the cabin door, and the latches on the windows had all rusted shut and would not budge. He probably wouldn't try to intrude upon America tonight, but she felt better with a chair jammed beneath the doorknob of the small bedroom just the same.

The oddest sensation of falling assailed her, and she lowered herself to the bed with her head reeling. She rubbed her forehead to ease the ache growing behind it. Her throat felt dry, even scratchy. Hopefully, she wasn't coming down sick.

Her arms felt empty without Liberty. She couldn't allow herself to believe her baby was dead. She had never felt so helpless in her life, not even when the buffalo wolves gathered around her while she dragged Richard's body away from them and into the barn.

America couldn't help but wonder if God's anger had brought her to this pass. She'd tried to make amends for her sins by doing her best by Liberty, but it hadn't been enough. From what Shane had said, redeeming herself in God's eyes wasn't necessary or even possible, but she couldn't fathom such mercy as he'd described.

So far, she'd relied mostly on her own strength, but her efforts to create a better life had all ended in defeat. She'd tried to rely on Shane, but he was gone too, just like everyone else she'd ever loved. At the realization that she included Shane in that number of those "she'd ever loved," she put a hand to her mouth to stifle her sobs.

As the night wore on, America tossed and turned. Her headache, sore throat, and stiffness from being so long in the saddle kept her awake. She fell into an uneasy sleep just before the first light of dawn penetrated the flimsy curtains at the window.

The door burst open, overturning the chair she'd propped against it. "Rise and shine!" Virgil commanded. "Time to move on."

America jerked awake and sat up blinking. "I'm sick." Her voice came out little more than a croak.

He screwed up a bloodshot eye to peer at her. "You wouldn't be pretending, now would you, darlin'?"

"I'm telling you the truth," she gritted out.

He strode toward the bed. America scrambled to her feet. The room tilted. She put out her hands, trying to stop her fall.

Virgil caught her by both arms, holding her upright. "Mercy, but you're hot to the touch. All right. You can have a few days to get better. That Indian won't want you in this condition, and no one will bother us while we're here." He sauntered from the room. A few minutes later, the key grated in the lock.

America sank down onto the bed, trembling. All she wanted

to do was slide into sleep. In her woozy state, she couldn't help but hope that Shane would come to her rescue. How he would do that—given his refusal to fight—she had no idea. Not to mention the fact that he had no idea where she was being kept.

The horrifying truth forced itself on her. *No one* knew her whereabouts. She moaned and slid from the bed onto her knees. "God, if there's a chance You could forgive me and help me escape this nightmare, then I ask You to do so."

Her whispered prayer vanished into silence.

CHAPTER TWENTY-TWO

SHANE STOOD AT THE BOARDING HOUSE window, looking out without really seeing the street below. A late wagon creaked down the street and faded into the encroaching darkness with Shane no closer to answering the riddle plaguing him.

Gusting a sigh, he swung away from the window. He could no longer delay. Right or wrong, the choice he made tonight would change his future. The lantern he lit cast a circle of light around him. He lowered himself to the blue velvet settee and leaned his head against the hickory edging that arched across its back.

How did America fare this night? As always in quiet moments, she inhabited his thoughts. Ignoring the urge to go to her wasn't really an option. He couldn't abandon her in an hour of need. She would do her best for her baby, of that he had no doubt. Whether or not Liberty lived, America would need someone to turn to for comfort.

Shane knew beyond a shadow of doubt that he wanted to be that person. With that knowledge, the paths before him narrowed to two. He could go to America in his role of a preacher . . . or simply as a man who loved her.

He wouldn't consider the second course of action, since a circuit rider was more likely to leave his wife widowed at a young age than to see her into her declining years. America had already been widowed once, and he refused to risk bringing her more sorrow. No, if he married her, there would be no going back to circuit riding.

But after talking with David, he couldn't turn away from his charges so easily. Reaching them with the gospel of peace had to come first--before a woman's love, his own comfort, maybe even life itself.

Shane needed divine guidance to succeed. So far, he'd trusted in his own strength more than God's. He had to stop manipulating others into listening to him and trust God to draw them instead. That would take a great deal of prayer and the faith of Abraham.

"You might reach a good sight more people, Saint Preacher, if your feet touched the ground now and then." Con's voice echoed in the corridors of memory. He smiled ruefully. His cousin's brand of theology could be so maddeningly right.

Shivering with fever, America huddled under the sparse covers. Her head throbbed, and her throat ached as if she had swallowed sand, but she couldn't summon the strength to climb out of bed and haul herself to the water bucket to soothe its rawness. Closing her eyes, she drifted away from wakefulness in a haze of pain.

Footsteps crunched the snow outside, rousing her. She thrust herself into a sitting position. Her fever had abated while she slept, but her thirst had increased. In the other room the key grated in the lock and the knob rattled. Hinges creaked and wood thudded against the cabin wall. Boots thumped toward the room where she huddled. The door swung inward but halted when it thunked into the chair she'd propped beneath the knob.

"What's this?" Virgil chuckled. "Let me in. I only want to feed you, woman."

America swung her legs out of bed. She'd rather meet him on her feet than lying helpless. Before she could rise, the chair scooted across the floorboards as Virgil shoved his way into the room. She squinted to see him, although he blocked most of the light streaming from the open front doorway. Balancing a plate of beans with a biscuit perched on top in one hand, he surveyed her from rheumy eyes. "You look a mite better. We'll ride out in the morning."

"I can't travel yet." America forced the words past the pain in her throat, although she spoke without much hope. Virgil had laid by for several days already. She had to try and delay him, though. Once he took her to the Shoshone tribe's winter encampment, she would be far from Virginia City and the possibility of rescue.

"Now you're playing possum." Virgil chuckled. "Got to happen sooner or later, darlin'. Might as well accept it."

"But why? I would think you'd be happier mining gold than kidnapping and selling me."

"That could have been so, if I'd made it to Alder Gulch with the stampede at the beginning of the rush. With the good claims snatched up, a newcomer has to settle on what's left."

"There's still enough gold from what I've heard."

"Maybe so, but sluicing takes a lot more work than I want to put myself to at my age."

She failed to see how dragging an unwilling person hundreds of miles in the snow was less exerting. He'd obviously made up his mind, so she saved herself the frustration of pointing that out.

"I've brought you some food." He slid the plate onto the table in the other room. "Eat hearty. There won't be the like of this once we leave. It'll be trail rations or nothing." He closed the front door, shutting most of the light from the room.

She dragged herself to the water bucket and drank two dippers full before lowering herself to a chair at the table. With her appetite stirring but her throat on fire, she choked down what she could of the meal. Virgil usually left her alone to eat but now sat across from her in a worn chair and watched her in a way guaranteed to put her off her food. "Even sickly, you're a good-looking woman. I'm surprised no one's snatched you up yet."

Ignoring him, she swallowed a morsel of biscuit that scraped her raw throat. She took another bite, determined to survive this ordeal and return to her daughter.

"I thought that preacher was sweet on you, but he up and left town. Never mind. There's one that wants you." He grinned. "I'm taking you to him."

America stared at him. Did he see himself as some sort of grizzled matchmaker? She had to disabuse his mind of *that* notion. "He doesn't want me."

"What?"" He screwed up an eye and examined her like a bug to squish. "Why do you say that?"

"Because it's true. Tendoy doesn't want me, at least not in the way you think. What you saw that day was simply him recognizing me from before."

Virgil's forehead creased. "What? How does he know you?"

"I met him while traveling in the wagon train."

He shrugged and pulled a plug of tobacco from a pouch. "Don't matter to me, whatever you say. If he doesn't want a pretty thing like you, we'll find someone else who does."

America stopped eating, unable to swallow any longer.

"Maybe I'll sell you for a dancehall girl."

"If it's money you want," America gasped. "I'll give you my savings in exchange for my freedom."

Virgil's tongue wetted his lips. "You'd sooner see me arrested as hand me your money."

"Please, I want my baby." She rasped the words out.

Virgil threw up his hands. "What do you take me for? I don't aim to go anywhere near Virginia City's jail with you by my side. I had a time talking myself out of it the last time I landed there."

His refusal struck America like a physical blow. Exhaustion washed over her, and she put her head in her hands.

"Get some sleep." Virgil's voice penetrated her sorrow. "We leave in the morning."

The front door creaked open and thudded shut. The key rasped, locking out every shred of hope.

Shane took to the road long before dawn stained the sky. Huddled in his jacket, he kept Archibald to the wagon ruts in the snow. He'd been several days in the saddle now and accustomed to the cold, but he would welcome the chance to stand before the hearth at Addie's restaurant.

He restrained the temptation to urge Archibald faster. He needed to pace him through the day's long journey. Winter travel required a man to depend on his horse for survival, and he needed to keep Archibald healthy.

He went on with a feeling of purpose, knowing he had made the right decision to take David's advice. Whatever God planned for his future, the way to it lay before him.

A herd of deer sprang across the road and into a stand of willows on the other side. A distance beyond the herd, two figures moved along the road in his direction. He would be glad to meet other souls on this desolate stretch of road, the domain of bitter winds that whistled in the night.

The familiarity of the riders snared his attention. Sitting taller in the saddle, he craned to see. *Could it be . . .?*

The woman riding the Indian pony and led by a man on a sorrel horse could only be America. He would know her blonde hair and that tilt to her head anywhere. The flop-brimmed hat on the man's head gave away his identity too.

Shane's heart pounded in his chest. Rage equal to what he'd felt at seeing America bound and gagged by Virgil surged over him. What did the man want with America? She wouldn't go anywhere with him without being forced.

Slumped against the cold, Virgil didn't seem to have noticed him yet. Shane slipped into the concealment of a willow stand, hoping for the advantage of surprise. He dismounted and led Archibald into the shade beneath a willow's drooping leaves before pulling the Colt Paterson from his saddlebag. Shane balanced the gun against his palm, and looked out through the snow-lined screen the branches provided.

Virgil appeared within range. Shane leveled the barrel of his gun at the man's chest. How easily he could take a life. All he had to do was squeeze the trigger.

His gut roiled and a sour taste made him want to vomit. He lowered his gun, and it slipped from his grasp. Not for his own life—not even for the woman he loved—could Shane bring himself to violate everything he held true. But he refused to let her go by undefended.

Virgil neared the willows, his horse's hooves thumping along the path.

Shane held himself in check, but one glance at America had him clenching his jaw. Worry lines seamed her forehead. She kilted to the side as she rode as if barely able to stay seated. He promised himself that whatever else happened today, she would go free.

Virgil glanced back to America as he neared Shane's hiding place.

Shane gathered himself to leap.

Archibald whinnied to the other horse. Virgil whipped his head around and went for his gun.

Shane leapt before Virgil could fire. Hooking an arm around Virgil's waist, Shane forced him out of the saddle and into the snow. Screaming, the sorrel horse reared and brought its hooves down inches from Shane's head. Virgil's gun flew from his hand. The two men rolled in the snow, battling with bare knuckles.

Virgil ploughed a fist into Shane's stomach, awakening the injury Atticus had inflicted.

Fighting dizziness, Shane blocked a second blow to his middle and aimed a punch at Virgil's jaw. The miner turned his head at the last second, and Shane's fist slid against his teeth. Virgil lurched to his feet, dabbing at a cut on his lip.

Shane thrust himself upright and faced off with Virgil. The miner darted glances about, no doubt searching for his gun. Shane spotted the weapon, lying dark against the snow. He dove for it but too late.

Virgil came up with the pistol in his hand. He aimed it at Shane's head. "Well, well, Saint Preacher. Looks like there's more to you than I gave you credit for."

Shane faced him without flinching. Out of the corner of his eye, he saw America slide down from her horse. "Let her go. She's done nothing to deserve what you're putting her through."

Virgil grimaced in place of a smile. "She's worth money to me."

"What price can you set on a human life?" Shane challenged him. "Did not our Savior die for each one?"

"You seem mighty taken with this Jesus of yours. Guess I'll do you a favor and send you to your Maker right now." Virgil cocked his gun.

"No!" America flung herself in front of Shane and shielded him with her body. She raised the Colt Paterson in both hands.

Virgil held his fire. "Aw, ain't that touching. Put the gun away, darlin', before you hurt yourself."

"Don't think I can't use this." She thumbed back the hammer and took aim. "I learned how to shoot snakes on my homestead. Put your gun away or I'll demonstrate."

"Now, now." Virgil's gun hand shook. "I'd rather not tangle with a woman holding a gun." He eased off the trigger but kept his pistol ready.

"That's wise," Shane murmured. "No one wins an impasse."

The grizzled miner backed toward his horse. "There's no arguing with love, I guess." He gathered the Indian pony's lead and mounted the sorrel horse.

"You forgot your hat." Shane swept it from the snow and

carried it to Virgil with slow steps.

"My thanks." Virgil accepted his hat but kept an eye on America, who still pointed the gun at him.

"Thank you for choosing peace." Shane stepped back, positioning himself to block their lines of fire.

"You never fail to surprise me, preacher." Virgil pushed back his hat with the barrel of his pistol then holstered his gun. "I owe you a favor for saving me when I hurt my leg. I always wondered why you did that. In your place, I'd have shot me."

"You needed saving." Shane gave him the simple truth.

"Maybe—" Virgil's face worked. "Maybe I still do. You once promised to pray for me, do you recall?"

Shane started at the memory of a hooded man riding out at him along a road at dusk. "I remember."

"Sometimes Buck Stinson took me along when he went out at night on certain duties. He wound up at the end of a noose. Guess I'd rather travel by a better route, after all."

"Make this a start to it then."

Virgil scrutinized him from his pale gray eyes. "Keep praying for me, preacher."

"That I will."

"Thank you." Virgil tipped his hat to America. "I knew she'd make a nice bride for somebody. Reckon that'll be you." He wheeled his horse and started off with the Indian pony trailing behind.

Shane relieved America of his gun. She watched him uncock the hammer and pocket the weapon. Her face went white and she swayed. He caught her in his arms. "What were you thinking, risking your life like that?"

She sent him a wounded look. "But he was about to shoot you!"

"That would be a reason to stay out of the way, I would think." Her lips so close to his own made him ache to kiss them.

Her pupils dilated, and she put a hand to his chest to ward

him off. "No, don't. You'll get sick."

He kissed her anyway.

America clutched Shane's chest to anchor herself as wave after wave of longing swept through her. Any lingering doubt about her feelings for this man washed away in a floodtide of emotion.

Every obstacle she'd raised between them crumbled to dust. She had never felt like this with Kyle or Richard. This kiss felt sanctified, holy, pure. The past faded, leaving only this moment with this man and the love she could no longer deny.

Shane lifted her into his arms. "You're weak as a kitten. Let's get you back to Virginia City." He whistled, and a nicker answered him. The roan stepped out from among the trees. He deposited her on Archibald's back and swung up behind her. She leaned against him, reveling in the strength of his arms. He nuzzled her neck but then gently pushed her upright. "I'd better behave myself."

His horse's swaying combined with the cold lulled America into drowsiness.

"Tell me, how is your baby?" Shane asked near her ear.

"I don't know." Tears sprang to her eyes. "Virgil made off with me before the doctor came."

"I'm sorry for all you've suffered." He pulled her back against his chest.

Resting against him, she filled him in on everything that had happened since her baby became ill.

He kissed her hair. "I'll reunite you with Liberty as soon as possible, I promise."

They rode past Robbers Roost after dusk, escaping unmolested. He waited until miles stretched themselves between themselves and the roadhouse before pulling alongside the banks of the Ruby River to water his horse and make camp.

He helped her out of the saddle. "I'd like to keep going, but Archibald needs to stop." The temperature had dropped as nightfall neared, but he couldn't risk lighting a fire to warm them. He dug a hollow in the snow, lined it with evergreen needles, and lashed together fir boughs above it. Then he laid out his bedroll in the improvised shelter.

He held back some of the boughs to make an opening. "Climb inside."

She held back. "I can't take your blankets. Where will you sleep?"

"I'll wait up and keep watch."

The memory of Richard's frozen body returned to haunt her. "I know you want to be a gentleman, but your freezing to death won't help either of us."

"It's doubtful I will in this coat, but I wouldn't sleep much either. Still, we need to think of your reputation."

America considered his last remark. The miners probably didn't care that she had spent several nights away from home in the company of a man, but the families settling in Virginia City had opinions on matters of propriety. The nights she'd spent at Robbers' Roost compromised her in their eyes despite the fact that Virgil Henry hadn't touched her. She shook her head. "I'm not so fragile that I can't share a blanket to keep you alive, and my reputation is already ruined."

Shane gave her a thoughtful look. "We'll have to do something to change that."

What did he mean by that remark? America had no idea, but he joined her under the blanket, and she forgot to ask him to explain. She snuggled against his chest, and the heartbeat against her ear matched her own in urgency. She wanted this man in the way of a wife, the same way she'd wanted Kyle. The pain a union unsanctioned by marriage caused was difficult to remember in this moment. How would she make it through the night with him so near?

"Warmer?" Shane asked gruffly.

"Yes." Her voice came out breathy.

"Shall we pray?"

She blinked. "All right."

He led the way. "Dear Lord, thank you for protecting us today. I ask that you protect us tonight as well. Please help me to honor this woman and keep her safe."

America warmed enough to sleep, but she lay awake until long after darkness fell. Shane's even breathing measured the passage of time. Her stomach knotted, and the terror she'd held at bay babbled in her mind. Tomorrow they would reach Virginia City and find out if her baby lived. Not knowing, she'd been able to pretend that Liberty remained alive, but she would soon learn whether she'd deceived herself. She wanted desperately to find out the truth, but her mouth went dry at the prospect of discovering that God had parted Liberty from her, just as He'd taken Richard and Gramma.

CHAPTER TWENTY-THREE

ADDIE WOKE WITH A START.

Where is Liberty?

Remembering, she rolled over and tried to go back to sleep. With the restaurant closed for Sunday, Addie could enjoy the luxury of a midday nap. Nate had stopped by earlier and had gone on a walk with Travis. One good thing had come out of this terrible situation. Nate and Travis had mended fences and were working toward a better understanding.

Something bad must have happened to America. She would never have willingly left her sick baby alone. Nate had organized a group of miners to search for her but to no avail. She seemed to have vanished off the face of the earth. Meanwhile, Doc Steele had called on Liberty. The little lamb had hovered close to death, but by God's mercy she had pulled through the crisis. A week later, her color had returned and she was making daily strides toward recovery.

With America gone, the burden of Liberty's care had fallen on Addie. She'd closed the restaurant but would reopen it soon to keep her regular customers. Managing a restaurant while caring for a sick baby who missed her mother would not be easy.

Nate now pitched in alongside Travis to walk Liberty during her crying fits, heat goat's milk for her nursing bottle, and cradle her while she fed. Caring for a baby with Nate seemed so natural, and Travis acting like a big brother made the picture of a small family complete.

Addie needed to remind herself of reality, however. She had rejected Nate's advances and, despite his assistance with the baby, they would part company after the crisis resolved. Hopefully, America would turn up alive and well. If she didn't, Addie would continue to care for Liberty.

She had changed. Everything she had thought and felt about building a life for herself on her own still held true, but excluding Nate seemed less important now. If only they could go on as friends. In her heart of hearts, she knew that couldn't happen. Like a door that locked after walking through it, trying to go back to yesterday never worked.

Thinking of what she couldn't change didn't help Addie's mood and kept her from sleeping again. She might as well get up and start supper.

In the kitchen, she punched down the bread dough she'd left rising and shaped it into smooth loaves, working with the ease of familiarity. Her bread had become one of her trademark items, and she handled each loaf with care.

The front door burst open and thumped against its stop. "Ma, we're home," Travis shouted above the baby's crying. "Liberty's hungry."

Nate looked into the kitchen from the doorway. "I can feed her while you work."

Addie gave him a grateful smile. "Thank you. I couldn't do this without you."

He smiled back, his gaze lingering on hers. "You don't have to. I'm not going anywhere." He warmed the baby's milk and carried her bottle from the kitchen. Liberty's cries soon quieted.

Travis came into the kitchen and hovered behind Addie. "What's for dinner?"

Her son had a bottomless stomach these days. "Wilted red cabbage and bacon, potatoes, greens, and apples." She spoke absently while dicing onions.

Travis didn't move away as she expected but remained standing behind her. She glanced over her shoulder. "Something on your mind?"

"While Nate and I got to talking."

"Oh?"

"Yes, and I realized I have something to say to you."

She put down her knife and turned around to face him fully. "What is it?"

"I already told Mr. Whalen, but I need to tell you too. I'm sorry for what I said the other day after I saw you two . . . after—"

"Oh, Travis—"

He shook his head. "No, let me go on. I shouldn't have carried on that way. I know you loved Pa. I was wrong to say you didn't. I worried that Mr. Whalen might take his place."

"No one could ever do that."

"I see that now, but I couldn't then. You were sad when Nate didn't come around anymore, and it's my fault. But Pa wouldn't want you unhappy, and I don't either. If you want to be with Mr. Whalen, I won't stand in your way any longer. I kind of think Pa would have liked him, anyway."

Addie hardly knew how to respond. She'd burned that bridge, or so she'd believed. Recent events had cast some doubt on that subject.

In the other room, Nate's voice raised in a melody. Her lips curved as she recognized "When Summer Flowers Are Blowing," her mother's favorite song.

America shifted in the saddle, trying to ease the discomfort of so much time in the saddle. Although her body ached dreadfully from the long ride and her illness, she refused to ask for any breaks. She would do nothing to delay finding out what had happened to Liberty. The yearning to hold her baby grew so strong that it troubled her as much as a physical ache.

The moon lit the sky, and stars littered the heavens by the time Shane turned aside at Addie's restaurant. They stopped in the glow from the window beside the front door. He dismounted and reached up to help her down.

America shrank back. Her breath choked in her throat. How could she go into the house and find her baby dead?

"Don't take on so." Shane's soft words reached her from the darkness.

America sheltered against him, grateful for his strength. She had none of her own. She turned her face into his shirt and wept.

He held her against him. "Do you want me to go inside and ask about Liberty while you wait on the porch?"

"No." She heaved a breath and scrubbed away her tears. "That would be worse."

He bolstered her with an arm around her shoulders and climbed the porch steps beside her. Shane opened the door and stood back.

"Addie?" America stepped inside. Travis and Nate stood up from chairs at one of the tables, but she barely saw either of them. "Oh, my baby—" Her voice strangled on a sob.

Liberty turned her head toward her mother's voice and squirmed in Nate's arms. He carried America's baby to her and smiled as Liberty leaned from his arms into her own. Sinking into a chair at one of the tables, she held her daughter close.

Liberty leaned back and hooked a finger in her mother's mouth with an intense stare.

Laughter bubbled up within America and overflowed to burst the dam holding back her tears. She cradled her daughter and wept.

Addie rushed in from the kitchen. "I thought I heard . . . My goodness, it is you!" She gaped at Shane. "Where did you find her?"

"With Virgil Henry. He took her a second time," Shane replied. "I brought her back."

America awarded him a grateful glance. She suspected it would be a long time before she could talk about the terror she had experienced at that man's hands.

"Where is Virgil now?" Nate asked as he and Travis sat across the table from her.

America held her head, which had started to ache. "I don't know or care, so long as he stays away from me."

Addie put an arm around her. "I'm just thankful he released you without serious injury. You're pale, though."

"I've been ill with a fever." America shivered.

Addie pressed a hand to her forehead. "You don't have one now, but you feel a mite cold. Shall I make you a hot cup of tea?"

"That would be wonderful, thank you." America breathed in the sweet scent of Liberty's hair, an antidote to the vile experiences she had suffered.

"How about you, Reverend Hayes?" Addie asked.

"I'd welcome some coffee, thank you." He smiled at Addie then returned his attention to America and the baby.

"Nate?"

"Sit down, Addie." Nate stood. "Let me do that."

She smiled her thanks and took the chair he'd vacated.

"Liberty looks much better." America kissed her baby's forehead. "Did Doc Steele come?"

"Yes, the next day," Addie answered. "He helped her through the crisis and stopped by to check on her every couple of days."

"I'm grateful. Thank you for caring for my baby when I could not," America murmured.

"I was glad to do it." Addie brushed tears from the corners of her eyes. "Travis and Nate helped with her too."

"Thank you, Travis." America rewarded him with a smile.

His face reddened, and he looked away. "You're welcome."

Nate looked out from the kitchen doorway. "Are you hungry? There are leftovers from supper."

"That would be wonderful." America stroked the soft skin on her baby's arm.

"Yes, thank you," Shane answered.

With her attention on Liberty, America hadn't noticed how tired Shane looked in the lantern light until now. Lines of strain etched his face, and his eyes lacked their usual liveliness.

"Stay there." Nate commanded when Addie started to rise. "I'm not such a bachelor that I can't heat food without burning it."

Addie laughed and relaxed into her chair again. "How did you find America, Reverend Hayes?"

"By God's hand, Mrs. Martin." His gaze rested on America with an expression she couldn't interpret. "I stumbled across her on my way back from Idaho City."

"I'm thankful you did." America touched Addie's arm.

Addie covered it with her own. "I heard something about your going to Idaho City for good. Will you stay in Virginia City for a while now?"

"I'm afraid I can't stay." Shane's jaw tightened. "Once I've rested my horse, I need to return to Idaho City."

America tried not to show how much his words troubled her. She'd thought he would remain in town a while before continuing on his circuit, but he seemed focused on leaving Virginia City behind.

Addie's forehead puckered. "That's not the direction you normally travel on your circuit, is it?"

"No, but I need to go to the church office on a private matter." Shane's glance flicked to America then away.

Shane cut into the steak he'd ordered in the hotel restaurant. After eating trail food on the lonely road to Idaho City, this fine meal of seared steak, potatoes swimming in butter, glazed carrots, and early greens came as a welcome treat.

"Nice meal, especially the part about you paying for it." Shane guided another tender morsel of beef into his mouth.

Con laughed. "Eat hearty, Cousin. I'll be able to afford

plenty of steaks once I start working at the Kohler Ranch."

"So, you're staying on here." Shane liked the idea of having Con nearby. Maybe he could hire on as a ranch hand too. After he talked to David, he was going to need a new job.

Con tilted his head. "Truth told, I've fallen in love with Deer Lodge."

"There are a lot of reasons to like the valley, one of the most important being that it isn't under dispute by an Indian tribe."

Con swirled a bite of potatoes in melted butter. "I'm finding that the ranching way of life appeals to me."

"Careful now," Shane warned. "Life as a ranch hand could make you into a drifter, going from one job to the next."

Con lifted a brow. "You can't become what you already are."

Shane made a face. "One day you may come across a woman who changes your mind about that."

"Is that what happened to you?" Con asked.

"It may have," Shane answered quietly.

Con cast him an amused look. "You'll be glad to know I've started attending chapel."

Shane's fork paused on the way to his mouth. "Really?"

"Don't look so shocked."

"I'm sorry." Shane recovered his composure. "It's just that you've always seemed so adamant against having faith."

"Are you going to eat that bite of food?" Con grinned. "I know it's hard to believe, but even I can convert."

"What made you change your mind?" Shane's fork continued its journey to his mouth.

"If you must know, it's your fault." Con watched him with a vulnerable expression.

"How so?"

"I kept this to myself for the most part, but I admired how you live life according to what you believe. The way you went back to your circuit when you wanted to give up on it spoke to me. And the courage of your convictions just plain made me jealous."

"Really?" Shane couldn't hide his surprise. It occurred to him that Con hadn't mentioned any of his attempts to persuade him. Somehow, he had won his cousin by living out his own faith. "I'm glad to have helped change your life for the better."

Con remained in high spirits throughout the rest of the meal, carrying the conversation without remarking on Shane's silence.

Shane worked his way through his food, hardly tasting it, his mind preoccupied. How would Con react to his news? He kept silent. He first needed to talk to David before mentioning his decision to anyone else.

Shane turned the hat in his hand and perched on the edge of the chair under the spinster Bradley's scrutiny while waiting for David to reach his office. Normally he would have arrived at the last minute to avoid this situation, but the matter weighing on his mind had distracted him from his usual circumspection.

"Shane? You've returned from your circuit early." David's surprised expression gave way to a welcoming smile.

"May I speak with you?"

"Of course." David gestured him into his office and shut the door behind them. "Have a seat."

Shane sat down in the same chair he'd occupied during his previous visit. "I have to confess. I've failed in my duty. I relied on my fists instead of on God."

David leaned back in his chair. "Go on."

Shane filled him in on the details of his fight with Virgil.

A silence stretched between them while David looked out the window. "I'm sure you are aware," he said when he turned back to Shane, "that Jesus defended His Father's house from the money changers and sellers. Have you considered the violence with which He overturned their tables and cast them out?"

Shane pictured the scene David described. "I hadn't thought of it that way before."

"We like to think of Jesus only as a gentle Shepherd, and certainly He is that to his flock. However, we can't ignore that He acted out of *righteous anger* to defend the purity of God's temple against those who defiled it."

"What are you saying?"

David folded his arms on his desk. "Given your background, it's no wonder you loathe fighting. I commend you for your aversion to violence. Blessed are the peacemakers, for they shall be called the children of God. However, in the interests of peace, there are times when it becomes necessary to defend yourself or another person."

Shane stared at him. "I don't understand. Aren't we supposed to act in God's love at all times?"

"That's true, but sometimes the most loving thing you can do for someone is force them back when they overstep. Jesus did this in the temple. He stood up to the money changers and sellers, but he killed none of them. It's not wrong to defend the innocent, as long as you don't do it from selfish, anger."

Shane pondered David's words. "That makes sense." He'd respond to an attack from Atticus differently next time.

David's face lit in a gentle smile. "I'm glad to ease your mind on the matter. Will you be returning to your circuit?"

"I'm afraid there's more." Shane took a deep breath. "I've compromised a woman."

Another silence ticked by. "I'm surprised to hear that," David said at last. "You've seemed so driven by spiritual fervor as to barely notice the fairest among us."

"We shared my bedroll in the snow," Shane blurted.

David's gaze swept his face. "Did you violate her?"

Shane shook his head. "I kissed her, but then I took her to prayer."

David smiled. "Is this the woman you defended?"

"Yes."

"Let me see if I have this correctly." David rubbed his chin. "You say you've compromised a woman but you haven't violated her."

"That's right. Through no fault of her own, her reputation became forfeited. We spent the night together after I rescued her, and now I'm wondering if I need to marry her."

David's gaze pinned him. "Is that what you want to do?"

Shane had asked himself this question ever since. The only way he could spare America shame following her ordeal would be to marry her, assuming she would have him. "It's not that simple. I've come to love her, but I don't want her to endure the hardships of a circuit rider's wife."

"We've discussed this before. I can see how it puts you in conflict, but I have good news. The church is reorganizing, in reaction to the ongoing emigration into the West. We've decided to offer some of our ministers the chance to establish a church to serve a congregation in a single location. This would allow for a deeper relationship with your charges and leave more room for a family. We'd like to establish a church in the Bitterroot Valley. Is that something I might interest you in?"

America finished dressing Liberty in the dress she had sewn for her out of brown linsey-woolsey patterned with red and yellow butterflies. She carried her daughter into the kitchen. "What do you think of her new dress?"

"Oh, look at you!" Addie stepped back from drawing butterflies in different colors of frosting on Liberty's first birthday cake.

It hardly seemed possible that a year had gone by since she'd given birth, alone and frightened on her homestead. Her baby had grown into the solid little girl in her arms, and her hair had changed from fine down to golden curls that danced about her head.

Liberty wiggled to be put down. America set her daughter on her feet. She watched over her while Liberty took a few toddling steps then sat down abruptly. Liberty fussed, frustrated—as usual—at not being able to do everything she fixed her mind upon.

Travis arrived in that moment, snatched Liberty into his arms, and bounced her while speaking in the high-pitched voice he reserved especially for her. Liberty giggled profusely. Travis strode around the restaurant, which had closed since Liberty's birthday fell on a Sunday.

America had been saving a ragdoll she'd purchased while in Bannack. She smiled in anticipation of Liberty's excitement when she unwrapped the gift. "Is there anything I can do to help?"

"You can set the table." Focused on her task, Addie answered without looking back.

America took five crockery plates down from the shelf, including a smaller dish for Liberty. She toted the dishes into the restaurant, where they always took their meals on Sundays and special occasions, and began laying them out on top of a table covered by a red-checked tablecloth.

They'd invited Nate to attend Liberty's party. She wished she could have asked Shane too, but he hadn't returned from whatever errand had carried him off to Idaho City.

Nate visited Addie more frequently now. America guessed it would only be a matter of time before they settled the matter between them. Happy for her friend, she couldn't deny a certain reluctance to see the lifestyle they'd established—two widows raising their children together—come to an end. She'd planned all along to make her own way in life, but having grown accustomed to living with Addie, she would find it difficult to leave.

America had saved enough of her earnings to travel

somewhere else, maybe Idaho City like Addie had suggested. Living in a more civilized place appealed to America, especially a place where a drunken man wouldn't ride down the street whooping and firing a six-shooter, and end by galloping into the saloon. That behavior had earned Jack Slade a hanging. Some had protested, saying that the vigilantes shouldn't have executed him because he hadn't killed anyone, although he had terrorized them all.

America couldn't accustom herself to vigilante justice. At any moment, she might look out the window and see a lynching. One day while walking up Wallace Street, she'd approached a large cabin. Excitement from a small crowd gathered in front of the building charged the air, but she hadn't understood why until she saw the five men strung up by ropes around their necks from the rafters of the cabin.

Hayes Lyons, one of Dillingham's murderers, dangled among them. He had cheated the grave dug for him on Boot Hill during Dillingham's trial, but not for long. Now he would lie in the road agent's cemetery, a plot of ground outside the regular graveyard. Malcontents were not welcome to mingle with the town's decent folk in the hereafter.

Addie lifted the cake on a crystal platter with scalloped edges. "What do you think?"

America pulled her mind away from its gruesome train of thought. Such a happy day shouldn't be spent on gloomy reflections. "It looks wonderful." The smell of the dried-apple cake had made her mouth water while it baked, and the caramel frosting looked delicious.

A knock came at the door, and she went in answer, starting when she saw Shane with his hand raised to knock again. "What are you doing here?"

He smiled. "What a greeting."

"I'm sorry. You surprised me, showing up unexpectedly. Please, come in." She stepped back.

Shane slipped past her and into the room, studying her in a

way that seemed different from before, although she couldn't solve the riddle of why.

Addie came through from the kitchen, carrying a pot roast with carrots and onions surrounding it on a platter. "Reverend Hayes! It's good to see you. Can you stay to supper? There's plenty, and it's Liberty's birthday."

Shane sent America an inquiring look.

She found her tongue. "You're welcome to stay."

"Thank you. I'd be delighted." He favored her with a tense smile.

What on earth was wrong with the man?

Nate arrived a few minutes later, and they all sat down to eat. Happy chatter went around the table while they filled up on delectable food. Addie had outdone herself on the meal. Besides pot roast, they ate portions of Yorkshire pudding and cabbage slaw. Later, America cleared the table. Addie brought in the cake and cut a slice for Liberty.

America smiled as her daughter tasted her first bite of birthday cake. Liberty managed to paint her face with multi-colored frosting in the process. The child giggled in utter delight. When they joined in her merriment, she entertained her audience with peals of laughter and a game of peekaboo.

America helped Liberty open her presents, enjoying her delight with the ragdoll she'd given her, toy dishes from Addie, a miniature tambourine from Travis, and a Noah's Ark complete with pairs of animals from Nate. Not to be outdone, Shane had chipped in a buckskin pouch of gold dust that America suspected he'd mined himself using Con's sluice box and gold pan.

Liberty played with one toy after another until she fell asleep on the floor. America carried her to bed and tucked her in with a kiss on her cheek and a brush of her hand over her baby's downy hair.

Travis climbed to the loft with a lantern, ready to write in a journal he kept. Nate followed Addie into the kitchen to assist with the clean-up. America volunteered also, but Addie refused her help. "Shane will want someone to talk with."

She returned to Shane, who was finishing his after-dinner coffee at the table. Being alone in his presence left America feeling tongue-tied. Her shyness struck her as ridiculous, since they'd kissed a time or two and had slept in one another's arms. Nonetheless, she couldn't quite overcome it.

Shane drained his cup. "What a nice party. Thanks for including me, considering I showed up at the last minute."

"You're welcome. I would have invited you beforehand if I'd had any idea you were in town." She never knew when to expect Shane.

He gave her a searching look. "Care to look at the stars with me?"

Why did he sound so nervous? Maybe he felt the same way she did, tongue-tied and self-conscious. "That sounds wonderful." The darkness would hide her awkwardness.

The stars glinted like silver dust scattered across an ebony sky. Wisps of clouds clung to the moon. Beyond the houses, the swells wore a mantle of snow, but the thaw would melt it soon.

America tilted her head and gazed upward. "When I look at the sky, it's easy to forget evil inhabits the world."

"I wish it didn't." Shane's hand closed around hers. "Have you recovered from your ordeal?"

"As best I can. It helps to have Liberty to hold." Her voice trembled at the remembered agony of wondering if her baby had died. "I never want to go through such a trial again."

He turned her to face him. "Perhaps you should make a home somewhere safer."

"I have considered it, especially now that Liberty is getting older. The menace of the road agents may be ending, but other dangers present themselves around a mining camp. I swear, the miners must be turning over every square foot of earth along Alder Creek. It will be a long time before I allow my daughter to play outside without fear of injury."

Shane cleared his throat. "There's a reason I mentioned that. You can come and live with me. As my bride, of course."

America stared at him, caught completely off-guard. "I don't know what to say."

"I hope you'll consider the idea." He squeezed her hand. "It would save your reputation and ensure a quieter life for you and the baby."

He'd said nothing about his feelings for her. They'd established their physical attraction, but she wanted to be more to Shane than someone he married out of mercy. Besides that, she couldn't deceive another man into becoming her husband under false pretenses. If she accepted him, she would have to tell him about Kyle . . . and that would rip her heart from her chest. A preacher deserved better than what a tarnished woman who had destroyed her future had to offer. She pulled her hand out of his. "I'm sorry, but I can't marry you."

"Why not?" He gazed at her so longingly she yearned to change her mind. "I would do everything in my power to look after you and the baby."

"You don't really know me." She looked away, unable to meet his eyes.

"I know you well enough to want you always by my side." He cupped her face. "I love you."

"No!" She broke away and turned her back on him. "You don't understand. I can't be a preacher's wife."

"But I'm willing to settle down."

"I'm sorry." She held back tears. "I can't."

"I'm sorry you feel that way," He lifted her hand and closed her fingers around a small, metal object. *A ring?* It felt warm from resting against his body. "Save this for Liberty. Maybe one day she'll find the happiness her mother denies herself. Give my regards to Mrs. Martin."

Shane strode away and disappeared into the night.

CHAPTER TWENTY-FOUR

"OH, LOOK, LAMB'S QUARTERS." ADDIE BENT to pluck a handful of the green herb that grew in the mounds of earth turned over by miners. Spring had come to Alder Gulch. Along the road where she walked with Nate, wild roses turned their faces to the sky. Pink primroses, blue flags, the rosy petals of bitterroot, and sunny yellow bells clothed the tumbled hills. In watered draws between ridges, violets blossomed in shades of blue, yellow, and white. Now that the vigilantes had done their grizzly work, the townsfolk could wander farther afield without fear.

With so much beauty to feed the soul, Addie lingered over the pleasant task of foraging spring greens for her restaurant. Much to her delight, a supply wagon had driven into Virginia City last week with a load of potatoes from Hell Gate, a town to the west.

Today Nate carried her basket while she chose wildflowers to display in vases on the tables.

A striped badger darted from the brush, lifted on its hind legs to gape at her, then ran back into cover.

She laughed. "There's a curious fellow."

Nate's eyes gleamed, and his laughter merged with hers. "I would say so. He's done that twice already."

Addie liked the way Nate's voice vibrated on the air. Come to think of it, she liked most everything about Nate. She'd pushed him away because of Travis, but her son had removed himself as an obstacle. Now she didn't know what to think or do about Nate. It had been her choice to keep him at arm's distance, but now she wondered if he would speak of love again. They got along well. She could easily imagine continuing together as husband and wife.

Travis benefited from Nate's interest also. More than a year had gone by since Clyde's death, and her son might willingly accept a stepfather. She could tell from the way he looked up to Nate and beamed when accepting his praise that he needed one.

Nate tilted her face with a finger under her chin. "Penny for your thoughts."

Her face flamed, and she averted her eyes. "I don't need money that badly, but thanks all the same."

He chuckled. "Look at me, Addie. Please. I want to ask you something."

She peeked at him. "What is it?"

"Don't sound so alarmed. It's not frightening."

His anxious tone did nothing to reassure her.

"Well, at least I hope it isn't," Nate went on. "What I mean to say—oh, hang it all, Addie. Will you marry me?"

Hiding her amusement at his abrupt proposal, Addie leaned down and selected a violet. She needed time to decide what to say. A sweet fragrance wafted from the patch of blue. The blossoms would open their faces to the sky and bring forth their scent for a fleeting time. She couldn't keep them alive but might enjoy their beauty for a time.

How like life that seemed. Her thinking crystalized on one sparkling fact. She loved Nate with her whole being. She'd let Travis come between them out of guilt, but no more. Nothing else mattered as much as this. She could run the best restaurant in the territory, but if she lived the rest of her days lonely for this man, the happy life for which she yearned would surely pass her by. By helping build her restaurant and stepping in during Liberty's illness, Nate had taught her that he not only wouldn't stand in the way of her dreams, he wanted to make them come true.

Addie rose. She twirled the violet by its stem, smiling at the flower. "I think that would be fine."

Nate laughed. "Oh, do you now? Only *fine*?"

Her laughter joined his. "Well, how could I resist such an eloquent invitation?"

"Oh-ho! So the lady wishes to be romanced. How's this?" The basket thumped to the ground as Nate gathered her into his arms. "I love you to distraction, Addie Martin, and I want to spend the rest of my life with you. Marry me and make me the happiest man alive. Better?"

She gave him a teasing glance. "Much."

He tilted her face to receive his kiss, and the lamb's quarters she'd picked drifted down to mingle with the flowers strewn at their feet.

A little while later, they broke apart.

"We should start back." Addie picked up the basket and collected the scattered flowers and greens.

He stooped to help. "I suppose you'll want to wear a fancy gown."

She gave him a surprised look. "Who, me? I'll sew my wedding dress and wear a spray of elderberry in my hair."

"You'll expect to ride to the church in a carriage." He nodded at his own suggestion, but with a smile in his eyes.

She shook her head. "I don't mind the walk, and the restaurant can make do for the ceremony."

He folded his arms. "We'll honeymoon in St. Louis, unless I miss my guess."

Her lips curved. "Wherever you go, Nate Whalen, is where I want to be."

He captured her hand and kissed the palm. "Anything you want, Addie, is what we'll do."

She considered this. "I would rather have a real preacher instead of a judge."

Nate drew her back into his arms. "We'll send for Reverend Hayes." He lowered his head, and she raised hers to receive his kiss.

If the badger ran out again, she never knew.

A knock shuddered through America's bedroom door. "Ma wants you," Travis called.

America sighed. The preparations for today's wedding had gone on for weeks on end. She didn't begrudge Addie her happiness, but it highlighted her own loneliness.

If she had told Shane about Kyle, she might not be sad right now. They could still have a chance together if she would only throw herself on his mercy and confess the truth. She yearned to tell him and free herself from the secret that tormented her, but she couldn't bear to watch his opinion of her change.

America had made up her mind to leave after Addie's wedding. She had to. Running into Shane when he came to town on his circuit and possibly finding out if he married someone else would break her heart.

Liberty had kept the household up last night crying from teething pain, but she now sprawled across America's bed, blocked in by pillows to prevent a fall. She checked Liberty often and came away smiling at the delicate snores that arose from her baby. America would have to make sure she didn't sleep too long, or the same thing might happen again tonight. Addie had never complained about Liberty's crying, even when it robbed her of slumber. However, being kept awake half the night on the eve of her wedding had been more of an imposition than usual.

Addie greeted America with a sweet smile. Her eyes appeared only a little red, and excitement buoyed her step. She stepped back from one of the tables she had draped in linen and decorated with an unusual combination of elderberry flowers and lamb's quarters. "What do you think? Will this do?"

The arrangement, simple and beautiful, represented Addie very well. "They're perfect."

Joy for her friend warred with a sorrow she couldn't escape. She swallowed against tears, but they insisted on falling anyway.

Addie turned to her with quick sympathy. "I didn't mean to make you cry."

"Never mind me." She picked up a flower that had been knocked to the floor and trampled. She stared at the bruised petals, wanting to weep even more. They reminded her of the flower she'd crushed in her hand while kissing Shane.

"Why are you sad?" Addie asked in a gentle voice.

Tamping down her emotions, she shrugged. "I'm just . . . moody."

Addie's gaze searched her face. "Does this have to do with Shane leaving so quickly on the night of Liberty's party?"

"I always cry at weddings." Addie didn't need to worry about America's problems with Shane today of all days.

"He left town right afterward, and you've been sad ever since." Addie gave her a knowing look. "Did something happen between you?"

"We watched the stars together." She hoped Addie would let the matter drop, but her friend looked unconvinced.

"Maybe you two can work out whatever went wrong between you today."

Hope leaped in America's chest, but she ignored it. Expecting Shane to marry her would be selfish. As a preacher, he deserved a wife above reproach. She did not qualify for the position, plain and simple. "We'd better finish decorating the tables so we can dress for the wedding," she said in a voice that wasn't quite steady.

Addie gave her a fierce hug. "I hope you find the same joy I have."

America swallowed hard. She would *not* cry on Addie's shoulder on the morning of her wedding. Determined to celebrate with her friend rather than drag her into her own sorrow, she shoved her melancholy thoughts to the back of her mind, banishing them for the remainder of the day.

The decorations transformed the restaurant into a suitable location for wedding nuptials. Vases of elderberry and lamb's quarters graced the windows. A whisper of white lace bedecked with flowers floated above the place where the bridal couple would pledge their troth.

America woke Liberty and dressed her in the lavender gown she'd sewn for the occasion. With her golden curls glistening, her blue eyes shining, and color in her cheeks, Liberty glowed with health and high spirits.

America had worked hard fashioning a gown for herself from the length of chestnut silk Addie had purchased for her role as matron of honor. A row of mother-of-pearl buttons ornamented each cuff and the bodice of her dress. With her hair pulled back by combs to cascade down her back in curls and her crinoline belling the skirt of her dress, she almost felt carefree and ready for a party, like she had in the days before meeting Kyle.

Addie emerged from her bedroom wearing lavender silk shot with purple threads that formed a grid pattern in the cloth. Purple braid trimmed the sleeves, and the bodice came to a point at the front to show off her slender waist. She'd twisted her dark hair into a loose chignon held at the back of her head by a large comb to which she had attached elderberries. She twirled, making her skirt flare around her. "How do I look?"

Tears pricked America's eyes, this time for joy. "Simply beautiful."

"Thank you." Addie gave her a quick hug. "I must say, you are stunning. I'm certain Shane won't be able to keep his eyes off you."

America's smile wavered, but she forced it back to her lips. "I should check on Liberty." She skirted the room and went into the kitchen, finding her baby playing with her wooden blocks in the corner of the kitchen where they kept a basket of toys.

Travis, helping himself to a spoonful of frosting from the side of the wedding cake, gave her a sheepish smile. "Don't tell Ma." Handsome in a vest and jacket, and with a riot of dark curls springing from beneath the bowler hat perched on his head, it was easy to see the fine man he would become.

America smiled at him. "Are you looking forward to today?"

"I'm happy for Ma." He answered in a neutral voice, but then his grin broke out. "And I really like Nate."

She gave him a quick hug. "I'm glad you feel that way. I understand that the Taylors will be among the wedding guests today. Jenny will come with her parents."

His face went red. "I'll take Liberty around to say hello to everyone." He picked up the baby and hurried from the room. The guests would arrive any minute now. With people to engage, Liberty would be in her element.

America followed Travis from the room. She should see if Addie needed her, but Shane stood beneath the lace swag, discussing something with Addie. He hadn't glanced up yet, and America pivoted back into the kitchen. She busied herself with the washing up as long as she could, but when the chatter of arriving guests reached her, she had to leave her hiding place.

Without looking at Shane, America threaded through the crowd toward Addie's bedroom, where the bride sheltered out of view until the ceremony began.

Someone bumped her. "Oops, sorry. I was in too much of a hurry trying to get back to Nate."

She turned to discover Abe Williams at her elbow. Nate's best man gazed at her from his deep-set gray eyes.

"Oh, I'm glad it's you." Now that the too-familiar words had passed her lips America wished she could call them back. Relieved that he hadn't been Shane, she'd smiled more enthusiastically at Abe than she might have otherwise.

He surveyed her with masculine interest. "That makes two of us."

She took a backward step to put some distance between them. "If you'll excuse me, I'll check on the bride."

"I will if you promise to save some dances for me tonight," he murmured.

America didn't like Abe's suave approach. It reminded her too much of Kyle. Out of the corner of her eye, she noticed Shane watching them. Heat crept into her cheeks, and she forced a smile to her lips. "I'll gladly dance with a handsome man like you."

She couldn't call forth an inviting tone of voice, but at least she managed to say the words that would give Shane a reason to break free of the love he'd professed for her and go on with his life. She turned away from Abe. Tears blinded her eyes. She dashed them away and tapped on Addie's door.

Addie pulled her inside with an anxious expression on her face. "Thank goodness it's you. I can't go another minute without knowing if Nate is here yet."

"Don't worry. He's outside on the porch, ready for the ceremony to begin."

"Thank goodness!" The tension slipped from Addie's face. "I don't know what I'd have done if he hadn't come."

America smiled. "Since he's head over heels in love with you, that wouldn't happen. The best gold strike in history couldn't keep that man away from you today."

Addie massaged her temples. "Chalk it up to bridal nerves, I guess."

America took her friend's hands and warmed them in her own. "You're going to be all right."

Addie's face softened. "I wouldn't want anyone else to stand up with me today. I think of you like a sister."

"I feel the same about you." America held back tears at the thought of moving away from Addie.

"I want you to know that you have a home here as long as you need one." Addie squeezed her hand before letting go.

America blinked. It seemed almost as if Addie had heard her thoughts. "What about your new family?"

"My new family . . . I like the way that sounds." Addie beamed. "Don't trouble yourself about us. Travis and I will move into Nate's cabin, so you'll have the restaurant to yourself in the evenings and on Sundays. During the day, I'll come over and cook meals for the miners like always."

How America wished it could go like that. The fact that it couldn't had her wanting to weep all over again, but she summoned a smile for Addie's sake. "You have been kindness itself to me."

A tap came at the door. Addie moved out of sight while America opened it. Travis stood on the other side, bouncing Liberty. "It's time."

Red Hardy, one of the regular customers at Addie's restaurant, struck up "Auld Lang Syne" on his violin, the nearest his limited expertise brought him to the wedding march. Abe offered America his arm with his dark head bent attentively toward hers.

Walking down the aisle on another man's arm with Shane waiting at the end was one of the hardest things she'd ever had to endure. Shane looked so attractive in his frock coat and string tie that America's breath caught in her throat. She couldn't meet his eyes, so she diverted her attention to Abe. He guided her to the place where she would stand throughout the wedding and went to stand beside Nate. America turned to watch Addie coming down the aisle.

No bride ever appeared more radiant than Addie as she walked toward Nate. He waited for her with quiet reserve. They exchanged brilliant smiles, clasped hands, and faced one another.

Shane stepped forward. "Dearly beloved, we are gathered here today in the sight of God and in the face of this company to join this man and this woman in holy matrimony . . ."

Gripping her bouquet of wildflowers, America stole glances at Shane as, in his lilting Irish accent, he recited the words that united two lives as one in the sight of God and man. Nate and Addie repeated their vows with conviction.

Was it her imagination, or did a tremor run through Shane's voice as he declared them husband and wife?

Shane watched America walk away from him and back up the aisle on the arm of Abe Williams. Sorrow pinched his heart. If he needed any evidence that she didn't care for him, he had it now. She laughed with Abe, tilted beguiling glances his way, and rested her hand on his arm as if it belonged there.

He couldn't stop himself from stealing glimpses of them, despite the fact that seeing them together caused him pain. Since America had turned him down, he had spent days on end in solitude. Even tending the needs of his flock had not summoned his mind from grief. With a sinking heart, he wished America would have realized she loved him by now.

Truth be told, Shane had aspired to win her promise to marry him today, during the aftermath of Nate and Addie's wedding. His hopes now died a horrible death. He would do his best to bury them deeper this time so they couldn't rise again to wound him. His appetite vanished, and he ate little from the wedding feast. All he wanted was to go back to the privacy of Con's wickiup, where he could crawl into his bedroll and mourn the loss of the woman he loved.

He waited a decent interval before approaching Addie. "I'll take myself off now. Thanks for inviting me to officiate for you. I hope you and Nate have many happy years together."

"You're not leaving yet?" Addie's gaze darted to the crowd as if searching for someone. That would be a woman in a fetching chestnut gown, he suspected.

"I'm afraid so." He infused his voice with polite regret.

"Perhaps you would wait a few moments." Addie swung her attention back to him. "I'm sure America planned to visit with you, but she's busy at the moment."

He saw her dancing with Abe and knew that was true. "I'm sorry, but I need to leave."

Addie touched his arm. "Can we talk for a minute on the porch before you go?"

"Certainly."

The front door closed, and Addie turned to him "I'm concerned about America. She's so sad lately."

His lips twisted with wry humor. "She seems to have recovered nicely."

"Appearances can deceive, Reverend Hayes." Addie sighed, the small sound more eloquent than any persuasion she might have tried.

Shane had viewed the scene through the eyes of a rejected suitor, so he had seen what he feared most. Now Addie placed doubt in his mind. How easy to cave in to optimism and convince himself that America's laughter had sounded forced and that the glances she'd sent his way had meant more than nothing. But thinking that way would probably lead to more heartache.

"May I ask you a personal question?" Addie murmured.

"Go ahead, if you must." He braced himself for what she might want to know.

"Did something happen between you and America on the night of Liberty's birthday party?"

He thought about brushing off her question, but that would be rude. She'd taken time on her wedding day, after all, to ask it. "She didn't tell you what happened?" That hardly seemed plausible, considering the closeness of her friendship with Addie.

"No. She never let on about anything, but I suspected

something had gone wrong."

"I asked her to marry me, and she said no."

Addie gave a small gasp. "That makes no sense at all. She's completely in love with you. I'd swear to it."

He gripped the rough wood of the porch rail. "That's a little hard to believe with her attaching herself to Abe."

She rounded on him. "Reverend Hayes, a woman doesn't always do things for reasons that make sense to a man. America is acting tonight out of her pain, of that I'm sure. I believe she's battled heartache for a very long time. Whatever causes her grief is what held her back from accepting your proposal. I hope you won't give up on her."

Shane closed his eyes to shut out the sight of the stars, for they took him back to the emotions of the night America had rejected him. "It's hard to ask again once you've been refused."

She touched his arm, drawing him out of his suffering. "Nate asked me to marry him three times before I said yes."

"Poor man."

Her tinkling laugh lifted his spirits. "He took it in stride." She sobered. "In certain situations, it can be best to give up. But in these circumstances? If you love America, please be patient and give her time to sort out what she needs."

CHAPTER TWENTY-FIVE

AMERICA FOLDED HER QUILTS IN HER trunk as she did her best not to cry. She'd spent the past week preparing to leave. How ironic that now she had made up her mind to leave, Virginia City had moved beyond its wild days.

She was going to miss this town, the restaurant, and her small bedroom. Even more, she would miss living with Addie and Travis. Life wouldn't ever be the same again. The change that came favored Addie, giving her all she could wish for, but it had left America on her own once more.

Liberty awoke with a scream. America patted her back to calm her, but her own agitation seemed to have infected her baby's mood. Liberty finally quieted, and she put her down to play while she finished packing.

Gramma had always said America had a strong will. She'd mentioned it as an indictment sometimes but at other times as an endorsement. America had learned it could be both. If only Gramma hadn't gone to her beloved hills of Nevermore, she would have liked to talk to her now as an adult. Remembering back to little things she had told her, America could believe Gramma had understood what it took to survive in life, and that at times it called for a person to take a chance or two.

What Nate had told Addie about the Deer Lodge Valley when he'd tried to persuade her not to come to Alder Gulch had convinced her that she'd find a better life for herself and her daughter there. Robbers Roost had stopped being quite such a terror. Nevertheless, she hid her gold in the storage compartment beneath her mattress and kept Richard's gun loaded.

She couldn't become used to how quiet the restaurant seemed now that Addie and Travis had gone. They would return to reopen it to the miners, but by then she would have taken her leave of Virginia City, Alder Gulch, and Shane. She wrote a note explaining her decision to leave and promising to write from wherever she ended up. Propping it on the kitchen table, she brushed away a tear. She hated saying her goodbyes like this, but doing it in person would hurt too badly.

America finished her packing and settled Liberty for the night. Lying in the dark, she reasoned that she was embarking on a new adventure. If only leaving Virginia City didn't feel suspiciously like running away, she might convince herself of that.

She finally slept in the small hours and woke later than she'd intended. She busied herself at once, taking care of Liberty, preparing food for the journey, and packing the last items into her wagon. The thought of traveling alone with the baby for all those miles didn't appeal to her, but she had to do it. The Indian threat had calmed for the present, and travel had become safer in the wake of all the hangings.

Some people saw the vigilantes themselves as a menace, but others argued in favor of their activities. Whatever the truth, now that mountain justice had run its course, the road agents had largely stopped operating in the area. She could feel more secure on the road, she assured herself but couldn't escape a certain uneasiness nonetheless. What would she do if calamity overtook them on the road?

Thinking like that only sapped her will. She pushed the unsettling question away and went after the oxen. She'd hobbled them so they wouldn't wander far, and they came into sight in a draw along Daylight Gulch. She left Liberty playing with her blocks in the shade along her line of sight and attempted to yoke the oxen. This frustrated her to no end. The beasts revived their old tricks while Liberty called for her attention, but she managed it at last. Carrying her daughter on her hip, she led the oxen along Wallace Street and back to her wagon. Hitching them to the wagon proved easier, and she struck out at last.

With the first hint of copper light washing the sky and the sun slanting rays from behind the saddle of a mountain, she pulled off to make camp along the Ruby River. After the long day spent either outdoors or jostling in the wagon, Liberty fell asleep early. America could not follow her example, despite her exhaustion. Her body might want sleep, but she could not persuade her mind to rest. She sat on the banks of the river, watching the ruffled surface as it reflected the changing colors of the sky.

How would Shane react when he learned she had left? She'd tried to sever the bond they shared with her behavior at the wedding, but she might only have succeeded in breaking her own heart. If she hadn't alienated him completely, he might still grieve for her.

She swallowed against a lump in her throat at the idea of causing Shane pain. She had felt wretched when she turned him down, but even if she could have brought herself to tell him about her secret shame, he didn't need a woman with a past and a ruined reputation hampering his ministry. Allowing him to suffer now would become a kindness later. He would recover and find someone better suited to be a pastor's wife.

Her reflections did nothing to ease her body toward sleep.

Hooves pounded the road behind her. She looked back. Her heart raced as all her fears confronted her at once. A lone rider on horseback galloped toward her on the road. She hurried to the front of her wagon and opened the jockey box where she stored tools. Her hand closed on the handle of Richard's gun. Her gaze searched the dimness.

The rider neared, churning up the taste of dust.

Could it be? *Surely not . . .*

She withdrew her hand from the gun. "What are you doing out here?" she called when Shane came within hailing distance.

He reined his horse to a stop. "I wanted a word with you."

She stared at him, trying to gather her wits. The joy of knowing he'd cared enough to follow surged over her, drowning her protests, betraying her. She clung to any pride she could salvage like she might cling to a rock that could save her from the wild current threatening to sweep her away.

He dismounted. "I noticed you left town. Where do you plan to go?"

"I'm on my way to Deer Lodge Valley."

"Deer Lodge?" He walked toward her. "Why not the Bitterroot Valley with me?"

Her throat went dry. Unable to frame a reply or meet his gaze, she turned to look out at the river.

He stepped in front of her. "I love you, America, and I want your happiness. Please tell me why you feel the need to run away."

She tore her gaze from his. "You don't understand."

"That is true." He took her by the shoulders with gentle hands. "But I'm willing to listen if you'll tell me what's wrong."

She might have stood in the face of his arguments, but his tenderness tore down every defense. Knowing she had lost the battle made her want to throw up new barriers between them—anything to protect herself from his ability to crush her. He couldn't know how much his approval meant to her or what it would cost her to lose it. She knew, and it strangled the breath from her throat.

He shifted to watch the river next to her. "Do you know what I wonder about you?"

Not trusting her mind to form a reply or her voice to give it, she gave him no answer.

"I ask myself why you would try to sacrifice your life to save mine, as you did with Virgil ready to shoot me." He glanced sideways at her. "That was an act of love."

"Stop it." She clasped her arms around herself.

"Stop what? Loving you? I can't."

She rounded on him, provoked beyond measure. "Stop pushing me to say why I'm not worth marrying."

He stared at her, astonishment widening his eyes. "Tell me why you could possibly think that."

"Because it's true!" A sob tore from her very soul. She clapped a hand over her mouth to prevent more from escaping. Her face flamed, and she averted her eyes. She'd said too much, but she couldn't take her words back any more than she could erase her mistakes.

"America, look at me." Shane turned her toward him and lifted her head with his hand. His gaze caressed her. "Nothing you can tell me will change my love for you."

"You don't know—" She broke away from him.

"Then tell me."

Weariness dragged at her. She couldn't fight Shane and his God any longer. "Liberty wasn't my husband's baby," she confessed in a ragged voice.

A long silence followed, broken by the rushing of the river. When she couldn't stand the quiet any longer, she risked a glance upward.

Shane's eyes shone with love. "That lies in the past, America."

"Richard never knew. I lied to him about Liberty. That's why God took him from me." The words rushed from her like water escaping a dam.

Shane's gaze searched her face. "Do you truly believe that?"

"What else can it be?" She picked up a rock and flung it as hard as she could into the river, where it sank. She looked back at him. "Everything keeps happening wrong."

Shane rubbed the back of his neck and gave his attention to the river, where a fish jumped and splashed. "I have seen my share of sorrows, but one thing I've learned. You can always find hope if you want it badly enough. God takes vengeance on those without repentance, but He loves a broken and contrite heart. Have you confessed your sin to God?"

She folded her arms against the chill breeze lifting off the water. "More times than I can count."

"You only needed to do it once. After that, holding yourself guilty calls God a liar. He promises to forgive and cleanse us from all unrighteousness, if only we will confess our sins and trust in Him."

"Can it be that simple?" The beginnings of relief washed timidly through her.

He smiled and pulled her close. "Marry me, and I'll spend the rest of my life improving your understanding of love."

America turned from the mirror hanging on the wall of her bedroom at the back of Addie's restaurant. "There. I'm ready as I'll ever be."

Addie laughed. "Have you no idea what a beautiful bride you make? I'm so pleased for you and Shane."

"I can't believe this is really happening." She smoothed the silk of her wedding dress.

"I can. Nate and I both saw it coming a mile off. Now turn around and close your eyes. I want to give you my present while we're alone."

America gave Addie a questioning look but did as she asked. A chain touched her neck. She reached up and caught hold of the object weighting it.

"You can open your eyes."

America looked down at the gold filigree locket Addie had placed around her neck. From its tiny hinges, she could tell it contained a hidden compartment. "What's inside?"

Addie smiled. "Open it and take a look."

Her fingers shook as she tried to open the locket, but the hinge resisted her efforts. "I can't seem to do it."

"Here. Let me help." Addie took over. "It's brand new, but I expect the hinge will loosen over time. There." The locket swung open.

America gasped. One side of the inner chamber framed a picture of herself with Liberty. The other held a picture of Shane.

"Thank you so much. I'll treasure this." Moisture pricked her eyes at the thoughtfulness of Addie's gift. She had once put herself into jeopardy while searching for the cheap locket Kyle had given her. While grieving its loss, she'd never guessed the real riches that waited for her.

Addie beamed at her. "I'm glad you like it."

"I wondered why you insisted on my having a picture taken with Liberty when that traveling photographer came to town."

Addie dimpled. "Shane helped me convince you to pose, if you'll recall."

"I might have known you two would gang up to surprise me. I appreciate your talking to Shane at your wedding, Addie. He told me what you did."

"You two simply needed a little help sorting yourselves out. I'm glad you finally did."

America hugged her. "Thanks for letting us stay here until we set ourselves up elsewhere."

"Oh, goodness. Now we've mussed your hair." Addie arranged America's curls with gentle fingers. "You and Shane are welcome to stay as long as you need. It will be nice to have you near when he leaves on his circuit."

"Didn't I tell you his news?"

"I've been a little preoccupied lately." A blush crept across Addie's face.

America laughed. "The bishop Shane answers to has chosen him to establish a church in the Bitterroot Valley."

"Why, that's wonderful!" She picked up America's bouquet from the bed and pressed it into her hands. "It's almost time. Does this mean Shane won't travel anymore?"

America shrugged. "I'm sure he'll be called upon to travel as a preacher, but it won't be the same as before. He'll have a home now, and we'll see one another more often."

Addie retrieved her own bouquet, a smaller version of America's, with wildflowers providing a riot of color. "I'll have to visit you sometimes. You won't be that far away."

"Yes, do, and I'll visit you," America told her. "I never want to lose touch with you or Travis. How is he adjusting to life with Nate?"

"Quite well. He needed a father as much as I needed a husband." Addie's lips curved in a contented smile. "He's happy now, and I'm grateful."

Someone tapped at the door, and Addie answered it. "Auld Lang Syne" drifted into the room.

"Are you ladies ready to come out yet?" Nate asked with a lighthearted lilt. "There's a man out here who's mighty nervous."

Addie laughed. "Tell him that all the gold in Alder Gulch couldn't keep a certain woman away from him today."

This time when America walked down the aisle with Shane at the end of it, she didn't look away.

Now, A Sneak Peek at Book Two

Cheyenne Sunrise

Chapter One

THE ARM THAT CLAMPED BRY'S WAIST hauled her backward into the travesty of an embrace. HerBry's heart pounded so hard she could scarcely catch her breath. The carved rosewood door gaped tauntingly ajar mere steps away. She twisted, her fingernails gouging flesh.

Her assailant gasped in a breath. "Fight if it helps your pride, *Irish*," a voice she recognized snarled. Jeffrey Wainwright's arms tightened around her. "We both know you want this."

Bry turned her head to give her employer's son the glare he deserved. "You flatter yourself."

He slid moist lips over her cheek, but she ducked her head before they could reach her mouth. "Let me go." She struggled to free herself. "This minute!"

"Never mind trying to cozy up, now," he mocked. Laughing at his own joke, he turned her toward him, his hold loosening. He stroked her back. With his blond head tilted coaxingly and shadows carving hollows in his cheeks, he appeared older than his nineteen years. "I've seen the way you look at me."

He must have noticed her keeping an eye on him, something she'd done ever since he'd started watching her. "What would your mother say?" She spoke without conviction. They both knew that Audra Wainwright exerted little control over her son.

"Who's going to tell her? Not you if you want to keep your job." Jeffrey pulled her closer. "Slip away to my bed now and again. I promise you'll never find yourself cast upon the road."

"Like Deirdre?" Bry shoved against his chest. "Shame on you for what you did to her, Master Wainwright!"

He tugged her closer. "My, but you're a little shrew, aren't you?"

"And you're a bully."

"That's not what Deirdre said."

She drove her foot down onto Jeffrey's instep. He grunted, his arms slackening. She wrenched free but spun back. Her slap echoed through the bedchamber. She closed a stinging hand. "Never touch me again."

"Harpy!" He rubbed his cheek. "That will cost you."

She tossed her head in the doorway. "Deirdre O'Meara told me more than you'd care to have your mother know. Keep that in mind."

The smile that lit his face made him look almost charming. "If you think she'd take your word over mine, you're a fool."

Bry slammed the door between them.

She reached the bedchamber belonging to his mother, blessedly empty, before the shaking overtook her. She leaned against the tall door and clasped her arms about herself. Tears trembled on her lashes, but she brushed them away with a sigh. She wouldn't cry, not over Jeffrey Wainwright. She'd already shed more than her share of tears over a man even more worthless.

She caught sight of herself in the gilded mirror above the dressing table. A pale woman stared back at her with eyes sparking green fire. Fresh alarm jangled through her. She looked a fright. How would she ever conceal what had happened? And yet she must to keep her job. Jeffrey had spoken the truth. His mother would never take her word against his. She hastened to tuck her tumbled black hair into her cap and smooth her serviceable frock.

The door burst open. As if conjured by Bry's thought of her, Audra Wainwright swept into the room. Her gaze locked on Bry's. She halted abruptly, and her silk faille day dress swung about her ample figure. "What have you been doing? You should have finished the bedrooms by now. Instead I find you admiring yourself in my mirror."

Bry gaped at her employer, too stunned by her hostile tone to answer.

"Stay, however. I want a word with you." Audra settled into a rose velvet chair in front of draperies in the same unfortunate shade, which clashed with the woman's determinedly red hair.

"Yes, Ma'am." Bry waited with as much patience as she could muster. All she wanted was to shut herself into her little room in the attic.

Audra folded her hands in her lap and looked Bry up and down. "My son tells me you've made improper advances toward him."

Bry started. Jeffrey had lost no time in seeking his revenge. "*I* made advances?"

"Yes, well…" Audra smoothed her skirt. "Under the circumstances, I no longer require your services."

"But I'm innocent."

"That's not what Jeffrey tells me."

"Mrs. Wainwright, you are mistaken. Your son–" Bry choked on her outrage. "Your son—"

"Mind you, as another widow, I understand loneliness. And Jeffrey is handsome enough to tempt a saint. However that may be, I won't allow you to seduce my boy."

The urge to laugh burbled up within Bry. She fought to quell it.

Audra waved a plump hand. "That's all I have to say. Leave me."

"But—"

Audra's face turned as red as the handprint had on Jeffrey's cheek. "You are dismissed!"

Bry straightened her spine. She would leave all right, but not before she spoke the truth. "Your son made improper advances to *me*, Mrs. Wainwright, and I'm not the first to draw his eye. *He's* the one who ruined Deirdre and made Mary run away."

"*Liar!*" The veins stood out in Audra's temples.

Bry feared she'd suffered a stroke. "Mrs. Wainwright!"

Her employer waved a hand. "Go this minute or I'll have Grayson put you out. And don't think you'll receive any reference from me."

"I'll pack my things." Bry flung open the door and stumbled down the corridor to the back stairs. She climbed the two steep flights to the bedchamber she'd shared with Mary, the quiet blonde scullery maid from County Kerry who had run away to escape Jeffrey's advances. Bry had always found the view from the dormer window fascinating, but today she didn't linger to watch tall ships ply the sparkling waters of Boston Harbor. Holding back tears, she placed a clean shift, a change of clothes, and a few oddments in her satchel. She glanced around the small room she'd called home for more than two years, then slipped down the stairs and let herself out by the servant's door.

The harbor wind scoured her face in an icy blast. Bry turned her back on the manor that had seemed a haven when she'd first come to it in the days after Ian's death. The disastrous marriage she'd made to escape a life of squalor had left her battered and destitute. But she'd survived to stand over Ian's grave, delivered by his death from the violence of his life. She would endure now, even if it meant returning to the slums of Manhattan.

Author Notes

My Search for the Hills of Nevermore

We can't fully understand with our finite minds the mystery of creative inspiration. We might name its triggers and obstacles, but where does it originate? As an author, I'm aware that story ideas can form without effort. Once while on an anniversary trip with my husband, I gazed through the passenger window across a wild river that ran through the Willapa Hills of Washington. A title dropped into my mind seemingly out of nowhere: *Hills of Nevermore.* Aware of a touch of the divine in the moment, I treasured it in my heart. The title teased me with possibilities. What would the story theme be? Who were the characters? I assumed the location would be the present setting.

I figure that if I can ignore a new idea, I should. After returning home, I moved the prospective title to the back of my mind. Once in a while it would surface, but I couldn't sort out what to do with it.

Two years later while on another trip my family was returning home from Yellowstone when we drove through Virginia City, an inhabited ghost town. I learned in a tourist brochure that this town had been the capital of Montana Territory. Excitement rushed over me as I realized we were passing Robbers Roost, a notorious road house. Popular tradition has it that outlaws watched from the balcony for stagecoaches carrying gold between Virginia City and Bannack, another gold rush town. I reveled in the drama of this tale, ripe fodder for an author's imagination.

Other accounts state that Robbers Roost wasn't used for nefarious purposes, but I didn't know that then. The road house now standing on the site, which I visited on a research trip, was built after an earlier building by the same name burned down. I've wondered if the reputation of the first building attached to the second. Whatever the truth, by the time my research turned up the discrepancy, the story events were already cast. I claim creative license.

While gazing across the Ruby Valley to the enfolding mountains, a title flashed across my mind. *Hills of Nevermore?* Here? I couldn't deny the whisper of inspiration that told me my book had found its true home. I believed at the time that fictional events would somehow move from Montana to the Willapa Hills.

I didn't understand yet.

Several more years went by. At some point, I applied for a scholarship to a local writing conference. The hosting organization required authors to submit several paragraphs judges would review to award scholarships. My entry, entitled *The Hills of Nevermore*, later formed the foundation for the scene where Gramma describes the hills of Nevermore to America, using them as an analogy for heaven. I won a scholarship to the writing conference based on my paragraphs, a small nudge from the Author of my life to write the book.

My search for the hills of Nevermore came to a rest, but I hope the story inspires others to begin their own.

True Historical Events in the Book

Apart from condensing events in the miner's trial, which really occurred over several days, and the arguable inclusion of outlaws at Robbers Roost, I stayed close to historical records for background events.

Regrettably, the murder of Chief Snag actually happened.

A group of men from Bannack did ride out by night to bring in a wagon train following Chief Snag's murder. For purposes of the story, I made this into America's wagon train. As in my story, local Indians passed peacefully by the wagon train as it traveled toward town.

Tendoy rode into Bannack on a war pony to inquire into his uncle's death.

Bannack miners 'stampeded' to Alder Gulch in huge numbers after the discovery of gold by Bill Fairweather and Henry Edgar.

The murder of Deputy Dillingham, noted as an 'honest man' in historical records, happened as described in Virginia City.

The miners' court trial of Buck Stinson and Haze Lyons occurred much as I've described it. Deputy Jack Gallagher actually rode into the crowd at their trial, brandishing a gun. Buck and Haze escaped on a horse stolen from an Indian woman at the spur of the moment

Popular opinion held that Buck Stinson and Haze Lyons resented the fact that Charley Forbes gained his freedom by obtaining a separate trial for himself in Deputy Dillingham's murder. I described the later disappearance of Charley Forbes from historical records. He was never found.

Judge Bissell changed the town's name from Verona to Virginia City for political reasons.

A circuit preacher (Brother Van) shut down a saloon to sing hymns for an hour on Sunday. I wrote the scene where Shane does this in tribute to this Wild West legend.

Road agent activity in the area took place (although some accounts may have been exaggerated). Sadly, the murder of Nicholas Tbalt did happen, and George Ives hung for the crime.

The Virginia City and Bannack Vigilance Committees formed in response to a need for law and order.

I followed historical records in describing the hanging of Sheriff Henry Plummer, Buck Stinson, and Haze Lyons.

A rash of lynchings, including that of Jack Slade for shooting up the town (while hitting no one) did occur.

Want more?

Read the true-life stories behind this story. Learn how to make spotted pup, bacon stew, vinegar lemonade and other Oregon Trail recipes mentioned in this book. Receive book extra feature articles on topics related to historical fiction novels by Janalyn Voigt, cover reveals for her upcoming novels, personal updates she shares only with readers, and early notice of her new releases. Go here:

http://janalynvoigt.com/hills-of-nevermore-readers.

Book Club Discussion Questions

America believes through much of the story that God took her husband away to punish her. Does God make us pay for our sins?

Shane brought Travis to Addie after the boy fought with Pete. Shane urged her not to be too hard on her son. How does Shane's request contrast with his own aversion to fighting?

America and Addie chose to follow the miners to Alder Gulch, potentially exposing their children to the hardships and violence of a mining camp. They wanted to earn money in order to survive and make better lives for their children. Did the end justify the means?

What did Shane mean when he wondered how to save people without *striving* to save them?

How did Shane come to understand what it means to do the work of God without *doing* God's work?

After Addie refuses Nate's advances, he determines to ease her burden, regardless. He hopes she will later accept his proposal, but if not, decides to "show her love in the ways open to him." How could he accomplish this?

Given the isolation and violence of the western frontier, were the vigilantes justified in their actions when they lynched Sheriff Plummer and his two deputies?

Do you agree with Shane's eventual conclusion that he should fight back to protect himself or another innocent person from harm? Why or why not?